ARRANGED WITH THE EARL

SAVING THE SPINSTERS
BOOK TWO

JACKIE KILLELEA

WILD HEART
BOOKS

Cover design by: Carpe Librum Book Design

ISBN: 978-1-963212-28-0

To God and all my English teachers.
Thanks for everything.

CHAPTER 1

1818, CUMBRIA, ENGLAND.

*L*oftus Cromwell, Fourth Earl of Hardwicke, strode toward the conservatory, the only place in this blasted house in which he could find peace. Frowning portraits stared at him from their places on the walls. His jasmine needed tending, and his melissa needed to be watered. What other plants needed attention? His booted footsteps marked each distracted thought.

"Loftus."

He stopped in his tracks at the sound of his brother's voice, a frown pulling at his lips. As he turned toward that blood relation of his, the other man grimaced. Loftus was used to the reaction by now. He cleared his throat and eyed the man's rumpled cravat. He was wearing the same coat as he had yesterday. "Gilbert." He checked the time on his pocket watch, then slipped it back into his green waistcoat. "You're awake...early."

Gilbert stood taller, his light-brown hair disheveled from what Loftus assumed was the previous evening's carousing. "It's one in the afternoon. Don't act so surprised." His voice was rough, as though he'd woken up only ten minutes before.

Loftus tilted his head, eyes narrowed. "Indeed. Is there something you wish to speak with me about? I was just—"

"Going to the conservatory? Yes, I thought you might be. Really, Loftus, must you always be tending to your plants? It's dreadfully embarrassing to have a brother whose sole interest is in leaves and vines. You wouldn't believe the ribbing I got about it last evening from Lord Templeton." Gilbert propped his hands on his hips and shook his head, light flooding in from the window behind him.

Loftus stretched out his arms, irritation bubbling within him. "What care I for Lord Templeton's opinion? His reputation is as clean as a chimney sweep after twelve hours of labor."

"You know, this continued behavior of yours isn't what Father wanted." Gilbert crossed his arms, his dark-blue eyes flashing. The corridor seemed to narrow around them. "He thought your foolish hobby would go away. When he sent you off to war, he thought you'd come back a hero. Not like..." Gilbert raised a hand in a gesture toward Loftus's face. "This."

Loftus's hands tightened into fists at his sides, his jaw clenching. "There was every possibility I wouldn't come home at all." Indeed, perhaps his brother would have been better suited to the fight. "But I agree. I wish he would have let me be. I would never have had to see what I have seen, nor to see what I have to every day when I look at myself. You do not realize how difficult Badajoz was. It is not only the physical marks that I have but the—" He swallowed past the thickness in his throat. "Do you believe I want these scars?"

"You still don't understand, do you? You needed to secure the line. No woman would have married someone as obsessed with plants as you, which is why Father sent you away." He eyed Loftus, a pitying twist to his mouth. "But now the situation is doubly impossible."

Loftus's heart sank. Must his brother state the obvious? "It's been three years since I came home from the war to find that my brother was no longer as I knew him, and you have remained that same changed man—that same stranger in my home. Will you ever return to the kind sibling I knew?" He couldn't keep the longing from his voice.

Their father's death had done something to Gilbert. Perhaps he attempted to find solace in vice and hide away from his grief in drink and cards. Perhaps it was the uncertainty of his own future now that his mooring point—their sire—had been washed away. Gilbert had always idolized the man, after all. Whatever the case, Gilbert had only grown more distant over the years.

Gilbert stepped forward, his handsome visage animating. "I *am* trying to be kind. To give you what you want...peace and your plants. Father taught me about how to run the estate when you were recovering, you know...before he died, that is." His brother looked away and shrugged. "If ever you wished to relinquish your title, the estate would be in good hands. It can be a lot of weight on one's shoulders, I understand." Gilbert shifted on his feet. "The title needs heirs to continue the line. You'll never marry, whereas I—"

Anger and disappointment mixed in his stomach. "I am not relinquishing my title. I do not care what you believe, brother. I will be married, and I will carry on our family's name." For his brother to suggest such a thing proved how much he had changed. Loftus might be scarred, yes, but did his brother really think so little of him? It only served to make Loftus more determined to prove him wrong.

Gilbert's expression twisted. "Do you truly believe a woman of the *Ton* will marry you?"

Loftus raised his hand. "Enough! Go back to sleep before the next round of spirits takes you off."

He turned on his heel and departed, heading for his study

instead of the conservatory. He'd need to send a note to his solicitor. As much as Loftus didn't wish to marry, he'd need a wife and heir if he was to keep his cad of a brother from becoming the next to inherit. Loftus wasn't about to let Gilbert run Blackfern Manor and the surrounding lands into the ground—not with his record of debts.

Surely, his solicitor could find some woman who wouldn't mind a marriage of convenience in exchange for land and title —even if that marriage happened to be to a man with a face as marred as his.

~

Catherine Blynn sat down at her vanity, her maid reflected in the looking glass as she pulled back Catherine's long brown hair. Each tug and push of a pin readied her for the evening to come. She slid her round-rimmed spectacles higher up her nose and examined her well-proportioned face. She was pretty, she supposed, though no diamond of the *Ton*. Gentlemen were introduced to her—that wasn't the problem. What *was*, was that they didn't seem to enjoy listening to what came out of her mouth thereafter. That was, of course, besides the fact that she was four-and-twenty. Would anyone ask her to dance tonight?

"Do you think this one will be like the last?" She met her maid's eyes in the mirror, tension threading through Catherine's shoulders.

Susan pinned a few violets here and there. They were a good match for Catherine's light dress. "I can't see 'ow it would be, miss. Ye were engaged at the last ball. Ye won't be at this one."

Catherine's arms tingled where the bruises had been. When she'd been betrothed, Lord Balfour had certainly left his mark on her—and not in a good way. "What if he's there?"

"'E may well be, but 'e can't 'arm ye no more, miss, and thank the Lord for that!" Susan blew a wayward strand of dark hair from her face, ruffling the edge of her white cap in the process. "I don't know why yer parents arranged that match in the beginning, 'twas so terrible."

Catherine sighed. "You know as well as I, Susan. I am nothing but a pawn to them—simply a thing to be traded to get connections and status."

Susan set the hairpins aside and moved to the jewelry box, reaching in to pull out Catherine's pearl necklace. "Well, I'm mighty relieved that Lord Balfour called off the betrothal."

Catherine nodded. While the scolding she'd received from her parents had been horrible—them blaming her for his calling it off—she'd much rather face their wrath than spend a lifetime with such a man as he.

The door burst open, and her mother entered the room, a storm of silk and jewels. A scowl was on her face, framed by golden curls. "Catherine! How are you not yet ready? We must be going immediately if we are to be on time for the ball. Come!" She reached for Catherine's hand and pulled her from the seat, Susan clasping the necklace onto Catherine's throat as they hurried out of the room and down the hall.

Not long after, Catherine was unceremoniously pushed into her family's carriage, and they were off to the ball, her heart thumping louder with each *clop* of the horses' hooves upon the ground.

If Lord Balfour was there, would he speak to her? Would he attempt to reconcile? She shuddered. Kenneth had never pretended to be a good person nor a loving betrothed. He only wanted her dowry. He had made it clear her eccentricities would not be tolerated. Her hand lifted to her cheek of its own volition, a phantom sting on the skin.

"You must be on your best behavior tonight." Her father furrowed his eyebrows, his voice gruff. "If you're to ever make a match, , the *Ton* must forget about your failed engagement. Let us hope Lord Balfour hasn't been spreading the news to all of his friends."

"Yes, Father." Catherine ducked her head, her voice quiet.

His black mustache twitched, and his brown eyes flashed. "None of your eccentricities. If you make a fool of us again, there will be consequences. I don't know what you did to make Lord Balfour call off your engagement, but you won't get out of another one, I tell you. Your mother and I have worked too hard for this."

Catherine lifted her chin. "I didn't do anythi—"

"It was surely your bluestocking tendencies that sent him running. What an ungrateful child you are." Her mother sniffed, turning her head to look out the window. "We have done so much to ensure you could marry a titled man, yet all you do is complain."

Catherine wasn't the one who wished for a title, and she was hardly a child at the age of four-and-twenty. Yet she bit her tongue.

The carriage ambled down the busy London streets, eventually stopping in front of Lord Fifett's large brick townhome. Candles were aglow in every window, and footmen stood at attention on either side of the front door, waiting to greet guests.

Catherine followed her parents into the house and was welcomed by the hosts, a large man and woman with great smiles on their faces and bright eyes. Catherine's shoulders loosened. How did these people come to be friends with her parents? She bobbed a curtsy.

"Welcome! We're so glad to have you here." Lady Fifett spread her arms out and gestured around the expansive foyer at the few lingering guests, nodding her head in the direction of the ballroom. "There are many people to meet, for it is a crush this evening." She leaned toward Catherine as though imparting a secret. "There are many young men, as well."

Heat rose in Catherine's cheeks, and she clutched her skirt with both hands. Lady Fifett studied her for a moment, then turned her head to a nearby servant. "Where is Roger?"

The man straightened. "He is—"

"I am right here, Mother." A man who looked about a few years older than Catherine entered the foyer through a side door, a drink in hand. His hair was the color of rust, and his features pleasing, with a smattering of freckles along his nose and cheeks.

"Ah, so you are." Lady Fifett's smile widened as her son neared. "Come, meet the Blynns and their daughter, Catherine."

The man—Roger—moved across the marble floor and bowed at the waist. "It's a pleasure to meet you all." He picked up Catherine's gloved hand, his face hovering over it. "Might I have your first dance, Miss Blynn?"

Her eyes were wide. Never had she so quickly secured a dance—and the man seemed genuine too. "If I might have the pleasure of knowing who I am dancing with."

Roger's chin dipped. "Ah, please forgive me." He looked past her to her parents and then his gaze darted to hers once more. "I am Lord Fortescue."

Catherine nodded. "I'd be pleased to dance with you, my lord."

Her mother's tight voice sounded from behind her. "You'd better let him escort you to the ballroom, Catherine, for I am sure we are the last of the guests and the dancing is soon to begin."

Catherine allowed herself to be led away from her parents, her shoulders easing as the distance apart from them increased.

"Might I say, you look lovely, Miss Blynn." Lord Fortescue leaned forward, his head tilted in her direction.

A flush heated her cheeks. She mustn't say anything her parents would disapprove of.

"Thank you, my lord." She settled on giving him a smile. Surely, her parents wouldn't find fault with that.

As he led her through the doorway into the ballroom, he took one last sip of his drink and handed the glass to a nearby footman. He turned to her and said with brandy on his breath, "Let us join the throng, then."

The first dance was a minuet, which Catherine knew very well. She promenaded with Lord Fortescue, then danced in slow circles while other couples watched. Whenever the dance brought them close, his eyes brightened and her steps were lighter. He was a fine dancer, truly. He held her gloved hands in a soft yet warm grasp.

When the dance was over, he bounced on his toes. "Would you like to take a turn about the room?"

Catherine lifted her lips, though hesitation pulled back on the reins of her enthusiasm. This was how Lord Balfour had acted when she'd first met him. Her stomach tightened. "I would, thank you." No matter her anxiety, she wasn't yet prepared to return to her parents. They'd always find fault in her, no matter what she did.

Lord Fortescue wrapped her hand around his arm and circled the ballroom. The dancers in the middle skipped about with their partners, the sound of their feet tapping beneath the steady thrum of the musicians' instruments.

"Why is it we've not met before?" Lord Fortescue cast her a sidelong glance. "I've never seen you around London."

Catherine fingered her pearl necklace. "I attend events, but I do not stay at them for long, if my parents have any say." And she wouldn't say more, though they normally blamed

Catherine for their leaving early—saying her behavior was causing them embarrassment.

Realization crossed his face. "You must have to get up early for callers, then. It's no wonder your parents wouldn't have you stay out too late."

Let him think what he would. Catherine wouldn't have him believing her to be some sort of oddity among her sex—which is what her parents would claim, if he asked. "What of you, my lord? I haven't seen you about either."

"I've just returned from a stay with my friend in the country." A half smile crossed his face.

"Indeed?" Catherine tilted her head, interest coloring her tone. "What area, my lord?"

"He has an estate in Kent. It's beautiful there. A perfect place to escape the city crowds. The lords here are too akin to peacocks for my tastes."

He plucked a glass of lemonade from a footman's tray and offered it to her, pausing right before the glass left his fingers. A look of concern crossed his face. "As much as I wish to keep you in my company, I should return you to your parents. They are looking in our direction with rather undecipherable stares. Your mother, in particular, has quite the scowl." Lord Fortescue frowned. "I've no ill intentions toward you, Miss Blynn. I promise, I will not steal you away."

Catherine took a sip of her lemonade. This man seemed to share her same views, and he was good company so far. "Do not fear, Lord Fortescue. I do not mind, for it would be a blessing if you would."

He reared his head back. "What?"

"'Tis nothing, my lord." She waved his concern away. "You may take me to them. I would be most grateful." She placed her hand on his arm, and they moved toward her parents, sliding around giggling groups and men slapping each others' shoulders.

"I do not want our acquaintance to end." Lord Fortescue tilted his head down to whisper in her ear. "Might I take you for a ride in my barouche tomorrow? We could go to Hyde Park."

"What time of day?" She hated to go during fashionable hour. It was so slow then. It was nothing more than people parading themselves around for the sake of being seen—absolutely ridiculous.

"Anytime you like." His breath brushed her ear, sending tingles down her spine.

Her parents, of course, would wish for her to go, but this time, Catherine wished to as well.

"Meet me at two." She gave him her address as they stepped to her parents' sides.

"What is this?" One of her father's dark eyebrows rose in question.

Catherine cleared her throat. "Lord Fortescue has invited me for a ride in his barouche tomorrow."

"How wonderful!" Her mother's face transformed in an instant from a dislike for Catherine to an eagerness to see the outing go well. "Thank you, Lord Fortescue, for doing our daughter such an honor."

Lord Fortescue's eyebrows furrowed, his mouth twisting to the side as he bowed. "'Tis an honor she accepted, madam. If you'll excuse me, I must check on my mother." In a blink, he was gone, and Catherine's parents stared her down as though she held the weight of the world on her shoulders.

Her mother grabbed her arm, her lips pulling into a thin line. "You must make him like you, Catherine. Our family depends on it."

Her arm began to ache as her mother's nails dug into Catherine's skin—her cold blue eyes without emotion. "Yes, Mother."

Finally, the woman released her, only for Catherine's father to move closer, a furious look on his face. "While you were dancing, your mother and I were trying to find you prospects. As it is, Lord Balfour has slandered our name because of you."

Catherine's mouth dropped open. She took a step back, her heart racing. "I—I didn't do anything to discourage him, Father —I promise. I always bent to his whim as you told me..." Her voice was a murmur. How could her father be blaming *her* for Lord Balfour canceling their betrothal? It had been *his* decision, not hers.

"What does it always come down to, girl? What is it that always gets you in trouble?" He didn't wait for her to answer. "Your behavior!" He huffed, pulling on the lapels of his coat. "You can never act as your mother and I have instructed. Instead, you spout what that governess taught you and what my sister taught you after that. It's a good thing we replaced the former and sent the latter away, or I suppose you'd be even worse than you currently are, eh? My sister never learned, and neither will you, it seems. No man wants an odd wife, Catherine, and Lord Balfour's been telling all who will listen that's exactly what you are. Says you drove him away with your vulgar ways."

Tears stung the back of Catherine's eyes. Her father was keeping his voice low, but she felt as though many eyes were upon her. Now that Lord Balfour had spread these rumors, perhaps there were. "I was always refined in his presence, Father." And she had been. She'd never been her true self around him—not that she wasn't refined in her normal behavior, but by the *Ton*'s standards, she was not yet the pure gold that could be made into a ring. It had been difficult, yes, but necessary, according to her parents.

So, then, why would the man use her behavior as a reason for canceling their betrothal when it clearly hadn't been? Unless... There had been one time Catherine had stoked his ire to a greater degree than others. The anger on his face was burned into her mind, and she'd received more than one slap for denying him what he wished.

Catherine met her father's eye, her stomach churning. "I know why Lord Balfour canceled our engagement."

Her father crossed his arms. "We already know the reason."

"This isn't about my unladylike behavior, Father. Lord Balfour broke our engagement because of my Christian behavior—the behavior that he views as meaningless."

"What are you talking of?" Her mother narrowed her eyes.

Catherine's heartbeat increased. This was not something she was comfortable talking about—especially not in the middle of a crowded ballroom—but her parents were sure to force it out of her one way or another.

She lowered her voice to a whisper. "During our betrothal, Lord Balfour wished to...lie with me...in a carnal way. I told him I would not do so."

Her father's eyes widened, and her mother clutched the jeweled pendant at her neck. Catherine's shoulders fell in relief. At least they cared about this.

"Why did you deny him?" Her father's voice was all fury as the words spewed from his mouth.

Catherine's gaze lost its focus. Her limbs went numb. "You... want..."

Her mother shook her head. "You foolish, foolish girl." Her voice was all venom.

Catherine came to her senses, her gaze flicking from her father to her mother. "You would have me go against God and... and *lie* with a man before marriage? I cannot disrespect Him in such a way. I cannot disrespect *myself* in such a way."

The music seemed to get louder. Her father rubbed a hand down his ruddy face. "You could've entrapped him, Catherine. Don't you see? He'd have to marry you then. You'd be titled, and all of the fellow merchants would be crawling to me, asking to merge businesses. Lords would finally be willing to work with me."

Her mother waved her fan in an erratic motion. "I would finally be able to show to the other ladies that not only do I have the wealth they do, but the relations, as well. We told you what to do in the simplest of directions, yet you couldn't even follow those. Our only hope now is that Lord Fortescue doesn't hear of these rumors before you can convince him to marry you."

Catherine felt sick. Never before had she known her parents to be willing to stoop to such levels in order to get what they wanted. Inwardly, she sighed. Lord Fortescue, though she hadn't interacted much with him, seemed kind and genuine. He didn't deserve her manipulative parents for relations. On the drive tomorrow, she would do what she hadn't done in some time with a suitor—be herself. If that scared him away, then at least he was safe from her parents' schemes.

CHAPTER 2

*C*atherine tied the pink ribbons of her bonnet in a bow beneath her chin as she stood in the foyer of her townhouse, Susan beside her. Afternoon light spilled in through the windows, glazing the beige tiled floor in a gleam of white. A variety of weapons her father had collected over the years adorned the walls, arranged in spirals and other impressive manners to intimidate anyone who entered. The sun's rays glinted off the metal in stripes of gold, reflecting along the opposite wall.

"With them hung on the wall, one almost forgets what these weapons are capable of. I wonder if they'll scare Lord Fortescue off."

Susan followed her gaze, her mouth drawn to the side. "I find that the unseen can do far more 'arm or good than that which is seen."

Catherine's eyebrows furrowed. "What do—"

"That's what you're wearing?" Her mother's pinched voice came from behind.

Catherine turned around, her stomach dropping. "Indeed. Is something wrong?"

Her mother wrinkled her nose, stepping closer to finger Catherine's light-green day dress. "The color does not become you at all. Why, you'll blend right in with the foliage. I insist you change at once."

A knock sounded at the door, and the butler, Tetley, entered the room to open it.

Catherine's mother tapped her foot on the floor and huffed. "What you're wearing will have to do, for today." She leaned closer. "Remember, you must be on your best behavior. He must not find out about your previous engagement to Lord Balfour. Catherine, if you do not do this—"

"I am aware that our family depends on my success." At least in her parents' eyes, it did. "I will be on my best behavior." Of sorts. She would behave as she normally did—her true behavior.

Before Tetley opened the door any farther, her mother pinched Catherine's cheeks and turned her around, pushing her forward.

Lord Fortescue entered, his green eyes alight. They matched his waistcoat perfectly. His coat was black, and his trousers were a slate color. His cravat was tied neatly around his throat in a waterfall style. "Miss Blynn." He bowed the minute he laid eyes on her.

Catherine curtsied and looked over her shoulder, but her mother had gone. "Ah, Lord Fortescue, what a pleasure it is to see you again."

He escorted her out the door and down the steps of her townhome to his waiting barouche—the driver sitting up front with the reins in his hands. Lord Fortescue helped her up and sat in the seat across from her as she arranged her skirts, the day bright and warm. Susan climbed in as well and sat next to Catherine.

The coachman set the horses into motion. Other vehicles passed on the busy London street, but Catherine couldn't focus on that now with her chest tight and shoulders tense. She hated to see it, but the interest in Lord Fortescue's eyes would inevitably flee as soon as she began to act like herself. That was how it always went when she acted as she truly was, and how it always would be, it seemed, but she was done with trying to change herself to fit with her parents and society. Aunt Marjorie had taught Catherine to be herself, no matter if society frowned upon her. Her aunt had always done so, and she'd lived a better life for it, with a loving husband and three cats in a cottage in Shropshire.

"You seem troubled, Miss Blynn."

Catherine tilted her head up. Lord Fortescue's brow was drawn down as he looked at her. She inhaled. She might as well drop the act now. "To be honest, my lord, I do believe you'll soon come to dislike me."

He blinked. "Why would that be?"

She clasped her hands in her skirt. "Because my parents were forcing me to behave last night, and I no longer wish to behave. Not today. For your sake and mine."

"For my sake?" His mouth twisted to the side.

The coachman pulled into the main park entrance, following the path inside. Few carriages passed, given that the time of day was not popular for park goers. A few mothers were out with their children, and some servants walked dogs. Wildflowers dotting the ground near trees and benches and on vines and bushes sweetened the air.

"Indeed. You should not like to have my parents for relations. If I continue with this charade, then you very well might." Catherine bit her lip and looked away, a light breeze caressing her face and cooling her cheeks.

"You're presuming quite a lot, you know." His tone was affronted.

His words drew her eyes to him once more. "I know I am. I am only attempting to help you, my lord."

Lord Fortescue tapped his fingers against his knee and slumped back into his seat. "Are you always so forthright?"

"Yes—when I'm not pretending to be proper, that is. Does it bother you?"

"It does, actually. Can't you show some tact like other ladies of the Ton? It isn't befitting a young woman to be so direct."

Her heart fell. This was what she'd never understood about society—one of the things, anyway. How its members danced around a difficult topic, stepping around it as though it was a shard of glass, while she wished to stomp on it and be done with the dance. That way, she'd feel the pain, and the blood would be drawn, but then she'd be able to move on and heal. There'd be no more dread of the pain to come or the mess to follow.

"You will be disappointed with me, then, my lord."

"You cannot be disappointing in all respects, Miss Blynn." Lord Fortescue flashed her a small smile. "After all, I enjoyed dancing with you last evening." He called to the coachman and ordered the man to pull the carriage to the side of the path. "Come, let us walk a while and see if we are not better company on our feet."

Lord Fortescue helped Catherine and Susan down from the barouche and wrapped Catherine's hand around his arm. They strayed from the path and walked through the lush grass, their footsteps cushioned as though they stepped on pillows. Susan followed but left ample space between her and them.

Catherine removed her bonnet, letting it hang at her side.

Lord Fortescue eyed her. "Surely, you don't want freckles?"

She raised an eyebrow. "Such as yours?" A blush crossed his face, and she shrugged. "My mother finds them unfortunate, but I rather like them."

He cleared his throat but said nothing in response.

They meandered down a small dirt path, grasses poking out from each side. The branches overhead became denser.

Catherine spotted a flat rock about the size of her hands and dropped Lord Fortescue's arm, bending to lift it.

"What are you doing?" He spoke behind her in an almost accusing tone.

She peeked beneath the stone, her breath stilling. A smile came to her lips. "*Lissotriton vulgaris.*"

A huff. "I beg your pardon?"

Catherine didn't move, her eyes pasted to the small creature before her. "A smooth newt, my lord. Come see."

"I shall do no such thing, Miss Blynn." His tone was fraught with irritation. "Truly, you should stand before anyone sees you. They would think you mad."

Catherine gently settled the rock back into the place, recovering the newt. "If this is madness, my lord, then let them think so." She stood and brushed her skirts off.

"So you possess a fondness for amphibians." He wrapped her hand around his arm once more and continued down the path, facing ahead with his mouth in a straight line. "Tell me of your more ladylike pursuits, Miss Blynn."

Catherine straightened her shoulders. Here was where she was to ring off all of the qualities he'd find enticing in a prospect for marriage. It never ceased to make her feel like a cow at market. "I love embroidery and drawing. My parents ensured I was taught to paint and draw by the finest art teachers in London."

Lord Fortescue nodded, some tension seeming to leave his shoulders.

"I speak French and Italian—my mother insisted on both—and I play the harp. You've already seen that I can dance, of course." She pushed her spectacles up her nose. At what point would he view her as qualified to be his wife? Was being skilled at the harp very high on the checklist of qualities? "If you wish for me to go into further detail, my lord, I prefer muslin gowns to silk—"

He coughed. "You need explain no further, Miss Blynn."

Fine. She had some questions for him, then. Catherine tilted her head to the side. "Very good. Tell me of your manly pursuits."

Lord Fortescue paused, Catherine nearly pulling him along. She glanced back. His face had turned cherry red, and he rubbed the back of his neck. "My—You would like me to tell you of my...*manly pursuits*?"

Catherine nodded. "If you should know how I spend my time and what I enjoy doing, then why should I not know the same of you?"

Lord Fortescue exhaled, his shoulders dropping. A look of relief came to his face. "Oh. Well, you needn't know what I enjoy doing. I'm sure it would bore you, anyway."

Catherine lowered her eyebrows. "How am I to see if you are qualified to be my husband? If you can adequately run an estate?"

Lord Fortescue snorted. "Have no fear of that, Miss Blynn."

Catherine bit her lip. "Why? You know how marriageable I am. How marriageable are you?"

The path grew wider as they came to a clearing, the earth less tamped down by footsteps. Instead, grass reached up, and yellow and white wildflowers bloomed toward the sky, darting from the earth in spontaneous patches. The sun filtered through the leaves more generously, as though drapes were slowly being pulled apart.

Lord Fortescue straightened his shoulders, a haughty turn to his lips. "Very marriageable. If you *must* know, I enjoy hunting, and I *do* know how to run an estate. I attend the occasional house party and do my duty in the House of Lords, of course. This, however, is none of your concern, Miss Blynn, as this is only our first outing."

And likely to be their last. He didn't have to speak the words, for she caught the underlying tone.

"And yet you asked me about my feminine pursuits, my lord —a thing a man does when he wishes to know how marriageable the woman he is speaking to is."

He scoffed, but she paid it no mind, her attention caught by the gleaming of the sun along the water. They had walked to the bank of the Serpentine River.

The tree line stopped five feet from the edge, the grass turning into a sandy bank that sloped into the blue waters. Catherine stepped closer, mesmerized by the soft patterns in the surface as a breeze blew, the sweet song of a chaffinch on the air.

A motion to her right caught her attention. A man in shirt-sleeves stood not twenty feet away, a small cloth sack in his hands. Ah. Today would be the perfect day for a picnic.

"Miss Blynn, we ought to return." Her companion's voice was strained as he turned his gaze downriver.

Catherine faced Lord Fortescue, confusion rising within her. "But we've only just arrived."

A splash sounded from behind, and she looked over her shoulder. The man no longer held the sack. Bubbles surfaced from the water near him.

That was no picnic. Something alive was in that bag.

CHAPTER 3

*C*atherine made to sprint down-shore, only for her wrist to be caught by Lord Fortescue.

"Don't, Miss Blynn. You will not convince that man to get the animal."

All at once, memories of Lord Balfour's violence surged into her mind. She felt trapped like a wild animal in a cage, Lord Fortescue's hand tight on her wrist. Her breathing became heavier, and her head grew hot. "Let go of me!"

She wrenched her arm from his grasp and ran in the direction of the air bubbles—or where she'd last seen them. The man backed away, but she paid him no mind.

Lord Fortescue called her name from the path's end as she rushed into the cool water, the spring air not yet warm enough to make it comfortable. Reaching into the murk, she grasped at the water, desperate to pull out whatever creature the man had so cruelly tossed in. Her heart raced, beating ten times its normal speed. Panic overcame her as the seconds ticked by and still, no bag had been found. The water's chill made her shiver, her skirts sinking down and pulling at her legs.

Finally, her forefinger brushed against the rough edge of

something. A manmade thing. She grabbed and pulled. A small brown sack emerged from the river's surface, water droplets running from it in a stream. Moving as quickly as she could toward shore—dragging her skirts along with her—she collapsed on the grass and pulled at the soaked-through knot that tied the bag shut.

"Oh, miss!" Susan came running up the shore, her skirt in her hands. "Ye've ruined your dress."

"It matters little, Susan. Help me, please."

The maid's fingers worked at the knot, and she soon yanked the top of the bag open to reveal a limp brown-and-black puppy, its fur wet and youthful skin wrinkled. Catherine picked it up in both hands and cradled it against her chest, the poor thing chilled through and just as big as a skein of yarn.

She closed her eyes. *Please, God, let this little creature live. I know You care for all of Your creatures, large and small. Please, Lord, raise this one up from death's fingers if it be Your will. Renew his life.*

She rubbed her hands up and down its back and placed the pup on the ground, patting it with vigor. A gurgle sounded, and it gave a small cough, water dribbling from its mouth and onto the sand.

Thank you, God. Catherine continued her ministrations, and the poor thing was soon giving a few weak yips, attempting to struggle to his feet.

Footsteps on grass preceded Lord Fortescue's arrival. "What were you thinking, Miss Blynn? You might have drowned—and all for a mongrel!"

She stood and picked up the puppy, his fur quickly drying in the sun. "I know how to swim, and he's not a mongrel, my lord. His name is Roger."

Lord Fortescue took his hat from his head, his arms spread wide. "But that's my name!"

Catherine lifted a finger to her lips. She'd forgotten that detail. "So it is. We can't very well have him named after a fine gentleman like yourself. You wouldn't even save him." She wrinkled her nose.

Lord Fortescue threw his hands up, but Catherine's eyes were on the creature in her arms. "I shall call him Giles."

A scowl marred Lord Fortescue's face as Susan attempted to straighten Catherine's skirt. "We will return, Miss Blynn, unless you've any other creatures to save?"

Catherine walked back to the path's end and picked up her bonnet, a tangle of emotions within her. She was glad to have rescued Giles from certain death, though how disappointingly cold Lord Fortescue's demeanor had become after he witnessed her behavior. Was rescuing a puppy really so objectionable? Or was it merely lifting up the rock to find the newt that had changed his opinion so swiftly? He *had* mentioned his dislike for her forthright speech, so perhaps it was everything combined.

Catherine sighed. Well, this *had* been her plan. She'd expected him to be scared away, and he had been. She wrinkled her nose. They wouldn't have suited, anyway.

Dread flooded her at the thought of facing her parents in her bedraggled state. Her gown was sopping and sandy, with mud streaks on the back. Her white gloves were covered in brown fur, and her hair was spilling from its pins. With every step she took back toward the carriage, water squeezed from her stockings and was reabsorbed like a rag being wrung out at the bedside of a fevered patient. And how would her parents take the appearance of Giles? Would she be able to keep him?

The trip back home was all too quick, with Lord Fortescue silent the entire time. Passersby took in her disheveled appearance with wide eyes. Catherine's cheeks heated, but she never once felt the sting of regret for what she'd done.

The coachman pulled up in front of her townhouse, and Lord Fortescue hopped out, his shoulders straight and head up. He helped her out and assisted Susan before giving a brief bow.

He leaped back into the barouche without so much as a backward glance and ordered the coachman to be on his way, not even hesitating to see if Catherine had made it safely inside her home. It wasn't evening, but it would have been nice.

She sighed. "Thank you for coming, Susan. Please meet me in my room in a few minutes. I'm sure my parents will have a lot to say before then."

The maid gave a sympathetic smile and disappeared behind the townhouse to enter through the servants' entrance. Catherine cradled the puppy closer and knocked on the front door.

Tetley gasped as he let her in. "Miss! What has happened?"

"Tetley? Who is at the door?" Her mother's voice echoed down the hall, her footsteps growing louder. "Tet—Catherine!" Her mother's exclamation bounced off of the foyer's walls. "What have you done?"

Catherine's stomach dropped. This was only the beginning. Her palms began to sweat.

"Harry! Come quickly! Harry!" She called out to Catherine's father. The dread in Catherine's stomach only churned more violently.

A slam came from down the corridor, followed by loud footfalls. "What, woman? I'm dreadful bus—What the devil?" Her father roared the words, leading Catherine to cover Giles's soft ears. "You look as though you've fallen into a pond!"

"'Twas a river, actually, and I jumped in of my own accord."

Her father looked as though he was about to suffer apoplexy.

Catherine hurried on. "It was for good reason, Father. I was saving this puppy." She held up Giles. "He would have drowned if I did not."

"Put down that flea-infested rat this instant!" Her mother's voice was shrill, her curls shaking with her fury. "You stupid

24

girl. You should have let the thing drown. Where is Lord Fortescue?"

Catherine pulled the puppy back into her arms, her gaze darting to the floor. "He left. I—I do not believe he will be returning."

Her mother's palm delivered a stinging blow to her cheek. Catherine held her breath to avoid crying out, knowing that a reaction would only provoke the woman further. When it felt as though she was truly suffocating, she inhaled again.

"You stupid, stupid girl!" Her mother's eyes blazed. "You will ruin us." She stomped her foot. "Put that *thing* down before I take it from you."

Catherine's eyes stung, tears threatening to fall. She had to be strong. She straightened her stance and lifted her chin. "I wish to keep him."

Her mother's hand raised again. "If you do not throw that dog outside right now—"

"You may keep it." Her father stood in the corner, watching the two of them. His mouth was curved to the side, his eyebrows furrowed.

"Harry!" Her mother turned on her heel, her mouth agape.

"She may keep it, Matilda. There will be no further arguing on the matter."

Catherine's mother's face twisted into an ugly scowl as she lowered her hand and her fists balled at her sides.

Catherine had no idea what to make of her father's newfound generosity—but she would not question it while it lasted. She scurried up to her room with Giles, dearly hoping her father didn't change his mind. Would this generosity come at a price?

~

$\mathcal{L}$oftus watched as Mrs. Stonehill directed several chambermaids down the hall, each with a bucket and rag in hand. His wife would be here in only a week's time, and serious preparations needed to be made if this manor was to be a comfortable home.

Gilbert sidled up to him, one hand in his waistcoat pocket. "What's all this, then? I didn't think Mother was having guests."

Loftus turned toward his brother, a sense of satisfaction blooming within him, followed by unease. How would his brother respond to his news? He cleared his throat. "She's not."

Gilbert's eyebrows raised. "Surely, you're not having a house party. Not considering..." His lips curving up in a grimace of a smile, he waved his hand toward Loftus's visage.

He tightened his fists at his sides and gritted his teeth. He might actually get a sense of pleasure in revealing the truth. "It is no house party I prepare for, but my wife."

Gilbert's chest had been rising in a breath, but it froze with Loftus's words. His mouth became a thin line. "A wife, you say? Who would take you?"

The comment was like a stickpin to the chest, but Loftus answered, regardless. "My steward made a few inquiries and found a woman in London."

Gilbert scoffed. "'A woman in London?' All you have to do is go to Covent Garden to find a woman in London. One of those birds of paradise would be pleased to live here, I'm sure."

Heat flushed through Loftus's stomach. "You know that's not what I meant. This woman is no common prostitute. She comes from a good family."

Gilbert raised a brow. "And yet she would marry you without seeing—"

"I am done speaking of this." Loftus turned from his brother and strode down the hall in the same direction the maids had gone. The tones of their soft humming reached his ears as he passed the rooms they were working in, swiping their rags across the windowpanes and batting at cobwebs in the corners of the ceiling.

Though he moved away from his brother, his comments lingered. How would Loftus's wife feel about his scars? Would she run away at the altar upon first seeing them? Had she the temerity to stay, could she ever grow to love him when he had such a face?

He wished for everything to be perfect for her, but he could never be perfect himself.

CHAPTER 4

*O*ne week later, Catherine was summoned to her father's study after the morning callers had gone on their way. Her mother had forced Catherine to keep Giles in her room, no matter how Catherine wished to have him at her side to greet Mrs. Colborne and Mrs. Hill. Those women held a ferocity as tangible as her mother and would unsheathe their claws in the blink of an eye if Catherine merely clinked her teaspoon against her cup.

Catherine walked straight from the drawing room down the hall to her father's study with its dark oak door. Knocking lightly, she waited for him to bid her to enter, her nerves flaring to life.

Why did he wish to speak with her? Was this about Giles? She'd been taking turns with Susan to tend his daily needs. So far, he really wasn't any trouble at all. He was proving to be a rather quiet pup, with the occasional howl escaping if he was left alone too long. Had her father changed his mind about her keeping him?

"Enter!"

Her father's bark startled her from her thoughts. She took a deep breath in an effort to calm herself and entered the room she rarely visited.

"There you are." Her father eyed her from behind his regal mahogany desk—the thing nearly taking up the entirety of the room. He glanced back down at a piece of foolscap before him and scribbled something down. "Sit."

It was no friendly invitation, but a command. That was the case with all of her father's words. Indeed, Catherine had come to wonder if he had ever spoken anything else. Perhaps he'd never even asked her mother to marry him—simply ordered it.

She did as he told her and sat in one of the dark-green cushioned chairs before the desk, gripping the sides in preparation for what he was about to say.

Her father continued writing, the gold-leaf clock on the mantel ticking away. Catherine's gaze darted this way and that, from the curiosity cabinet in the far corner of the room to the tortoiseshell snuff box perched precariously on the edge of the desk. Waiting was unbearable.

"Father?" Her voice was only a murmur.

"Hmm?" He tipped his head up, flicking his gaze in her direction. "Oh, you. Yes. You're to be married." He turned back to the foolscap again, the scratching of his quill now almost deafening.

The air in Catherine's lungs flew out of her. Her whole body stiffened. A chill came over her as though she'd just jumped back into the Serpentine River. "M-married?"

Her father remained quiet. He didn't even look at her.

Her hands began to ache. She looked down at them. Her knuckles were white as she gripped the chair arms. She forced herself to let go. "T-to whom? Who has sought my—"

"The Earl of Hardwicke."

Catherine's mind reeled, her arms trembling. "I've never even heard of the man. How—"

"It doesn't matter." Her father set his quill aside and clasped his hands together. "You will be married to him. He has a title, and through your marriage, your mother and I will finally get what we desire."

Tears stung the back of Catherine's eyes. "When? When am I to marry this earl?"

"In three days." His voice was cold.

She raised her hand to her chest, her breaths coming quicker. The tears began to flow from her eyes. She had desired a love match since she'd learned of Aunt Marjorie's. Her aunt had been her true self and had found someone who loved her all the same. Now, it seemed, Catherine would never be given the same chance at love, for she'd be pawned off in a marriage of convenience. She scoffed inwardly, bitterness flowing from the depths of her body. It was very *inconvenient*—for her.

Would she take the hand she'd been dealt? Could she not attempt to change her father's mind? Never had she been able to before. She had to try, or her life would never be the same. After all, she had no idea what the Earl of Hardwicke's disposition was. What if he was terribly cruel? Somehow, he'd managed to get into a business arrangement with her father, and that didn't speak well for him, certainly.

"Father, please. *Please*, Father. Do not make me marry him."

Her father shook his head. "You will marry him, Catherine. Do not try to sway me."

"I do not wish to marry him, Father. I will marry someone else, but I do not wish to marry someone I do not know." She wiped the tears from her face.

"Such as Lord Balfour? Or do you mean Lord Fortescue? No, Catherine. You have missed your chances to marry here. All of London knows of your folly."

She stood and reached across the desk, grabbing his arm in a desperate attempt. "Please, Father! Please!"

He wrenched away, knocking the snuffbox to the ground. Its

contents spilled onto the carpeted floor. "It is done! All is finalized. You are to be married in three days."

He jumped from his leather chair and pulled the bell on the wall. Tetley popped his head into the room, his face a mask of politeness. Her father scowled at Catherine before flicking his gaze to the butler. "Tell Catherine's maid to begin packing Catherine's trousseau at once. She will be leaving this evening."

Catherine ran to her room, hardly seeing where she was going past the blur of tears in her eyes. How could this be happening to her?

She entered her room and pulled the chamber pot out from under her bed, falling to her knees and leaning over it, but nothing came. She closed her eyes. The nausea was the sort that could not be gotten rid of by casting up one's accounts—it lingered only to torment, and only heaven knew when relief would come.

A quick tapping preceded something cold and wet pressing against her arm. Catherine peered to the side and raised her arm. Giles sat on the floor, the excess skin over his eyes drooping in an adorable manner. He laid down next to her and gave a quiet bark, his long ears almost touching the ground. Catherine pulled him into her lap and leaned back against the side of her bed, resting her head against her mattresses. She stretched her legs across the floorboards, and he settled immediately.

God, let me be as content and as at peace as Giles is. I fear this marriage may prove to be the end of my happiness. Let it not be so, God. Please, let the earl be a good man. Let him treat me well, and let our marriage be one based on respect and friendship—maybe even love. Let my husband not turn out to be like Lord Balfour. Please.

Susan knocked on the door and entered, followed by two footmen carrying Catherine's trunks. She stood and brushed off her skirt.

Susan's face was grim. She didn't speak until the footmen

had set the trunks down and left. "Tetley told me we're to leave at four. We'll stay at an inn tonight—"

"Do you know where the earl lives, Susan?" Catherine swallowed, her shoulders easing slightly.

"According to John, the coachman, we're driving to Cumbria. The day we arrive is the day ye are to be wed."

Cumbria? My, but that was a distance to travel. 'Twas no wonder, then, that her father was having her leave this evening. "Have you ever been up north?" Catherine undid the latches on her trunks and opened the lids.

Susan shooed her away from the task. "I haven't, but we'll soon see it with our own eyes." She opened Catherine's armoire and began to fold her gowns, placing them within the trunk with care.

Hours later, Catherine stood on the front steps in her traveling gown, Giles in her arms and Susan next to her. Footmen loaded the trunks onto the carriage, the horses stomping their feet, eager to set off. Neither her mother nor father were there to see her go, though Catherine wasn't particularly bothered by that.

As the footman strapped the last trunk onto the back of the carriage, Catherine gave him a brief smile of gratitude and turned to Tetley, who'd been overseeing the entire process. "Thank you, Tetley. I do hope your days are not monotonous after I leave."

He bowed, clasping his wrinkled hands behind his back. "I hope for the same. You will be missed."

Susan hugged the man and whispered something in his ear, then rejoined Catherine, tears in the girl's eyes. "He's been like a father to me." She straightened the white cap on her head.

Catherine patted her arm, her heart sinking. She dipped her chin. "I'm sorry you have to come with me and leave your family and friends. I am, however, very grateful for your presence."

Susan pulled a handkerchief from her sleeve and wiped her eyes. "It will be a change for us both, miss. It might not be an unpleasant one."

One of the footmen let down the steps to the carriage and helped Catherine into it, followed by a sniffling Susan. Not long after, they were on their way toward the North Country.

Countryside greeted them sometime after, for the outskirts of London could never last forever. She'd only been outside of the city a handful of times and, then, only to a neighboring county. The thought of traveling to such a distant one as Cumbria was almost overwhelming, but she was eager to see new sights, if nothing else.

Giles slept soundly in her lap, his head on his paws. Susan had pulled out some knitting and was currently working on that. Catherine peered back out the glass pane of the window, her mind unable to focus on the beautiful landscape. The expanse of lush grass would have to be admired by some other traveler, for all she could think of was her impending marriage to a man she had never before met—in a place she had never before been. She was expected to live her life with the Earl of Hardwicke, but she hadn't the foggiest idea as to what he looked like, what his temperament was, or how he spent his time. What if they got on terribly? What if he hated her from the start?

Lord Balfour's cruelty came back to her with shuddering clarity. His rude remarks. His harsh comments. The violence he used to control her. She'd become a puppet under Lord Balfour's command. Had her spirit been so weak that she'd been easy to crush? Keeping him pleased had become her goal —above all others. It was easy to lose interest in the fight when one saw the results so clearly on the body.

That was when she'd decided that she'd bend—when the violence had become physical. For if she didn't act the willow, she'd break like the oak.

Would it be the same with the Earl of Hardwicke?

CHAPTER 5

"*M*iss."

Catherine groaned.

"Miss, wake up."

Catherine opened her eyes at Susan's added shake. The sky was almost dark on their second day of travel. She never knew that sitting in a carriage for hours on end, only stretching when they changed horses, could be so wearying.

She licked her dry lips as Giles squirmed in her lap. "Where are we?"

"The Hogshead Inn. We'll be staying here for the evening."

She hugged Giles closer and alighted from the carriage, then brushed a few stray hairs from her face. Lanterns illuminated a path leading to the door of the inn and the ostlers who rushed forward to tend to the horses and carriage.

Catherine strode down the path, covering a yawn with her gloved hand, and entered the inn, Susan on her heels. The inside smelled of ale and beef and the fire that was lit in the hearth at one end of the room. Men sat at tables and in corners with glasses in hand, some of them looking the worse for wear. Their eyes seared into her as she moved forward.

The innkeeper—a thin man with a greying beard and bald head—greeted them by displaying a mouth full of crooked teeth. "Good evening. Welcome to the Hogshead. I'm Mr. Browne. What can I provide ye with?"

Catherine straightened her shoulders, trying to appear more confident than she felt. "We'd like a room, please, and dinner as well."

"Certainly." He looked over her shoulder at the door. "Ye may settle yerselves at a table, and I'll give yer brother the key."

Catherine's eyebrows furrowed. "I don't have a brother."

The man blushed. "My apologies. Yer father, then."

Catherine hugged Giles closer to her. "My father did not come with us. We traveled alone from London."

Mr. Browne's eyes widened. "You mean to tell me that yer father let you come all the way to Cumbria without male protection?"

Catherine ducked her chin. Her voice lowered. "Well, we have our coachman..."

"Pah! Much good a London coachman is against the likes of one of these men." He nodded toward the men in the tavern. "Ye'd best be careful, miss." He handed her the key to a room and bid them to sit anywhere they'd like. "My wife'll be out with yer dinner in a short while."

Catherine and Susan stepped over to a small unoccupied table in the corner of the room, far away from the other occupants. She tried to make herself as unnoticeable as possible—pulling her pelisse closer around her shoulders and leaning into the shadows. None of the people at the other inns they'd visited had made her feel so conspicuously alone, nor had they questioned her lack of a male companion. The inn they'd stayed at the night before, of course, had also had many other female patrons.

Minutes later, the innkeeper's wife—or the woman Catherine assumed was her—came out with two steaming bowls of beef stew and crusts of bread. She followed this with two mugs of ale and a cheery smile. "Is there anythin' else I can get ye?"

Catherine gave her a grin, her stomach rumbling at the sight of food. "No, thank you. This looks lovely."

After Mrs. Browne left, Catherine and Susan spared no time in feasting. When they were done, Catherine sat back in the worn wooden chair, her stomach full and body beginning to feel the drowsiness that comes after ingesting a large meal.

A new person entered the tavern wearing a dark-green cloak, the hood shadowing his face. Strange. It was a cool spring night, yes, but not so cold as to necessitate the wearing of a cloak.

The man sat in the adjacent corner, and Mrs. Browne bustled over and took his order, depositing a glass of ale in front of him not long after. The person lifted the mug to the shadow where their face was, but Catherine was never afforded a view. How odd. Mrs. Browne had seemed unfazed. Was this a regular patron here?

Susan was nodding off in her chair. They'd better be going upstairs before they fell asleep right there at the table. No one wished for an empty bowl as a pillow. Just as Catherine stood up, a man appeared at her side.

"What is a pretty lass like you doin' here?" He stepped close to her. Too close.

Catherine backed up a step, bumping into her chair. Her shoulders tensed. "I...er...I'm traveling through."

His breath reeked of ale as he leaned forward, his eyes unfocused. "Travelin', eh? Well, you could travel with me a little way down the road to my home—"

"N-no." A shiver ran down her back as her stomach tightened, anxiety flaring within her. She held her breath against the pungent odor that seeped from his person, leaning backward as far as she could from him. She was cornered, just as she had been those months ago in the drawing room with Lord Balfour.

He placed a hand on her arm, and every inch of her skin seemed to scream. Her breathing became shallow. If she fainted, she wouldn't be able to protect herself.

"Are your ears full of dust?" A rich voice sounded, the tone dry.

Her antagonist turned to the side, revealing the cloaked person, now only feet from them. She could only just make out the man's eyes in the dim lighting. He wasn't looking at her.

"This woman said no, and yet you continue to behave in such a manner toward her. Are you deaf? Perhaps just incomparably stupid?" The cloaked man propped his hands on his hips.

The drunk one dropped his hand from Catherine's arm and pointed a finger at the cloaked man. He scowled. "You'd better stay out of this."

The cloaked man shrugged. "Not when you are disturbing this lady. Now, will you leave her alone, or will I be forced to do something I'd wish not to do?"

The drunk man lifted a fist and aimed at the cloaked man's head.

Susan jumped from her chair, giving a small shriek.

The cloaked man avoided the punch, but his hood fell back. Catherine almost gasped, for two long scars ran across the left side of his face—one from his eyebrow to his chin and the other from his cheek to the corner of his jaw. They intersected like an X in the middle, reminding her of a mark on a map where treasure would be found.

In retaliation, the scarred man threw a punch of his own. His fist connected with the drunk man's nose with a crack. The man sprawled on the floor with a groan, blood pouring from his now-crooked nose.

Catherine's savior lifted his hood over his head again and moved closer to Catherine and Susan. "Are you all right, miss?"

Catherine nodded, her heart racing inside her ribcage. When she'd been able to see his face, the man had been handsome. The scars had added a mysteriousness that made her want to know more. It was a shame he'd covered them up. Did he have a reason to hide his identity? "Thank you. I don't know how I would have gotten myself out of that situation without your help."

The man bowed. "'Twas nothing. I am glad I was able to be of service."

The commotion had caught the notice of all the other patrons, their conversations having ceased once the drunkard had fallen.

Mrs. Browne rushed out of the kitchen. "Out! I won't have fighting in my inn." She poked a finger in the direction of the scarred man, a stern set to her frown. "You must leave at once. Won't have the Hogshead formin' a reputation of brawlin'."

The cloaked man locked eyes with Catherine for a moment, then turned, mumbling his apologies to Mrs. Browne. He paid for his ale and left. Mr. Browne, who'd been cautiously watching the scene unfold, strode over and nudged the drunk man with the toe of his boot. He urged him to leave while his wife reprimanded the lout, blood still dripping down the man's face. He eventually got up with a few curses and stumbled past tables, managing to find the inn door and letting himself out into the night.

"I'm sorry ye ladies had to witness that." Mrs. Browne heaved a sigh and placed a hand on her chest. "The gentlemen who come here don't succumb to fisticuffs too often, but it does happen on occasion. It's a bout of misfortune that it had to be on the night of your arrival."

Catherine stepped forward, giving the woman a small smile. "It's quite all right, Mrs. Browne. Susan and I haven't seen anything so exciting since we left London." Although the maid wrung her hands and bit her lip. "However, we are a bit tired from our travels. Might you show us to our room?"

"Oh, but of course! Follow me." Mrs. Browne grabbed a lit candle and led them up the stairs to a long hall with dark wooden doors on either side. With each step they took, the floor creaked.

Mrs. Browne stopped and gestured at the fourth door. "This is your room." She retrieved a key from the ring attached to her apron and inserted it into the lock, turning it with a small click. She pushed the door open and put the key back into her pocket. "Ye'll wish to keep your door locked, of course—especially after what ye've just seen downstairs." She gestured to the corner of the room. "Yer coachman brought yer luggage in earlier, as ye can see. I'll have our maid Hannah bring in warm water in the morning. Is there anything else ye require?"

Catherine straightened her shoulders and gave the woman a smile. "I do not believe so. Indeed, you have been very helpful. Thank you."

"Ye are very welcome." Mrs. Browne's grey skirts swished as she left, shutting the door quietly behind her.

Catherine yawned and began to pluck the pins from her head. "Help me undress, would you, Susan?"

Susan soon had Catherine in only her chemise. Then the maid brushed out Catherine's hair and tied it in a braid.

Catherine got into the lumpy bed and pulled the coverlet over herself. Tomorrow was her wedding day. In the morning, she would travel to the church and be wed to the Earl of Hardwicke.

She closed her eyes and prayed, Susan's steady breaths coming from the other side of the room.

Please, God. If I am not meant to do this, let me know now. I will go back. I will go against my parents if You do not wish for me to do this.

Nothing. No words came to her. No voice. No sign that she should turn back.

So, then, You wish for me to go forward with this? This is something I should do?

An overwhelming sense of peace came over her. No longer was she worried about what was to come. God would never let anything happen that she could not handle, for He was her father, and He knew what she was capable of.

She leaned her head into her pillow. If only the image of the cloaked man could go from her mind as easily as her worries.

CHAPTER 6

$\mathcal{T}$he next morning, Catherine woke to the sound of an elephant crashing around the room. She opened her eyes. Oh. It was Susan.

The maid was bright-eyed, her fair skin almost white in the morning light that flooded through the windowpanes. She crossed the room to Catherine, a pink dress in her arms. "Oh, ye're up! Good. Do ye think this one fitting for today?"

Catherine rubbed her eyes and sat up in bed. "I do love that rosy hue. Yes, it suits me very well, I think." In truth, it was her favorite dress. She might as well wear it for her wedding day.

Susan squealed. "I thought ye might say that. Come, miss, there's little time."

Catherine washed her face, arms, and neck in the basin, and Susan assisted with her clothing. She then sat in a wooden chair in front of a faded mirror, and Susan brushed out her hair as she had the night before, this time pinning up most of it into a low bun at the base of her neck and leaving two large curls to frame Catherine's heart-shaped face.

She also pulled Catherine's clover perfume from her trunk and dabbed it on her wrists and neck before clasping her pearl necklace around Catherine's throat. "Ye're ready, miss."

They went downstairs, and as they made their way across the tavern, John stood up from a table, having just finished his breakfast.

Catherine greeted him with a smile. "Good morning. Would you please see that the carriage is readied and my trunks are brought down?"

"That I will, miss." He nodded and went about doing so, setting a few coins on the table for his meal.

Catherine found Mr. Browne at the table near the front of the inn. "Good morning, Mr. Browne." She lifted the key to her room from her reticule and handed it to him, along with payment for the room. "Thank you for your kindness."

Mrs. Browne appeared at her husband's side, her eyes wide. "It's been a pleasure havin' ye—but, no breakfast, dearies? And where are you goin', lookin' so lovely?"

Catherine's face heated, and the butterflies within her took flight. "I'm to be married today. We'll eat breakfast after with our guests, I think." That was normally what happened at the weddings she'd been to.

"Married?" Mrs. Browne's jaw dropped.

Catherine nodded as John lumbered down the stairs with a trunk. "I've only one more to get, miss. The carriage has been brought around. We'll be ready to leave in a minute."

Catherine thanked the Brownes again for their hospitality and turned on her heel, exiting the inn. Thankfully, they hadn't asked who the groom was, for if they knew him, they'd likely share their opinions, and Catherine wanted to go into her marriage having no opinions formed about him at all. She would form her own, based on her experiences with him—not on the stories people told her that may or may not be true.

Shortly thereafter, Catherine and Susan were back on the road, the horses pulling the carriage at a steady clip. Catherine looked out the window, eager to see the landscape of the county she was now to be living in. She'd missed it yesterday, as she'd been sleeping, but now she was able to take it all in.

Grass-covered hills dotted with trees and boulders greeted her, the morning air filled with a peaceful fog that stayed low to the ground. On their right, they passed a small lake, its dark blue waters like a mirror in the morning calm. An egret carefully waded in the shallow area near the banks.

They trundled along, the scenery something out of a storybook. Catherine had never seen its match—London could not compare.

Susan inhaled sharply next to her. "Miss, we must stop the carriage!"

"Wha—"

"The flowers along the road, miss. They'd look perfect in your hair." Susan's tone brooked no argument, so Catherine leaned her head out of the carriage window and called for John to stop.

As soon as the carriage wheels had ceased moving, Susan hopped out and rushed over to the flowers, picking small pink and white ones from amongst the tall grass. She returned to the carriage, and as soon as she stepped inside, began to weave the pretty petals in a sort of crown atop Catherine's head. What was left over, she handed to Catherine with a smile. "For ye to hold as ye walk in the church. They smell very nice, don't they? It isn't fancy, but it'll do."

Catherine placed her hand on Susan's arm. "Thank you. They are wonderful." The petals were soft and delicate, the pink blooms matching her dress almost exactly. "You make an excellent bridesmaid, Susan."

The maid's cheeks flushed, and she ducked her chin.

Catherine called for John to continue toward the church, now truly feeling like a bride.

CHAPTER 7

*L*oftus stood at the front of the church next to the vicar and twisted his signet ring around his little finger, uncomfortably warm even in the open space. He tugged at his too-tight cravat and tried to imagine what his bride might look like. Would she have dark-brown hair like him? Or maybe she'd have light hair? What color were her eyes? Blue? Brown?

When she entered the church and saw the scars marring his face, how would she react? She'd probably scream and run away, canceling their agreement. For all his luck, she'd not even make it two paces into this holy sanctuary.

His stomach tightened as Loftus caught his brother's smug smile from the corner of his eye...as if Gilbert discerned his fears.

Loftus groaned inwardly. Had this been a terrible mistake? He certainly didn't want Gilbert to inherit the earldom after he was gone, but to set himself up for such unequivocal humiliation seemed foolish, indeed. He shook his head. He couldn't fail in this. Not when his brother was the other option for the estate, with his IOU's and devil-may-care attitude.

Loftus ran a hand through his hair.

"Do stop your fidgeting." His mother's tone was harsh and unyielding from where she sat in the first pew. She wore a dark-purple gown and matching bonnet, her face all deep lines and stricture. It definitely wasn't the look of excitement one would expect from a mother on her son's wedding day.

Loftus clasped his hands behind his back, the sound of horses' hooves and the jangle of metal coming from outside. His limbs seized. She was here.

The church seemed to get even warmer. The pews before him stretched on forever toward the double doors. Light peeked through the large circular window on the back wall, illuminating the path down the center of the church that his bride would walk—if she wasn't frightened away, that was.

Feminine voices sounded from outside the doors and then the click of the handle. Loftus's heart beat fast, only getting quicker by the moment.

Finally, one of the doors was pushed open, and a short woman wearing an apron and cap stepped into the church and held it aside. Loftus could see nothing in the rectangle of light that was revealed. He held his breath.

In the blink of an eye, the silhouette of a woman was there, light all around her. This was his bride. Seconds passed before she moved through the doorway and began to walk down the aisle.

Loftus exhaled slowly. Before him was the woman from last night, and she was just as beautiful now as she had been then. She held a bouquet of *Lychnis flos-cuculi* and *Convallaria majalis*. Both were also strung in a crown around her head, her dark ringlets framing her fair face.

Her pale pink gown had a modest neckline with white embroidery decorating the top and the ends of her puffed sleeves. The woman moved with a graceful determination, her steps quiet and her head held high. She met Loftus's eye, and her lips pulled up into a small smile. His heart did a flip in his chest as his eyes widened.

Where was the screaming? Where was the running away? Where was the fainting at the sight of his ugly scars? This woman appeared entirely unfazed. Truthfully, there seemed almost an excitement in her eyes as she moved toward him. Was she looking forward to marrying him? That couldn't be.

He glanced over at his brother, whose mouth was open. Was he as surprised as Loftus was?

According to the woman's father—a Mr. Blynn, or something similar—the girl had been jilted by her previous betrothed and was also considered too old to marry into society. From what Loftus was seeing, however, the men in London must be imbibing too much. This woman was more than pleasing to the eye and couldn't be much above twenty. If she'd truly been jilted by her betrothed, , then it'd likely been the man's own pride that had caused him to separate himself from her, for this woman seemed as though she could do no harm.

All too soon, she stood before him and his scars were visible to her in all their unpleasantness. She turned to face him. He listened to her steady breathing, waiting for some sort of sharp inhale or pause that would indicate she'd taken notice of them. Nothing of the sort occurred.

He lifted his eyes to her face. Her hazel gaze was upon him, and her cheeks were a rosy hue. Her nose was small and rounded at the end, and her lips were pink and full. The desire to step closer to her was immediate, but he ignored it, turning his head to the vicar.

The man nodded and opened his book before him. "Dearly beloved, we are gathered here in the sight of God…"

The rest of the vicar's words faded as Loftus studied his soon-to-be bride once more. With her nearness came the sweet scent of *Trifolium repens*, known as white clover to most. The pleasant scent had always been one of his favorites—a simple, earthy aroma of the countryside. She remained where she stood, steady on her feet. It didn't appear she was going to be fleeing, after all. How would it be to have a wife at his side? Would it be enjoyable to have a feminine presence near throughout the day?

Loftus shook his head inwardly. He was being foolish. Surely, she was marrying him only for his title and money. A woman as beautiful as she didn't marry someone with a face like his. He wouldn't harbor any hopes of theirs growing into a love match.

"'...to prove his allegation: then the solemnization must be deferred, until such time as the truth be tried.'" The vicar paused, eyeing Gilbert and their mother. When neither spoke up, he continued. "Loftus Albion Cromwell, Fourth Earl of Hardwicke, wilt thou have this woman to thy wedded wife, to live together after God's ordinance in the holy estate of matrimony? Wilt thou love her..."

As the vicar listed out all that Loftus must do, he promised to himself he would take care of his wife to the best of his abilities, even if their marriage did prove to be one in name only. He and this woman were binding themselves together permanently, and that was not a decision he made lightly.

"...so long as ye both shall live?"

"I will." Loftus met his bride's eyes, his tone earnest.

The vicar turned to look at her. "Catherine Theodosia Blynn, wilt thou have this man to thy..."

Catherine. That was a pretty name. Loftus's pulse began to race as the vicar told Catherine of her responsibilities. Would she cry off? Was this the point where she'd realize what a terrible mistake she was about to make?

"I will."

Loftus stilled. She'd agreed. His mind was in a daze as the vicar made them to join right hands. She placed her small hand into his, and he held it with care. It was warm through the fabric of their gloves. His anxiety ebbed as he promised to love and cherish Catherine in sickness and health, for richer and for poorer.

She repeated the words—albeit with a few differences—and plighted him her troth. A warm feeling grew within him.

The vicar stared at him, and it was a few seconds before Loftus realized what he was supposed to do next. He stuffed his hand into his coat pocket and fished out the ring he'd had made—a simple golden band with a leaf engraved on the top. He handed it to Catherine.

Her eyes were wide as she took it from him, and she seemed almost hesitant to hand it to the vicar, but she gave it over. He placed it on his holy book and handed it back to Loftus, allowing him to place it on Catherine's ring finger. Loftus hadn't expected for it to fit properly—after all, he hadn't known the woman's ring size—but it fit perfectly. Everything seemed right as he slid the ring onto her slender finger.

"'With this ring I thee wed, with my body I thee worship, and with all my worldly goods I thee endow. In the name of the Father, and of the Son, and of the Holy Ghost. Amen.'"

They knelt, and the vicar prayed over them, Catherine's skirt brushing Loftus's knees. His hand felt empty. He wished to hold hers again and to feel its warmth. Loftus scoffed inwardly. Was he so starved for affection that this was how his body responded to the merest touch?

It didn't matter, for they were soon up again and holding hands.

The vicar spoke. "'Those whom God hath joined together let no man put asunder.' Forasmuch as Loftus Albion Cromwe..."

The vicar's words were drowned out by Loftus's pulse as he realized the ceremony was nearly over. Soon he would be on his way back to Blackfern Manor with Catherine as his carriage companion—along with his mother and brother, of course.

Catherine squeezed his hand, and he looked down at her, her eyes bright. A small smile twisted her lips, and Loftus fought to smack the butterflies in his stomach back down.

There'd be an entirely new person living under his roof. A woman. A wife.

~

*C*atherine's heart was beating so hard as the vicar sang Psalm 128, surely, the others could hear it. To think, in mere minutes, she'd be married to the dashing man who'd so boldly saved her at the inn—the man with the mysterious scars on his face that only added to his appearance. It was enough to make her swoon.

After the vicar led them through Psalm 67 and she learned that Loftus had a wonderful baritone, the vicar blessed them and their future children—though Catherine wasn't quite sure how many of those there were going to be. He hadn't looked at her for more than two minutes since she'd entered the church, so they had work to do before this union could become a marriage in the true sense of the word.

"I now declare you man and wife." The vicar gave a great smile, and the woman sitting in the first pew clapped unenthusiastically. Catherine's husband held his arm out to her, and she wrapped her hand around it, enjoying being next to the man who had been her protector.

He smelled like...something difficult to describe. Plants? Earth? It was the smell of crushed leaves in autumn, when they scurried amongst the grass and along paths. It was marvelous.

They moved from the altar and signed their names in the parish register. His writing was long and close together, while her letters were short and rather looped. It was interesting how they contrasted. The parish clerk congratulated them and bid them good day as they walked out the door and into the sunshine, the two guests following. Susan trailed a little way behind, looking unsure of what to do with herself.

Catherine's new husband stopped a few steps outside the church and pierced her with his light-blue eyes, raising a hand toward the woman in the purple gown. "This is my mother, the Dowager Countess of Hardwicke."

The woman only nodded at Catherine. No hint of a smile raised her thin lips. Catherine swallowed and gave the woman a curtsy. Had she had higher hopes for her son's marriage than a merchant's daughter?

Loftus gestured to the man who stood next to her. He looked similar to Loftus but had lighter brown tresses and was shorter than his brother. This man's gaze was the sky, where Loftus's was ice. "This is my brother, Lord Berkley."

Lord Berkley—in contrast to his mother—bowed over her hand with a smile. "Blackfern Manor is blessed to have such a pretty countess at the helm. Loftus is a fortunate man."

A burning sensation rose to Catherine's cheeks, and she almost thought Loftus pulled her closer to his side. "Thank you, my lord."

After a moment of awkward silence, Catherine spoke up. "Shall we be going to the wedding breakfast?"

The dowager crossed her arms in front of her, her tone disapproving. "There is no wedding breakfast."

"Oh." Catherine flinched at the woman's scowl. The ceremony had taken some time, and her stomach was empty. She'd rather looked forward to a hearty meal, though now she'd been made to look the fool in front of her husband and new family. As though it had been waiting for this very moment, her stomach gave an embarrassing grumble. Pangs of heat skittered around her face and neck.

Lord Berkley fought back a smile, his lip quirking, and the dowager's fierce expression only seemed to worsen.

Loftus put his hand on hers where it rested on his arm and

tilted his head in her direction. "The manor is only a short distance away. Come, my mother and brother can take my family's carriage whilst you and I can take yours, along with your maid." His voice was calm as he began to lead her toward her carriage.

Thank goodness. "Susan." Catherine nodded toward her maid.

"Hmm?" He raised an eyebrow as he helped her inside.

"My maid's name is Susan." Catherine straightened her skirts around her legs.

"Oh, indeed."

The commotion as they opened the door of the carriage startled Giles, whom they'd left sleeping on the floor of the carriage when they went into the church. Now that they were back, he gave a happy howl.

Her husband's eyes widened at the noise. "You have a dog."

She picked up Giles, holding him close. "I do." And she wasn't about to be parted from him either. If her husband tried to make her get rid of him, she'd...well, she didn't quite know what she'd do, but she'd do it.

Surprisingly, he didn't make any move to take the dog from her. "What's his name?" He reached out to the pup, scratching him between the ears.

"His name is Giles. He's only a few weeks old now." She raised Giles up to show him.

Her husband nodded, examining the dog more closely. "He's some type of hound, I think. He'll be a handsome dog when he grows."

Giles howled and squirmed in Catherine's arms, nipping playfully at Loftus's fingers.

She laughed. "He's taken offense to that, my lord, for he believes himself to be rather handsome right now."

Her husband's lips quirked up, and he patted Giles on the head, avoiding his little teeth.

The earl helped Susan into the carriage and jumped in behind her, settling himself across from the women before knocking on the roof to set the vehicle in motion. "I'm sorry about the lack of a wedding breakfast. I'll be sure to have food brought up for you when we arrive at Blackfern." He rubbed a hand across the back of his neck.

"That would be much appreciated, my lord." Catherine examined his face. His clean-shaven jaw and his long, stately nose. His cheekbones were high, and his lips were a pale pink —not thin nor wide, but just so. He appeared as though he were a statue that had walked out of the museum in London, but he was flesh and blood.

"Loftus."

His voice brought her out of her thoughts. He was looking directly at her. She cleared her throat. "Pardon me?"

"You may call me Loftus. We are husband and wife, after all."

A light of hope pricked in her chest, spreading outward from there. Her lips couldn't help but rise as she tested his name on them. "Loftus. A unique name. Might I say it suits you? You may call me Cate. It is what my aunt calls me."

"Then Cate it shall be." The barest of smiles crossed his face, and a surge of triumph buzzed through her.

Shortly thereafter, they arrived at her husband's home— Blackfern Manor—which was built of grey stone with wings on either side and countless windows looking out like eyes. Beech and ash trees surrounded the home, though the front lawn was expansive and held the beginnings of a beautiful flower garden.

As the carriage slowed to a stop in front of the grey stone steps, a footman dressed in dark-blue livery came forth to open the door and let the steps down. Loftus hopped out and held out his hand for her. Susan held Giles behind her, waiting for Catherine to step down. As Catherine placed her hand in her new husband's and alighted from the carriage, sparks seemed to run through her fingertips—a sensation she'd never felt before. How strange that a man she'd never met until yesterday could make her feel such a way.

Servants lined the steps, their hands clasped behind their backs, shoulders straight and heads high.

"May I have everyone's attention?" When her husband raised his voice, the staff stood straighter, if that were even possible. "I'd like to introduce you to my wife, the Countess of Hardwicke."

Suddenly, all of their eyes were on her. Her stomach tensed, and she held a little tighter to Loftus's arm. Countess... Would she meet their expectations, or would she disappoint them?

Loftus escorted her toward a middle-aged man with a grey mustache and thinning hair. "This, Cath—Cate—is Blackfern Manor's butler, Bromley."

The man smiled, his eyes bright. "'Tis a pleasure to have you here. If you need anything at all, I am at your assistance."

"Thank you, Bromley." His earnest manner eased the tension in her shoulders.

Next, Loftus led her to a plump woman—perhaps a bit older than the butler—with grey hair and rosy cheeks. The corner of Loftus's lips quirked up. "This is our housekeeper, Mrs. Stonehill. She's borne witness to many of my mishaps over the years and would be happy to tell you about them, too, I'm sure."

The woman chuckled and reached out to pat his arm. "That I would, dear boy. That I would."

Catherine's own lips raised, her heart lifting as she watched her husband interact with his staff. This was not a man who would treat her unkindly. "Then I suppose you and I will be in company quite often, Mrs. Stonehill. I'd like to hear more than a few of those."

Her husband turned his head at this, his lips parted. He almost appeared surprised at her response. Had he not been serious when he'd said the words? Did he not think Catherine would want to get to know him better? Why wouldn't she?

At that moment, the carriage conveying Lord Berkley and the dowager pulled up the drive and rolled to a stop, the two of them exiting with their feet crunching on the pebbles. They stood to the side, Lord Berkley with a look of boredom on his face and the dowager with an expression of irritation as Catherine met the rest of the staff. Never once did her new husband treat them as though they were his inferiors, and never did Catherine receive the impression that they were afraid of him. That spoke very highly of him, indeed. She didn't forget the way Lord Balfour's servants had flinched around him, scurrying around corners whenever he entered a room.

So far, the two men seemed very different, but would that impression remain once she got to know her new husband better? Lord Balfour had not seemed a devil upon first acquaintance either.

CHAPTER 8

The dowager and Lord Berkley left them as soon as they'd entered the foyer with its dark oak-paneled walls and black-and-white checkered floor. A suit of armor stood in the corner of the room, as if waiting to defend the inhabitants of the manor at any moment, and a tapestry portraying a hunting scene hung on the wall opposite the entrance.

"The footmen are bringing your trunks up to your chambers."

At her groom's words, Catherine froze in the act of handing her bonnet to Bromley, her gaze darting to Loftus. Chambers? Her pulse increased. Her breathing came quicker as she thought of what she'd have to do when they got there. Her aunt had once told her—very vaguely—about what to expect, but her mother hadn't prepared her at all. She wasn't ready. She didn't even know him. Her heart thumped heavily in her chest as she thought of what had happened with Lord Balfour. Her eyes began to sting with the oncoming of tears. She—

Loftus pulled her aside, concern written in his eyes. "Your chambers are attached to mine. Our rooms share a door. But I promise, Cate, I do not expect for you—for us—to... That is...I do not expect you in my bed this evening, nor any other evening. I also don't expect to be in your bed, if you understand my meaning."

Catherine blinked rapidly, her face going up in flames. Was she hearing him correctly? "My lord?"

He grunted and pinched the bridge of his nose, closing his eyes for a moment. "I'm making a muddle of this. Forgive me. What I mean to say is that I understand that this is a marriage of convenience. It is not a love match. I suppose someday we will need heirs, but now is not that time. For the foreseeable future, the marriage can remain unconsummated."

His face was all seriousness, with nary a lifted lip or playful gleam in the eye. She clasped her hands together before her, unsure of what to say. He was being very thoughtful in allowing her time before bearing his children, but how long would that actually be? For now, her heart slowed its pace.

"Thank you."

He nodded, pressing his lips together. "I'll show you to your chamber."

He led her up the wooden stairs at the side of the room, their footsteps muffled by a vibrant red carpet that ran their length and continued down the hall. A shield hung on the wall, and nearby was a large painting of a woman in expensive dress, its frame ornate and gilded. They passed multiple doors, all made from the same dark wood, and eventually stopped at one at the end of the corridor.

Her husband pushed it open and directed her inside. Dark-blue carpet covered the floor of the large room with gold accents. Tapestries covered the white walls abundantly in villages and dancing scenes. A sizable mirror gleamed on the wall next to the stately four-poster bed, its oak wood carved into symmetrical square shapes. She wouldn't have been surprised if Henry VIII had slept on it. It was certainly large enough to hold him.

Her trunks sat at the end of it. A table with a basin and jug of water waited beneath the mirror, and a dressing table with another mirror sat at the other side of the room. The large stone hearth sat empty on this warm day, with chairs gathered around.

"Do you like it?" Loftus's voice was soft. "If there's anything you do not see, I can get it for you."

She put her hands on her hips. "It is the finest room I have ever seen. From what I can tell, I shan't need a single thing."

There was that small smile again. That little quirk of the lips that made her heart pick up its pace. Why it had already become a need for her to bring it out of him, she did not know, but she would continue trying to do so.

He walked to the side of the room to a door she'd overlooked and turned the handle. As the door creaked open, she peeked inside, pushing her spectacles farther up her nose. It was another room—about the same size as hers—but all in red. The bed was as large as hers, with red velvet drapes. The carpet was a maroon as deep as hers had been in blue. This room, however, looked lived in. A shirt had been draped over a chair near the fireplace, and shaving items were laid across the dressing table. The room held the same earthy smell as Loftus.

"This room is mine. If you ever need to speak to me at night, I'll be here."

Catherine twisted her mouth to the side with a smile. "I'd imagine you would be. Where might I find you in the day?"

"In the day?" He looked at her askance.

She raised an eyebrow. "Certainly. What wife wouldn't seek out her husband during the daylight hours? Would you rather I ignore you?"

He shrugged. "Most people do. I doubt you'll come looking for me very often, but follow me, and I'll show you." He closed the door to his room and walked out of hers, striding down the hall once more. There was a nervous energy about him now. He pulled at his cravat. "My mother and my brother know of this place, of course, but not many people care to go in here. They don't find it as interesting as I do, I suppose."

Catherine was still reeling from his earlier comment. *Most people do.* Why would people overlook an earl? But then, she knew. It was for the same reason they'd ignored her and considered her beneath them. They thought she was deficient. Loftus' scars—to the *Ton*—made him deficient, as well.

Anger bubbled within her as she continued to follow him down hallways and around corners, portraits looking down upon them wherever they went. It was one thing to be insulted and another thing entirely to witness someone *else* be insulted. Did her husband deserve it? Not from what she could tell.

They arrived at a set of glass doors, and Loftus paused as he turned the door handle, taking a breath. He pierced her with a questioning look before pushing open the door and allowing her to go ahead of him inside.

As she stepped across the threshold, the temperature of the air became noticeably warmer. Catherine's lips parted as she took in the view before her.

Windows ran all along the ceiling and walls, allowing the sun to flood through and shine its magnificent beams upon the greenery that flowed throughout the area. Plants of all sizes and shapes grew around the room, with some flowering in one corner and vines creeping up the wall in another. Short, scraggly ones lined benches, and spiked thistles poked up near the edges.

Plants she'd never seen before were all around, combined with scents that had never before crossed her nose. First, a smell of something almost exactly like what someone would imagine to be the color green, and then the woody scent of something else. Finally, the sweet scent of honey or sugar—or something in between. And nowhere the stench of London smoke or the malodorant Thames. Catherine could never claim to have been in a conservatory until now, but she'd never want to leave if they added birds and animals. It'd be like having one's own private forest.

Loftus's voice came from behind. "This is where I spend most of my time." He stepped to her left side with his unscarred cheek facing her, fingering an ivy-like plant that hung from a hook on the ceiling, and heaved a sigh. "You'll probably think it odd as my family does, but it is a hobby of mine to tend these plants. I've always had a fascination with fauna."

Catherine's pulse increased. There was so much more to this man than met the eye, and she was only scratching the surface. If only she could see his scars from this angle. She tilted her head. "I think it's a very worthwhile pastime. Are you a botanist?"

His eyes flitted from the leaf, widening slightly. "I-I suppose I could be considered so."

"And you could tell me the names of each of the plants in this room?" She raised her eyebrows.

He nodded, lowering his hand.

Catherine moved across the room to a flowering plant with a drooping head, the purple-red color mottled in such a way that it almost looked like the skin of a snake. She pointed at it. "What is this?"

"*Fritillaria meleagris.*" There was no hesitation in his answer.

Catherine moved to another plant with ridged leaves and small white flowers. "What about this one?"

"*Lamium album.* White dead-nettle."

Catherine straightened her shoulders. "A nettle? Cannot those be found in the wilds of England?"

Loftus joined her beside the plant, continuing to keep his scarred cheek turned away from her. "Indeed, they can—as can many of the plants within this conservatory. The reason I grow them, however, is to provide extra to the apothecary when he runs out. On occasion, these plants can be difficult to find, and when their beneficial properties are sorely needed in the village and he has no more to give, he buys plants from me at low prices."

She stared at him a moment. "How amazingly generous."

Loftus shrugged. "I am more than happy to give them to him, but he insists on paying. I also grow a few exotic plants and sell the medicinal parts to the apothecary, as well. There have been some cases of illness in the village that require more specific herbal remedies than simple *Achillea mille-folium,* and that is when growing those exotic plants is very useful."

Catherine leaned toward him, intrigued. "What exotic plants do you have?"

He walked around the flowers and past a small tree, then crouched near a pot of seedlings by the wall that were soaking in the light from the window. "These are some of them. They're *Coriandrum sativum* seeds that I planted only a week and a half ago. The plant originally comes from the south of Europe."

Catherine bit her lip. "What does it help with?"

"Indigestion." Loftus was standing again and moving in another direction. She followed him to a darker, more densely foliated area. He gestured to a large ceramic pot with dark-purple flowers within, the centers of them a pale yellow in contrast. "These are also exotic. They're called *Helleborus niger.*"

"They're very pretty." Catherine took off her glove and ran her finger along the silky soft petal of one.

"Indeed, but their intended use is not so pretty." Loftus scratched the back of his neck.

She flicked her eyes up at him. "Oh?"

His cheeks reddened. "When ingested, the powder makes one...erm...cast up their accounts—rather violently, at that."

Catherine's mouth dropped open, a quiver in her abdomen.

Loftus lifted his hands, running one through his hair. "I-I'm sorry. That was indelicate. I—"

A disbelieving laugh burst from her. "You mean *these* beautiful things do *that?*"

Loftus's shoulders dropped, and he brought his arms back down to his sides, a smile coming to his lips. He even gave a chuckle of his own, which served to make her heart beat as though she were just a child rolling her hoop down the grass and hoping it didn't topple over.

When their laughter abated, Loftus held out his arm for her to take. "Speaking of casting up accounts, I realize I never did have any food brought to you. You must be starving." He twisted his mouth to the side in a chagrined expression. "I apologize. I do tend to get distracted in here. I'll order a tea tray and have it sent to you. Where would you like it?"

Catherine wrapped her hand around his arm and shook her head. "Think nothing of it. Your collection of plants has distracted me as well, as has your knowledge of them. As for the tray...I should like to see the garden, I think. It's a glorious day, and to feel the sun on my face would be lovely."

"Then outside you shall go." He escorted her out of the conservatory and into the hall, where Loftus called to a nearby footman to bring a tea tray to the garden. From there, he led Catherine to the cultivated area to the rear of the home.

Winding stone paths crossed over one another, and spring flowers had sprouted up from the ground in purples, whites, and yellows. Birds sang above and from bushes, their chattering providing a merry background to the day's beauty. The air was fresh and clean.

Ahead sat an intricate iron table with two chairs, nestled in a circle of shrubs and blooms. When they came to it, Loftus pulled out her chair and pushed it in as Catherine seated herself. She arranged her skirts, waiting for him to sit. He didn't.

He bowed at the waist. "Enjoy your tea, Cate." He turned on his heel and began to walk back the way they'd come.

She frowned and looked over her shoulder. "Have I missed something?"

He paused and spun to face her, eyes wide. "Pardon?"

"Where are you going, Loftus?"

He glanced back at the manor, then to her. "I am leaving you to your tea."

Her heart dropped, disappointment edging in. She didn't know him well yet, but she wanted to. "You won't be joining me?"

"I—uh—have some business to attend to, unfortunately." His scarred cheek was facing away again. She had a feeling this was about more than business. He bowed once more and departed, leaving her to wait for the tray on her own.

It came moments later, and she poured herself a cup of tea with milk and sugar, keenly aware of her husband's absence. Shouldn't they be speaking to one another more and learning about each other's preferences? How did he take his tea? Did he like it strong or sweeter, as she did?

But then, it was only their wedding day. Perhaps she was asking too much of him. They had time to get to know one another. She didn't want to be a burden to him if it truly was business that had taken him away. Lord Balfour had always insisted she was far too interested in him—he'd reprimanded her on more than one occasion for asking him questions about what he did during the day, claiming that it wasn't her business.

Catherine pulled her gloves from her hands and picked up a scone from a plate, slathering clotted cream and strawberry jam liberally on top of it. She took a bite, closing her eyes. Delicious. Would married life be so sweet?

Footsteps crunched on the pebbled path behind her, and she turned around, scone still in hand. Hope raised within her. Had Loftus changed his mind?

It was not Loftus who greeted her when she looked over her shoulder, however, but Lord Berkley—a cheery grin on his face. "Has my brother left you out here all alone?"

Catherine cleared her throat and set down the scone, a gentle heat coming to her cheeks. "He had some important business to attend to. That is all."

Lord Berkley lifted his eyes to the sky and scoffed. "Yes, that sounds like him." He gestured to the chair across from her. "May I join you?"

Catherine nodded, giving a hesitant smile. "Certainly."

He pulled out the chair and sat down, picking a cucumber sandwich up from the tray.

Catherine lifted the teapot and looked at him askance. "How do you like your tea?"

"Milk, please."

She fixed him a cup and handed it over.

He took a sip. "Perfect. Now, where do you come from, Countess? I know so little about you. My brother has hardly told me anything."

She was unsurprised at this information. She didn't think her husband knew very much, himself. "I come from London, my lord."

He nodded. "Ah, my mother's favorite place. I do believe she'll be going there soon. She never does stay at the country estate for long." He took another sip of his tea. "And how were your travels here?"

Catherine tilted her head, remembering the way Loftus had felled the drunken man at The Hogshead Inn. "The country-side is very beautiful up north, and the people are very...eager to assist in any matter."

Lord Berkley chuckled. "Indeed, they are. The people in this county are some of the friendliest you'll find."

Catherine swallowed a bite of her scone and wiped her hands on her napkin just as a woodpigeon flew down from a nearby tree branch, its wings whistling in the air. It landed on the stones beside her chair, its head bobbing eagerly as it strutted toward her on orange feet. Catherine pushed her spectacles farther up her nose, her lips turning up at the edges as she watched the bird.

"Have you an affinity for winged things?" Lord Berkley's voice caught her attention. She dragged her eyes from the woodpigeon to his face. His mouth was twisted to the side in amusement, though he tried to hide it behind the teacup in his hand. His voice didn't seem patronizing—indeed, it seemed as though he was genuinely curious, albeit surprised at her interest in the creature.

"I do." She pinched a few stray scone crumbs from her plate and dropped them to the ground at the bird's feet. It pecked away with haste. "Winged things, things with four legs, things with tails... If it is a creature, it has caught my interest."

"And humans?" Lord Berkley raised an eyebrow, picking up a chicken sandwich the size of two fingers.

Catherine took a sip of her tea, shrugging her shoulders. "Those are interesting, as well, though I am less adept at understanding them."

Lord Berkley set down his cup and saucer and leaned back in his chair. "You will be pleased to know, I think, that I am also intrigued by creatures."

"Truly? Any in particular?" Others did not normally find animals and insects as interesting as she. For her new brother to share her interest was fortunate, indeed, and told of many interesting conversations and outings to come. Susan was not very fond of seeking out nature with her, but perhaps Lord Berkley would be.

"I like all of them, of course, but prefer..." He paused and picked up another sandwich. "...the local creatures the best. I... study them. I'm something of an expert, you'll find."

Catherine nodded as the woodpigeon took a few steps and

flew back to its branch. "I suppose you would be, having grown up here as you have." She bit her lip. Would she be overstepping by asking him to show her the places where the wildlife tended to congregate? He must know the spots and trails in the surrounding forest. She lifted her teacup to her lips while she debated and sipped, the liquid barely warm anymore.

Lord Berkley opened his mouth before she could speak. "I could show you some of them, if you'd like. There's a pond nearby where some frogs and snakes enjoy hiding, and in the forest, the deer enjoy a specific area. Of course, we'll find squirrels and other animals too." He spread his hands, his smile wide. "I've heard from my valet that you've a dog. We could even bring him with us as I show you the grounds. That way, my brother can get his work done, and you can see the landscape that's your new home."

Catherine set down her teacup and clasped her hands together in her lap. Surely, her husband would approve of this plan. He must be a busy man—that he couldn't even take tea with her—and it *would* allow him to work more if she were to take the tour of the grounds with his brother. She needn't even take Susan, now that she was married.

"I'd like that very much, my lord."

"Please, call me Gilbert. We're family now, after all." He sat up in his chair.

She quirked her lips. "Then call me Catherine. When shall we go on this tour? I must say that I am a bit tired after today's events."

He tapped the table with his fingers. "Tomorrow, then. We'll meet after breakfast and go on horse. You've ridden before, yes?"

"I have." Excitement tingled through her. She loved to ride, though her parents hadn't sent her horse from London yet. She tried to ride every morning, for that was when the birds sang their waking calls and the creatures began to come out from their holes in the ground and their nests in the brush. That was when she most often saw God's unique creations moving about.

"Good. Let's meet at the barn at half-past ten. Be sure to wear a riding habit."

With that, Lord Berkley took one last sip of tea and stood, bowing at the waist. With a grin, he turned toward the house and sauntered back down the path, leaving her with significantly fewer sandwiches than had been on the tray when it had come out.

CHAPTER 9

$\mathcal{L}$oftus stared out of the window from his bedchamber toward the garden, where his brother was currently sharing tea with his wife. They made a pretty pair. A feeling of unease grew within his abdomen, a sort of twinge that ceased to go at the sight of them together.

Cate straightened in her chair, appearing very interested in whatever Gilbert had to say. A piercing heat struck Loftus. What was his brother sharing to so intrigue her?

Within moments, Gilbert was moving back toward the manor, his footsteps light. Loftus grunted, running a hand down his scarred cheek. If only he could have his brother's confidence. Truly, he'd had no business to attend to, but he couldn't bring himself to sit across from her for so long in the full sun. What woman would want to face him over a tea tray? He would ruin her appetite.

She was entrancing, with a cheerful demeanor unlike any he'd witnessed before, but no matter how polite she acted around Loftus, that was exactly what it was—an act. He had to remember his own appearance. She hadn't seemed surprised at his scars at the wedding, but many young women were skilled at artifice. He couldn't let himself get attached, no matter how kind she seemed. He wouldn't soon forget the look of horror on her face when she'd believed they'd be sharing a bedchamber.

He turned from the window, clasping his hands behind his back. He needed to tend to his plants.

That evening, Loftus was seated at the head of the dinner table, his bride to his right. His mother and brother occupied their correct places, according to rank. Candelabras lined the table, their light setting the dishes to gleaming. Cook had prepared Loftus's favorite—roasted duck alongside savory vegetables. But it was not the meal that was an issue.

"You have brought a dog." His mother sniffed, eyeing Cate over her duck.

Cate shifted in her seat. "I have, yes. He's very well-behaved."

His mother scoffed. "We'll see about that. I've never seen a dog behave well in a home. They're much better suited for a kennel. That mud-colored *pet* of yours will only cause a mess."

Cate frowned over her peas. "Dogs make very good companions. As such, they should be kept closer than in a kennel, wouldn't you say? It is much easier for me to see him if he is in the next room over than in a completely different building."

His mother's lips pulled down. "A hound for a companion instead of a group of ladies your age." She raised an eyebrow. "How old did you say you were?"

"I didn't, but I am four-and-twenty." His wife prodded a piece of duck with the tines of her fork. His brother's eyes widened, and he straightened against the triangular back of his upholstered chair, suppressing a cough with his fist. Apparently, this was news to him.

His mother's lips thinned. "I see now why it was so needful for you to marry my son."

Loftus's chest tightened. How dare she insult both of them

over Cate's first meal with her new family? It was beyond the pale.

Before he could defend her, Cate's hazel eyes flashed. "'Twas no *need* that caused me to marry Loftus, but my father's will and my mother's greed. Indeed, I wished to marry for love and naught else. That I was forced to marry before love found me is unfortunate, but if love blesses our marriage, I will be eternally grateful that I was bound to your son to receive it."

The room was silent. No one breathed.

Loftus felt as though the air had been knocked out of him. Who knew that his new bride was so outspoken? He didn't mind, of course. Truly, it was like a breath of fresh air. It wasn't often that a person spoke against his mother. But to hear that Cate hadn't wished to marry him? *That* was something he hadn't expected.

When his solicitor had spoken to her father and they'd written back and forth, Mr. Blynn had made it seem as though Cate was very amenable to the match—even eager to marry. To hear that she'd actually been forced into it made his heart drop. He'd never wanted to force anyone into matrimony. Especially not with him. But the rest of what she'd said...

Love? Surely, she said it only for his benefit. She couldn't truly believe that love would come in their marriage.

He appreciated her attempt at defense, but it rang hollow to his ears. He'd heard enough from his mother, brother, and father, when he was still alive, to know he wasn't truly a catch even when he'd been without scars—physical and mental.

His mother cleared her throat, her face unreadable. "I'm leaving for London tomorrow. Town is calling to me once more, and I must heed it."

Gilbert raised his wine glass, slapping a hand against the white tablecloth. "Enjoy your travels, Mother. I, for a change, will be spending my time here."

Alarm started from the bottom of Loftus's feet and spread

throughout his body. His brother never stayed in the country for long, always opting to spend his time carousing in London at the gaming hells. Why wasn't he doing so now?

Their mother raised an eyebrow. "Indeed?"

Gilbert nodded, swirling the liquid in his glass around. "I should like to get to know my new sister better, and I find that the city tires me. A few more months of northern air and time spent away from the bustle will do me good, I think."

Loftus's wife actually smiled at this. A frown crossed his mouth, and a displeasing jab poked at his abdomen. He lifted a spoonful of custard to his lips to keep himself from saying something rude about the man. It wouldn't do to act the fool in front of Cate on their wedding day—or any day, really.

In the drawing room after dinner, Cate played a few pieces on the harp. She was very good on the instrument, her fingers deftly moving from one string to the other. It was easy for Loftus to close his eyes and imagine that the gates of heaven had opened up, this beautiful music flowing out from behind them. Even his mother looked mildly impressed, though she regularly examined her nails and attempted to put on a bored air.

After Cate finished, Gilbert leaned forward from his place on the settee. "Do you sing?"

Cate's cheeks grew as red as rubies. "I do not."

Gilbert waved a hand. "Surely, you are being modest. Anyone who plays the harp like an angel must sing like one, as well."

"I sing like no angel, my lord, though I happen to know someone who does."

"And who is this person? Would I know them?" Gilbert raised an eyebrow.

An amused smile lifted Cate's lips as she pierced Loftus with a stare. "I would hope so, my lord, for he is your very own brother."

Loftus froze.

Gilbert's other eyebrow rose. "My brother? I've heard his voice. He sings well enough, but I've never stood after his performance."

Cate's smile widened. "Ah, but only today in the church did I hear his voice ring with the richness of Midas and warmth of a London summer. I will not sing, but if *he* will, then I will be very glad to accompany him on the pianoforte."

Loftus's heartbeat quickened. No one had ever complimented him in such a way. His shoulders tensed. He also wasn't used to singing in front of anyone. He'd only done it a few times, and it had been nerve-wracking then, as it was now.

He pulled at his cravat, but the hopeful look on his wife's face made it difficult to deny her. It wasn't as though he would be singing in front of a large audience—only his mother and brother, and they had heard his voice before.

He swallowed before standing from his seat at the side of the room and moving toward the stack of sheet music at the pianoforte. Cate joined him, and they sifted through the selection together, their fingers occasionally grazing and sending tingles through his hands and arms.

Why was his body responding in such a ridiculous fashion to her? Her scent of clover wafted over him once more with her proximity, and he couldn't help but take a deep breath. How he loved the smell.

Finally, they selected a piece they both knew, and as she settled on the pianoforte bench, Loftus stood tall and cleared his throat, clasping his hands behind his back. She played the opening section and he began. That he was already doing things he normally avoided simply to please her did not bode well for keeping his emotional distance from the lovely woman at his side.

≈

*C*atherine smiled to herself. Each note that came out of her husband's mouth washed over her in dulcet waves. Her fingers leapt over the keys. She swayed gently with the tempo, his voice growing louder with the rising of the music and softer as it ebbed.

> *"Hark the din of distant war,*
> *How noble is the clangor. Pale*
> *Death ascends his Ebon car,*
> *Clad in terrific anger. A*
> *Doubtful fate the soldier tries..."*

He continued on, telling the tale of "Death or Victory" by Charles Dibdin. Why had he chosen this song? Had he lost a friend to the war? Catherine knew many people who'd lost siblings across the channel. She'd ask him later. For now, she'd enjoy his lovely voice, full of emotion and strength.

> *"Perhaps on the cold ground he lies,*
> *No wife, no friend, to close his eyes,*
> *Tho' nobly mourn'd; perhaps, return'd,*
> *He's crown'd with victory's laurel."*

As he finished the song, she pressed the final ivory keys and let their notes ring through the room, a cathartic sort of feeling tangible in the air. She swung her legs over the bench to look at her husband as Gilbert and the dowager clapped. Loftus's eyes were closed, his shoulders tensed.

Perhaps he was one of those people who truly disliked performing. A pool of guilt grew in her stomach. She stood from her bench and curtsied, giving her little audience a smile before stepping over to him and wrapping her gloved hand around his. His eyes opened at her touch, and he promptly bowed to his family. He squeezed her fingers and directed her back to her seat, neither saying anything. The grateful look he gave her as she sat down was enough.

In bed that night, Catherine twisted her wedding ring around her finger. The gold was warm against her skin. How odd that only hours earlier, she'd been married to a man she'd never met—an earl, at that. Time would tell what type of husband he would be. Perhaps he'd not wish to have anything to do with her. Maybe he would be traveling most of the time, like her father.

He didn't seem to mind her behavior so far, although that might prove to be an act. The worst scenario of all would be if Loftus ended up behaving as Lord Balfour, for that man was akin to the stubborn mud on someone's shoe. The staining it left once it was removed was unfortunate and unpleasant, and would take a long time to fade, if it ever did.

Catherine knew, for she was that shoe, still stained from his insults and violence. The marks, while invisible, were upon her still, no matter how hard she tried to wash them away. It hadn't been that long, of course, since he'd broken their engagement, and time, surely, would help fade the dirt he'd left behind.

For now, however, she couldn't see men in the same way. Loftus probably wasn't as he appeared, no matter how she wished him to be. She would count herself lucky if he left her alone for the remainder of her days in this manor, for any attention from a man—no matter how gentle they might seem —brought danger.

~

*L*oftus woke abruptly, his eyes on the pitch black of the wooden canopy above him. Some sort of sound had woken him up, but what? He pulled the drapes of his bed aside. It was still dark in his room. Still night—or very early morning.

The sound came again, and he sat up in bed, tilting his head. Was it coming from his wife's room? He threw his legs over the side and was rushing through the dark when she cried out as though she was in pain. He stumbled to the door separating their rooms and opened it to see her dark silhouette thrashing in bed, her limbs tangled in her sheets and coverlet. He hastened closer.

Her chest heaved, and her long hair stuck to her face. Her eyebrows were scrunched up, her mouth twisted. "No! Let go of me! I'm sorry!" She fought against her invisible attacker, her arms and legs only getting more tangled in the bed coverings. "I won't do it again....I won't do it again..."

Loftus's heart broke to see her having such a terrible dream. He'd certainly had his fair share after the war. He took a hesitant step toward the bed and rested his hand on her arm. "Cate...wake up. It is only a dream. You are safe." With a little more shaking, her eyes popped open, followed by a sharp intake of breath.

"Loftus?" She sat up in bed and pressed herself against the headboard, pulling her coverlet and sheets in front of her like a shield. Her words came out quick and frantic. "What are you doing here? You said...you said that..."

He held his hands out—about to explain—but she shrank away from him. "Is that why you're here? It must be." Tears began to stream down her face. "I don't want to, Loftus. Don't make me. *He* tried to make me, but I wouldn't let him. Please. Please—you said you wouldn't." Her shoulders shook, and she began to gasp. She buried her face in her coverlet.

He? Who was *he?* Loftus shook his head. He could get the answer to that question later. For now, he needed to calm his wife and assure her he was not about to go back on his promise. He made his voice as soft and reassuring as possible. "Cate, I am here because I heard you having a nightmare. I was worried. I thought, perhaps, that you had gotten hurt."

Her crying quieted somewhat.

He ran a hand through his hair. "I am not here to consummate our marriage. I meant what I said earlier. I do not wish to do so until a later date. Of course, I would not wish for either of us to be uncomfortable."

Finally, she lifted her head from the coverlet, her eyes shining bright in the darkness. "P-promise?"

His heart nearly tore at the crack in her voice. Who had hurt her? Who had so tormented her to make her react in such a way? He'd wager it was the reason for the nightmare. "I promise."

She sniffed. "Thank you. I'm s-sorry for behaving in such a way. I don't normally have nightmares like this. To wake up and see you in my room was so surprising, I—well, I just ran to conclusions. You do not deserve to have such unfounded aspersions cast upon your character, all because of a dream." She shook her head, her tone self-deprecating.

Loftus bit his lip, wondering whether he should ask about it. Would she even tell him if he did? He straightened his shoulders and took a breath. "What was this dream about, anyway?"

She dropped her gaze, her voice lowering. "What it always is about."

That wasn't a complete dismissal. He forged on. "And that is?"

Cate raised her hand to her mouth and opened it in what looked like an acted-out yawn. "Your brother is giving me a tour of the surrounding land tomorrow. I should be going back to bed if I'm to be well-rested. You should be, too, if you're to complete all of your business."

Loftus knew when not to push. He nodded, inwardly troubled at the idea of his brother showing her around the estate. Was that why she had looked so excited during tea?

He stifled a sigh. "I'll see you in the morning. I hope the rest of your dreams are better."

"Thank you." Her voice was soft. She made no move to stop him as he turned and reentered his own room, closing the door behind him with a soft click.

He made his way to his bed and got under the covers, his mind on the woman only a wall away from him and the secrets she held. He didn't blame her for not telling him about her past. They were still practical strangers, after all. Perhaps she would tell him in the future, but—was it only this past that had made her so averse to Loftus's presence in her room, or was it his appearance? He feared very much that the latter played a large role in her frantic pleas. Many young ladies had been made afraid by his appearance. Why should his wife be any different?

A desolate feeling broke over him as he once more stared at the black canopy above him. He placed his hands on his chest, an ache there. Tomorrow was only the second day of his marriage, and his wife would rather be spending time with his brother than himself. That certainly didn't bode well for their future marital bliss. Then again, Loftus hadn't exactly made himself available to Cate today, having run away at tea and keeping out of sight in the hours following.

He pounded a fist into his mattress, huffing a breath. It was what he had to do. No one had ever borne the view of his scars for more than a few minutes with a smile on their face, and he wasn't anticipating that his wife would be the first. To see the exact moment when her facade cracked and the look of disgust finally broke through—that was too much for him to witness on someone whom he was now forever tied to.

He'd rather run away at every chance, content in the illusion that his wife could tolerate him than stay longer in her presence and realize the truth—that he was only some man she had been forced to marry. That she only stayed because she had nowhere else to go. That her kindness was an act and she, like all the others, wished she could have married someone else. Anyone else.

He closed his eyes, a weight pressing against him. Though he wanted to hide, how could he bide his time tomorrow, aware his brother was escorting her around the grounds? He had accounts and correspondence and plants to tend to, yes, but now that he was married, wasn't his first priority his wife, regardless of how she felt about him?

CHAPTER 10

*A*t breakfast the next day, Catherine helped herself to eggs and toast from the side table in the breakfast room, the morning sun shining through the large rectangular windows and past the golden curtains that lined them. It was half-past nine, but she was the only one in the room, besides a footman. Catherine placed a few rashers on her plate and moved to the table to sit down, laying her napkin over the skirt of her lilac riding habit.

She eyed the young servant with curiosity as she passed him. "Where is everyone?"

He straightened his shoulders and cleared his throat. "The Dowager Countess of Hardwicke left for London some hours ago." The tension in Catherine's shoulders eased. It was a balm to know she wouldn't be running into that woman anytime soon. The dowager's frown never seemed to leave her face. The footman continued. "Lord Berkley, I believe, has not yet left his chamber."

She hummed. He was a late riser. "And my husband?" She was in the midst of pouring herself a cup of tea when the door creaked behind her.

"What of me?" Loftus's soft voice pierced the quiet.

Catherine struggled to lift the spout in time, almost filling her cup to overflowing. How shamefully she'd behaved the night prior. Truly, she'd thought she'd prepared herself for the marriage bed. After all, it was something married women must do. But when he'd entered her room, the darkness had set in and all she could see was Lord Balfour.

She set the pot down and looked over her shoulder at her husband. He wore an umber-colored coat with a dark-blue waistcoat and buff pantaloons. A snowy cravat was knotted around his throat, and polished Hessian boots reached his knees.

Her eyes widened, heat coming to her cheeks. "I...was... wondering where you were."

A small smile came to his lips before he headed to the side table. "You need wonder no longer. I lingered abed later than usual, I'm afraid. My sleep was quite restless."

That would be her fault. "I'm sorry to hear it." Catherine spooned sugar into her tea and poured in the milk. "I-I'm truly sorry about how I behaved last night. I fear my nightmare got the better of me."

Her husband brought his plate to the table and sat beside her. "Nightmares often do that to a person. Do not let it bother you any more, for I understand well."

She exhaled, grabbing a teacup and saucer for him. They would forget last night. "Thank you. Now, how do you take your tea? I wasn't able to find out yesterday, but I'm quite determined to today."

Loftus chuckled, his dimples appearing. Her heart beat faster all of a sudden. "Just a bit of milk and sugar, please. Not as light as the color of your own tea."

Catherine grinned. "I can do that." She fixed it for him and handed back the cup and saucer, nearly dropping them both

Before she could say a word to stop him, he'd left the room —with only the earthy scent of plants unique to him left behind.

Her lips turned downward. She'd rather have spent more time with him before he went about his day. She took another sip of her tea, tapping her fingers on the tablecloth. Was it truly his business that took him away, or had she said something to upset him?

The footman cleared Loftus's plate from beside her.

"Good morning!" Gilbert entered the room, wearing buff pantaloons and a bright red riding coat. His boots sounded across the floor as he strode to the side table and helped himself to what was there. "I see you're ready for our outing— and a riding habit suits you very well, if I might say." He sat next to her, where Loftus had just been, and she poured him a cup of tea.

"Thank you. I must admit that I am excited for the day."

Gilbert swallowed a bite of kidney and shot her a dazzling smile. "And well you should be. I'll be showing you all of the places where the wildlife thrives."

Catherine raised an eyebrow. "What is your favorite creature native to this area? You mentioned yesterday that you are particularly intrigued by the local animals, but which ones specifically?"

Gilbert coughed on a bite of egg and reached for his cup of tea, taking a few sips before looking at her. "I like...deer. Yes, I believe...deer...are my favorite."

Catherine bit down on her smile. Deer were always a sight to behold, with their eyes that stared for miles and their perfect stillness amongst the greenery. She'd only witnessed a few on her family's trips outside London. The thought of seeing such a large creature again was thrilling. "What species of deer do you have around Cumbria?"

when the back of her hand brushed his. What was h
to her? She was never this thoughtless.

He brought the cup to his lips and tilted his head. "
preparing skills need no improvement, my dear."

She giggled. "That is high praise, indeed." Pushing
into a lump of egg, she bit into it and began to enjoy he
fast. The rashers were savory and delicious, and she s
butter and marmalade onto the toast in equal measu
perfect sweet to balance the salty. This certainly b
kippers her father insisted on at home.

"You know my plans for today, but what are
Catherine dabbed at her mouth with her napkin and su
Loftus, who was cutting into a piece of ham.

He looked up, silent for a moment. "Well, I'll be n
with my steward, Mr. Liltbury, this morning..."

Catherine nodded. "And then?"

"Erm...I'll be tending to the plants—but there's not very
to do at this time of the season. Not yet, anyway." Loftus shru

Catherine frowned. "Your brother seemed to be und
impression that you'd be very busy today. He didn't think
have the time to show me about the grounds."

Loftus's fork stopped halfway to his mouth, a piece of
skewered on it. His eyes became hard. "Did he not?
thoughtful of him, then, to offer to show you himself."

Catherine placed her teacup down. "You could show me
grounds with him—"

"No, no, but thank you for the offer. I've actually just r
ized that there are a few other things that must be done to
He is quite right—I am busy." A smile came to his lips, thou
it didn't seem to reach his eyes. He stood from the table, half
his plate untouched. "I'm sure Gilbert will be a knowledgeal
host on the ride. If you have any questions afterward, of cour
you know where to find me."

Gilbert dragged his fork across his plate. "They're sort of reddish in color... I—"

The door to the breakfast room burst open, and Giles came running in, his tongue hanging out of his mouth in a happy puppy smile. Susan barreled in after him, leaning toward the floor with her arms outstretched. "Ye scamp! Ye've not been called fer yet!"

Giles paid the maid no mind, only rushing over to Catherine to lick at her ankles. She laughed and stood, lifting him into her arms to hold him close. The dowager had relegated him to the stables for the first night of his stay, but now that she was gone, Catherine would make sure he was free to explore the manor as he pleased—within reason, of course. She definitely didn't need him harassing Cook belowstairs.

Susan straightened and bobbed a curtsy. "Sorry, my lady. He could not wait to see ye."

Catherine waved a hand. "Do not apologize, Susan—Giles *is* a scamp. It's no matter that he's early, for he'll be going with Lord Berkley and me on our exploration of the grounds."

Gilbert rose and eyed Giles, who was squirming in Catherine's arms. "So this is the pup I've heard of." A flash of something crossed his eyes before a small smile lifted his lips. "He is even more charming than they say."

Catherine patted Giles on the head and beamed. "Isn't he? We're ready for adventure."

Susan fitted his lead around his neck as Gilbert sat back down to finish his breakfast. Excitement thrummed through Catherine. She couldn't wait to explore her new grounds— especially with someone who would enjoy them as much as she.

CHAPTER 11

*C*atherine hurried to her room to retrieve her riding bonnet, and not long after, she met Gilbert at the stables with Giles bounding at her side.

"Ah, well met!" Gilbert stood beside a saddled chestnut stallion. At his side, a bay mare was fitted with a side-saddle, the reins held by a sandy-haired stableboy. The mare attempted to nibble at the grass at her hooves, reluctantly raising her head when the stableboy pulled at the reins, her steps slow. Was this mare to be her horse? It certainly looked that way.

Disappointment crawled up her throat. Catherine should be happy she was riding at all, but she considered herself more learned than a beginner rider. Her horse in London was a stallion, like most gentlemen's. She could hold her own in the saddle. That Gilbert had assumed otherwise was miffing, but perhaps he gave all of his friends use of this mare. Indeed, she should not be so quick to pass judgment. He likely only had a care for her safety.

Catherine picked up Giles and stepped closer, holding her hand out to each of the horses. "What beautiful animals. What are their names?"

Gilbert puffed out his chest, propping his hands on his hips. "The chestnut I've had for a few years now—his name is Trafferth. I'm not quite sure what it means, but I heard the word once, and I like how it sounds, so I named him that. I think it's Welsh for waves, or ocean." He turned his head to the bay, his nose scrunching up. "My mother named the mare. Juliet—after the dead girl from that play."

The mare gave a toss of her head. It seemed she didn't like to be reminded. Catherine didn't blame her. She pulled Juliet to a mounting block and jumped on, holding Giles close with one hand and gripping the reins in the other. Fortunately for her, he remained still in her arm this time. She'd considered putting him down and letting him follow the horses but didn't want him getting underfoot and being trampled.

She rode after Gilbert at a slow pace toward the first location where he claimed there was an abundance of wildlife. Their horses trekked through the forest, weaving around trees and in between rock formations, following a path that was just barely worn into the earth.

After about ten minutes of riding, Gilbert stopped ahead of her. Her eyebrows raised, her shoulders lifting. Had they reached the first spot? As Juliet moved closer to Trafferth, Catherine began to see why Gilbert had stopped. The type of vernal pool she'd only ever read about lay among the trees, formed from the collection of melted snow and ice that winter had left behind. Wildlife used them while they lasted, but the water didn't stay for very long. After a few months, the pool would evaporate.

The surface was glass-like, without any disturbances. Mottled, faded leaves in beige and black floated at the edges, but the mirrored surface reflected the new growth in the branches above. How beautiful.

Catherine dismounted, throwing Juliet's reins over a nearby tree branch. She took a few steps from the horse and set Giles down, holding tight to his lead. He immediately set his nose to the ground and began to sniff, his ears nearly touching the dirt. His tail wagged so fast that she feared it might fly off.

Boots thudded behind her, and she turned. Gilbert had dismounted as well, Trafferth's reins also tossed over a branch. She grinned. "I'm sure there are plenty of creatures that come here. What a pretty place."

He nodded, matching her smile. "I passed by it only a month ago. It was larger then, but it is still just as peaceful." He reached toward her. "I can hold the dog's lead if you'd like."

"Yes, indeed. Thank you." She handed it over and began to walk around, examining the sides of trees and listening for any rustling sounds.

As she stepped by a clump of leaves, they trembled. She bent down to get a closer look, and something brown burst out from them, leaping away from her. She was startled onto her backside, but a laugh erupted from her throat. "Oh, you!"

She got back onto her feet and searched the ground in an attempt to see what had just escaped her. A frog? Toads didn't leap like that. She gathered her riding skirts around her so she wouldn't trip, although she kept them at a modest height, and took a few careful steps forward, her head tilted toward the ground.

Her gaze fell on something out of place, but perfectly in place. A shiny brown frog. It blended in amongst the leaves and foliage, but its bright yellow eyes made it stand out. It looked up at her, remaining still with its legs crouched in a ready-to-jump position.

Catherine snatched the bonnet from her head, gripping it in both hands with the inside pointed down. "I only wish to look at you." Her voice was a murmur as she bent her knees, reaching forward. Just as the creature was about to leap again, she hurled herself forward and plopped the bonnet on top of it, capturing the frog within. "Gotcha!"

The entire front of her body was on the ground, her arms stretched out before her. Her hair was coming out of its pins. Susan would have apoplexy when Catherine returned.

She called to Gilbert over her shoulder. "Come here! Look what I've found. You must pick up Giles, however. Else, he'll frighten the poor thing." She peeked under her bonnet and gave a thoughtful hum. "The creature seems to fancy his temporary abode."

Gilbert crouched down beside her, and she tilted up her bonnet to let him see, grinning. "*Rana temporaria.* Isn't he magnificent?" She couldn't take her eyes from the creature.

Gilbert cleared his throat. "Erm...yes. Indeed." After another moment, he spoke again. "We should let him go now to take care of his offspring."

Catherine chuckled, turning her head to look at him. "Very clever, my lord."

He furrowed his eyebrows, making her smile fade as quickly as it had come.

She raised her bonnet from the ground and let the frog leap away. "Were you not jesting? *Rana temporaria* do not care for their eggs after laying them." He'd claimed to be interested in wildlife surrounding his home—had even claimed to study wildlife—and this type of frog was called "common" for a reason. Shouldn't he know that information by now?

All of a sudden, he slapped his knee and stood up, laughing. "Of course, I was jesting!"

He helped her to her feet. She tried to brush the mud from the front of her riding habit but failed miserably. It was silly to think this man could be lying. Why would he be? He had no reason to.

After a few more minutes walking around the vernal pool, they remounted their horses—Gilbert holding Giles this time—and rode to the next location. Gilbert led them back the way they'd come toward the manor. They passed it and went in a different direction through the woods, this section more mossy and flat. The path they traveled was well-worn, clearly ridden every week, if not every day.

The air was sweet with the nearby wildflowers that had sprung up along the swaths of mossy ground, the trees covered in lichens and shrouded in a light fog. The sun peeked through the canopies of the beeches, evaporating the dew on the ferns and grasses. Birds chirped all around, and the skittering of squirrels could be heard, followed by the dropping of twigs and leaves to the earth.

Gilbert pulled Trafferth up at a small clearing where the sun's rays illuminated a bed of grass and moss dotted by small fragrant blue flowers. Catherine closed her eyes, taking in the birdsong. If only she could lie down and spread her arms out amongst this bit of heaven.

They dismounted and Giles was able to sniff again. Gilbert was kind enough to hold onto him as Catherine searched for creatures.

"My brother often rides here in the morning, I think." He scratched his chin. "He studies the plants out here or some nonsense like that."

Catherine paused her steps, turning toward Gilbert with an eyebrow raised. "I see no nonsense in what he does."

Gilbert scoffed. "That will not last for long. He is forever fawning over his plants as though they are of great value. Tell me, what is a flower to a five-pound note? He knows nothing of how to run an estate and even less of the world around him."

Heat began to build in her abdomen. She straightened her shoulders. "From what I have seen, the estate is being run very well—enough so that it funds your mother's trips to London and your own without having you destitute. What could you need or want? Only this morning, the sideboard was filled with various foods beyond compare. I saw the wine you drank at dinner. You have expensive taste. You live in a mansion. And yet, you believe how your brother spends his time is meaningless? That he only focuses on his plants?"

"Well, I—"

She stepped toward him. "And, tell me, my lord, what about a flower is meaningless? What about Loftus enjoying the study of plants makes him unable to run an estate? What makes money more valuable than knowledge? I enjoy your company, Gilbert, but I'll ask you not to speak of my husband in such a way again."

He swallowed, his Adam's apple bobbing as his lips thinned. "Forgive me, Catherine."

A scuffling sounded to their left, and he turned his head, pointing in the same direction. "Look." A red squirrel hopped out of a bush, flicking its puffed tail. It began to dig at the ground with its paws, its fur a flash of orange amongst the viridescent vegetation.

Catherine couldn't help the smile that raised her lips. She saw squirrels regularly at Hyde Park but had never been this close to one. Its tufted ears were adorable, its feet appearing almost too large in comparison to its body.

Giles pulled at his lead, his nose pointed in the squirrel's direction, but Gilbert held him back. Giles gave a little whine, and the squirrel sat back on his hind legs, suddenly still.

Catherine patted her pup on the head, her voice a murmur. "Oh, Giles, you'll frighten him off. I cannot capture him under my hat as I did the frog." No matter how much she wished she could.

Without warning, the squirrel scurried off into the safety of a tree and was soon hidden from view.

Catherine walked around some more, her booted footsteps softened by the moss—as though she walked on carpet.

Giles circled something excitedly, his nose pressed to the dirt.

"Catherine! Look what I've found." Gilbert picked something up, a gleam in his eye.

She lifted her skirts and rushed over to him. "What is it?"

"See for yourself." He held his hand out, his chin tilted upward, and raised his fingers from over the creature.

A needle of delight pricked her. There, in Gilbert's gloved hand, was a large olive-brown toad, its skin rough with warts and its eyes a lovely copper color. It had short little legs and a stoic look on its face as though it should be in parliament. Toads, of all amphibians, were her favorite. Something about their undeserved poor reputation made her like them all the more. Perhaps because she could relate.

Everyone seemed to think that handling a toad would give them warts, but Catherine handled plenty of them, and she'd never gotten a single one. Did people believe that spending time in her presence would tarnish their reputation because hers was tarnished?

She shook the unfortunate thought away and pushed her spectacles farther up her nose, bending closer to get a better look at the *Bufo bufo*. She ran a gentle finger down its back and laughed with excitement. "How handsome you are!"

Imperfections had never repelled her. If only her husband knew that.

~

*L*oftus rode his bay stallion, Hedera, down the path they traversed each afternoon. He'd seen Gilbert take Cate this way, and he was hoping to catch up with them. With any luck, he'd join their tour of the grounds and prove to his brother that he wouldn't be pushed aside so easily.

As he neared the clearing he normally stopped at, feminine laughter reached his ears. He slowed Hedera to a walk and strained to hear anything else.

"How handsome you are!" Catherine's voice could be distinguished easily in the relative quiet.

His stomach dropped. Was she speaking to Gilbert? They were the only ones out here, as far as Loftus knew.

Her voice came again. "Your eyes are such a nice color too."

Loftus's chest tightened. Gilbert's eyes were only a bit darker than his own. Was there truly that much of a difference?

Her laughter rang out between the trees. "Oh, sir, you are very presumptuous, indeed! I'd rather you not go there. You must get off at once." Her laughter continued.

Anger boiled within Loftus. Was his brother taking liberties with his wife—and on the day after Loftus had married the woman?

Loftus urged Hedera forward and dismounted near the other horses, making haste toward the clearing. As soon as he stepped out from behind one of the beech trees, he spread his arms out and raised his voice. "What is the meaning of this?"

It was even worse than he'd thought.

Gilbert and Cate stood very near one another, with Cate's dress absolutely muddied from top to bottom. . Her chocolate curls were falling from their pins, and her bonnet was skewed to one side. A large smile wreathed her face. His brother reached for her shoulder.

"Loftus!" She smoothed the front of her skirt, her eyes widening. "Are you able to join us, then?"

"What is the meaning of this?" He took a step closer, his tone fierce as he glared at them.

Cate bit her lip, her eyebrows knitting. "I do not understand. You knew your brother would be showing me the grounds."

"That is not what I speak of." Loftus flicked his gaze to his brother. "What do you have to say for yourself?"

Gilbert shrugged, finally dropping his hand from Catherine's shoulder. "She was the one who jumped on the ground. I only followed when she bid me."

Loftus marched up to his brother and seized him by the lapels, pulling him away from his wife. His jaw ached, he was clenching it so hard. Cate gasped, but Loftus would confront her later. She had broken her vows only one day into their marriage.

"*That* is what you say to me, after so betraying my trust? After..."—he leaned close, seething—"*compromising my wife?*"

Gilbert pushed against his chest, alarm on his face. "I've done no such thing! I thought you were referring to her muddy clothing." He threw an arm out toward Cate. A dark splotch moved on her shoulder. Wait—was that a *toad*?

She stepped forward, the creature remaining still like some sort of ornate piece of jewelry from a bygone era. Her hazel eyes blazed. "Do you mean to tell me that you believed Gilbert to have..." She wrinkled her nose. "That I...that we..." She shuddered.

Loftus's brain began working again, the gears turning and clicking. "Do you mean to say— Have you not—" His mouth opened and closed as he struggled to make his tongue move. "I mean—"

Cate stomped up to him and jabbed him in the chest. "How dare you? How dare you presume such a thing? 'Twas only yesterday that I promised to remain with you in sickness and in health, for richer or poorer, and now you accuse me of this?"

His ire diminished, but he couldn't have been completely wrong. He crossed his arms, his voice raising a bit in volume. "I heard you calling him handsome. I heard you telling him he was presumptuous and to get off you!"

She pointed to the toad. "I was talking to this little gentleman, not to Gilbert. I'd rather not have a toad crawling into my gown, though he seems to be rather comfortable where he is... now." She scooped the animal from her gown and set it on the ground, where it hopped away. Tears began to form in her eyes. "Gilbert was only helping me get it off."

She picked Giles up and held him to her breast, flicking a glance to Gilbert. "Thank you for a lovely outing, my lord. I think I'd better be getting back now."

She led Juliet to a fallen tree and mounted her, piercing Loftus with a disappointed look before she rode down the path, away from them.

Loftus pinched the bridge of his nose and closed his eyes. He'd just made a colossal mistake.

"What a goosecap you are!" Gilbert ran a hand through his hair and threw his arm down at his side. "You should've swallowed your spleen before marching in here as you did."

Loftus heaved a sigh and stared at his brother. "Put yourself in my place. Had you heard the things I did and seen what I had upon coming across the clearing, you might also have presumed."

"Would I have? You have much too little trust in me, brother, to think that I—your very own flesh and blood— would ever even *think* of doing such a thing. She's your *wife,* man! Do you believe me to be without morals?" Gilbert straightened the lapels of his coat, heading for his horse.

Loftus bit the inside of his cheek and followed his brother. "I'm sorry, Gilbert. Of course, you have morals..."

Gilbert mounted Trafferth, his lips pulled into a thin line, his eyes hard.

Loftus met those eyes, so similar to his own. He had treated his brother unfairly. "Thank you for showing Cate around the grounds. I am sorry for the way I behaved. Neither you, nor she, deserved my ire."

Gilbert nodded. "I forgive you, brother, but I think you'll have a difficult time convincing her to do the same."

But Loftus could almost swear a smug smile crossed his brother's face as he turned his horse. Trafferth cantered down the path, and Loftus shook the thought away. It was nothing more than residual anger.

Loftus strode to Hedera and jumped into the saddle, inhaling the sweet forest air in an attempt to clear his mind. His wife had not been happy with him when she'd left—and for good reason. How was he to get her to forgive him?

CHAPTER 12

*C*atherine ran from the stables to the manor, Giles at her heels. She blinked away the tears that threatened to leak from her eyes, though they were dangerously close to dripping, anyway.

Bromley's brow furrowed as she passed him in the foyer, but she was already in another room when she heard him call to her. She needed to be alone. Well…Giles could be with her.

She raced up a staircase and found herself in an unknown corridor. As she searched for a refuge, she forgot to blink for a moment too long, and a tear made its escape, streaming down her cheek to her chin. She swiped it away, but others began to fall.

The distant click of footsteps sounded ahead. She froze.

No one must see her cry. From the time she was a child to the time she'd grown into a woman, her parents had always impressed upon her, among many other things, that tears were a sign of weakness—something to be used against the person they came from.

As quick as a bolt of lightning, Catherine scooped Giles into her arms and searched for a place to hide. She pressed herself flat against the wall, her hip hitting the wood paneling, and a *click* reached her ears.

All of a sudden, she was leaning backward instead of standing straight. A small rectangular door—a bit shorter than herself—had opened in the wall. It had blended perfectly with the paneling, but now that it was open, she could see the seam. Her mouth parted and she let out a breath. What was this? A secret passage? A hidden room?

The footsteps grew louder.

"Come, Giles," she whispered and pushed the hidden door open, escaping into the darkness before whoever was coming could see her likely blotchy face.

She closed the door behind her and exhaled, allowing the tears to come as she stood in a space the color of pitch. The air remained still around her. Quiet. She tucked her face into Giles's short fur, shuddering as the footsteps passed by.

Catherine fell back against the wall, resting one hand against it. Wood. Perhaps the same oak that comprised everything else in the manor. She dragged her fingertips along a knot, a new round of tears washing over her.

How could Loftus have thought she'd done such a thing? And with his very own brother! Had she given him any indication that she was such a woman?

"Why, Giles?" She whispered the words. "Why did he instantly believe the worst?" She brought her hand to her head, pain beginning to grow there. "Is it my reputation? Does he believe Lord Balfour canceled our engagement because of some sort of...indiscretion I committed? Could he believe me to be such a lightskirt?"

Giles whimpered, and Catherine set him down, keeping hold of his lead. "You saw his face as well as I." She pulled a handkerchief from her sleeve and wiped her nose. "Does he really think I have no respect for him, myself, or even God?" She flung out her other hand.

Giles pulled on the lead, dashing away with his nose as a guide. The loop Catherine was meant to be holding fell, and she was left on her own in the dark. "Giles!"

His paws scuttled on wood somewhere far ahead. How large was this hideaway? Catherine heaved an exhale. Should she go search for a servant to help her seek the pup? No, for her eyes were surely red still, and how would she explain her foray into a secret passage, anyway? "Blast," she muttered under her breath. She'd have to find him herself.

Lifting her skirts, she raised a hand to the wall and meandered forward, turning a corner now and again. She bumped into a few walls along the way, and there were more than a few areas where they stopped and it seemed she might be able to go in more than one direction, but she followed the sound of scratching nails and hoped her ears were leading her correctly.

The tapping of Giles's paws became louder, and she was soon able to catch him and recapture the lead. "Naughty puppy." She whispered the scolding, for they stood in front of the outline of a small door—a few feet shorter than she. While Giles, she was sure, would be happy to continue his exploration, Catherine had had enough of the darkness. Hopefully, this portal would open into another hallway, preferably near her bedchamber so she could escape there, after. But there was no knob...

She felt around until her fingers touched some protuberance. Exhaling a breath, she pushed it inward and quietly opened the door, moving into the light as quickly as she could in her desperation. She closed the passageway off behind her as the flash of a red tapestry caught her eye. This room looked familiar. She spun around.

There, standing in only a shirt and pantaloons—his boots strewn across the floor—was her husband—appearing as surprised as she. Neither said anything for a moment.

For a man who tended plants most of the day, his shirt was

rather tight around his arms and chest as he propped his hands on his hips. Catherine's cheeks heated as she took in his muscular form.

Loftus's valet walked out of the dressing room, holding two different-colored waistcoats. "This one or this one, my lor—" He stopped in his steps at the sight of Catherine.

If it was possible, her cheeks grew even warmer.

Loftus scratched the back of his neck, darting a glance to the man. "Might you come back in a few minutes, Verne? I must speak with my wife."

Verne nodded, setting the waistcoats aside. "Of course, my lord." He all but fled the room.

Catherine dropped Giles's lead and let the eager pup sniff Loftus. She made no move farther into the room.

Loftus bent down to pet Giles and tilted his head up toward Catherine. "I see you've found the hidden corridors."

She cleared her throat, sheepish. "They found me."

He nodded, a rueful smile on his face. "They were built in the last century. My grandfather had a few enemies and was somewhat paranoid, you could say, that he wouldn't be able to escape them. He built the passages so that if they came to collect on debts or settle whatever business they had with him, he'd be able to hide."

He picked up Giles. Now that the dog was at eye level, Catherine could see that he had more than a few cobwebs in his coat. Loftus moved across the room toward the fireplace and gestured at the chairs there, waiting for Catherine to sit before seating himself with the pup in his lap. He stared at her.

She looked back at where the door was hidden, her pulse increasing. She spread out her hands. "I didn't mean to come here, you know. Indeed, I was avoiding you."

He nodded. "I expected as much when Bromley told me you'd run through the foyer and I couldn't find you afterward."

He continued to stare. Would he say nothing of his behavior

in the forest? She ground her teeth. Her anger began to build again. She had to let him know how he'd made her feel. "And now that I'm here, you say nothing? Your behavior today was—"

"Reprehensible?" He scratched Giles's ear. "Disgraceful? Egregious?" He raised his eyebrows.

Catherine tilted her head to the side, her ire deflating. "Yes."

Loftus's mouth twisted to the side in a self-deprecating smile. "I'm aware, and I cannot apologize enough for it."

She sighed, still stung by the day's events. "Why, Loftus? Why would you believe that I would do such a thing? Do you believe me to be such a wanton woman?"

His eyes widened, his shoulders straightening. "Not at all. My brother..."

Catherine's lips parted. "You believe such a thing of him?"

Loftus shook his head. "I do not know what to believe anymore. Gilbert has always been the charmer—the one with the cheery grin that no one could resist. I was the lesser-liked brother, even before these scars were etched into my face. They only give people more of a reason to dislike me. But this isn't about me. This is about you and what I said today." He ran a hand over his eyes. "Please, forgive me. I should never have said what I said nor run to the conclusions that I ran to."

Catherine reached over and placed a hand on his where it rested on Giles's back. She softened her voice. "I forgive you— of course, I do." She raised her eyes to his, the icy blue of them seeming to see right into her soul. "I wish you to know, however, that I will always remain true to the vows I made to you. I did not cross my fingers behind my back when we married."

A small smile lifted his lips, lightening her heart along with it. "Thank you, Cate. I didn't either. I plan to remain true to my vows as well." He turned his hand over and captured hers in his grasp, running his thumb over her knuckles in a soft caress.

Bringing her hand to his lips, he pressed a soft kiss against it, scattering butterflies in her stomach.

When he released it, her hand tingled. She didn't know what to do with it anymore. It didn't seem to work like the other one. Should she tuck it into her lap? Rest it on the edge of the chair, perhaps? She settled the matter by dropping it onto her knee, although the action was floppy, as though she'd just lost all movement in her limb.

She grinned at her own observation, then realized once more where she was. "Oh—erm—I'd better let you finish dressing. I'm terribly sorry to have walked in on you in your state of undress—very impolite of me. I suppose it was partly Giles's fault, as he was the one who led me to your door, after all." She bit her lip, cursing her rambling.

Loftus's smile widened. "If Giles is the one who led you here, then I shall have to ask Cook to include a few extra sausages with his dinner."

Catherine pressed a hand to her cheek, covering the heat there. Her heart picked up its pace. Was her husband flirting with her? If so, she liked it very much. She rose, and he stood as well, handing her Giles. She got a whiff of that heady scent that was only his. She closed her eyes and breathed it in.

"Are you all right?"

Her eyes opened. He wore a look of concern as he looked down at her. She reached up hesitantly to straighten his collar, and he gave a quick intake of breath as she did so.

He was just as affected by her as she was him. Her lips quirked up, and she ducked her head. "Now I am."

With those three words and a lightness of step, she hurried from the room, nearly running into Verne who, it appeared, was just on his way in. She gave him a grin as he stood back from the door, eyes wide.

She nearly skipped down the hallway, a squeal stuck in her throat. Her husband had apologized—a thing neither Lord

Balfour nor her father had ever done—and he was attracted to her, even with her forthrightness and oddities.

For the first time in her life, Catherine was truly excited for a life spent with a husband, because it was no longer just a dream. No longer was it fiction. No longer was it something only others could have. Her marriage could definitely turn into love—it was only a matter of time and effort, and Catherine would give it both.

CHAPTER 13

*C*atherine took extra time preparing for dinner that evening, and it was a stroke of luck that Gilbert was dining at the neighboring estate. She would be alone with her husband for the entirety of the evening—a prospect that made her nearly giddy.

Susan finished pinning her hair in a low bun, leaving some curls around Catherine's face and tucking a daisy into the back. Catherine dabbed a few drops of clover perfume onto her wrists and neck and pinched her cheeks in an attempt to redden them. With any luck, the wine at dinner would stain her lips a nice red color too. A light flush was most becoming—or so she'd been told.

She stood from the dressing table and ran her hands down her skirts, tilting her chin up to glance in the mirror. Her pale blue gown almost appeared white when the evening sun hit it. She turned this way and that, her lips pursed. "How do I look?"

"Very well, my lady." Susan clasped her hands in front of her, her eyes wide.

Catherine looked over her shoulder at the maid. "But will he like it?"

"I do not know why he shouldn't." Susan shrugged.

Catherine exhaled. "If he and I are to fall in love, Susan, then I must look appealing to him."

Susan leaned back on her heels and narrowed her eyes. "You say he likes plants?"

~

*L*oftus waited in the drawing room for his wife, the room filled with a gentle light from outside. The sun was setting, but not very quickly. He stood by the empty hearth, examining a seedling he'd placed on the mantel. It was growing well here. The amount of sunlight it was getting appeared to be perfect, for the plant's leaves were a healthy green, and new ones were growing from the ends of it. He nodded, satisfaction stirring within him.

His attention turned from the plant to the window, however, when Giles barked outside. A footman was leading the pup through the grass for his evening walk.

Giles's owner was unlike any woman he'd ever met before, and not in a bad way. She was...intriguing. So many questions he wished to pose... She knew what he enjoyed, but what did *she* enjoy? Why had her betrothed canceled their engagement? Who or what had caused her to have nightmares like the one he'd witnessed the other evening?

Footsteps sounded outside the drawing room door, and he turned as it opened, much struck by what he saw. Cate entered the room as regally as a queen, with foliage of all kinds, flowers and greenery, pinned to her head in the shape of a turban. Curls had been left loose around her cheeks to frame her face, but the rest—as far as he could tell—was covered in material gathered from the garden.

The footman's eyes were wide as she moved past him and walked toward Loftus, a smile on her face. Loftus only just remembered to close his mouth as he tried to count how many varying species of flora she'd included in her coiffure.

He cleared his throat. "Y-your hair..."

Cate's smile widened, her eyes sparkling. "Yes, isn't it wonderful? I had Susan do it for me. I know you like plants, so I thought you'd enjoy it."

Loftus's brain struggled to interpret what she was saying. She'd done this...because he enjoyed plants? She'd made her head a veritable garden...for *him?* He blinked. No one had ever done something so thoughtful before, with him in mind. Was it out of the ordinary? Yes, but as Loftus's eyes traced over her, he knew very well that this woman must not be an ordinary woman, after all. Somehow, he'd married a princess from the forest. If, somehow, he could keep this princess for himself— with her crown of flowers and ferns—then he'd be a happy man, indeed.

"Do you like it?" Her voice faltered, and Loftus realized he'd been staring for too long.

He moved toward her and reached a hand up to finger the daisies at the crown of her head, their petals soft to the touch. "I love it. You look beautiful." His voice was a murmur. She truly did. No one else could style their hair the way she had and look so otherworldly.

A pink hue painted her cheeks, and she ducked her chin. "Thank you. I'm glad." She wrapped her hand around his arm, her touch light and gentle. He was keenly aware of where every finger pressed against him.

Time seemed to slow. Before anything else could be said, dinner was announced.

He led her to her seat and sat down after, then did his best to focus on the courses as each came and went. The fact was, if he didn't, he'd be staring at her all evening—and that simply wouldn't do. Cate, it seemed, was happy to be alone with him. She spared no question in between courses, or during.

"Have you always been interested in botany?"

He cut into his beef, thinking back upon his childhood. "I have. I was quite ill for a few weeks as a boy and was made much better by the apothecary's herbs. I became interested in what plant could make an ill person better and began to visit him often." He frowned. "Not long after, my father forbade me from doing so, but I continued to study plants and how they can be used to help others. God has put them on this earth for a reason, I believe. If we weren't meant to use them, He wouldn't allow them to grow."

Cate nodded. "Quite right. It is just like how all creatures have been put on earth for a reason. Some may seem like pests, but they are food for us or for other animals, or are simply beautiful to look at. Many also help maintain God's creation, just by living their lives."

Loftus swallowed his bite of meat. "Is that what you're interested in? Animals?"

Cate gave a wry smile. "'Tis partly why I accepted your brother's offer of a tour of the grounds. He told me of his love and study of animals and that he would show me where to find them."

Loftus bit the inside of his lip and nodded as he mulled over this new piece of information. Why had Gilbert told Cate such a thing? His brother was definitely no student of animals nor wildlife, and the only time he really looked at any creature was when he was ogling some woman or at the races. What motive had he to lie?

Loftus took a sip of wine. "He certainly loves his horses."

Unease coated the inside of Loftus's abdomen. What was Gilbert playing at? But then, Loftus *had* run to conclusions only that afternoon. Gilbert's words about trust came to mind. No. It could be no more than a simple mistake or a silly contrivance. And his wife was still speaking.

"I admit that I cannot resist observing any sort of creatures

—especially having grown up in London where the most common animals are horses and rats. I've always found it thrilling to interact with wildlife, large or small. Birds, butterflies, deer, and squirrels are among my favorites."

Loftus's lips quirked up at Cate's excitement. "You'll see many of those here. Pray, is that why the toad was on your shoulder today? You were attempting to observe him?"

Cate nodded, her curls bouncing. "Oh, indeed! He was a very fine specimen." She pierced a potato with her fork, lifting her eyes to him.

He fought the urge to shift in his seat as a warm feeling grew within him at being so tenderly looked at.

Her gaze remained on his face. "Might I ask you..." Her smile faded. "How did you get the scars on your face?"

Loftus closed his eyes, inwardly sighing. He knew that this question would come, at some point or another, but he'd been dreading it. If only they could both continue to act as though his scars were invisible—that there was nothing wrong with his face at all.

"I'm sorry. I..." Her soft voice made him open his eyes. Her cheeks were red. She looked as though she'd rather be anywhere else—with anyone else. Perhaps now that she'd acknowledged his scars, the full effect of them and realization that she'd be stuck with them and him for the remainder of her life was overwhelming. He understood well. He'd been told almost daily by his mother and brother what a sight he was to behold. Not a pleasant one. Never a pleasant one.

He raised his hand to stop her apology, though he kept his focus on his plate. "Do not apologize. Your question is reasonable." He gripped his wine glass, holding it near while he spoke. "I got them in the war."

She raised her eyebrows. "When you sang the song the other evening, I wondered if you mightn't have lost someone in the war, but you went yourself?"

He nodded. "I have lost many, Cate."

She shook her head. "Fathers do not normally send their heirs into war."

He took a sip of wine, reliving the discussion he'd had with his own. "My father did not approve of my study of plants. He called it 'embarrassing,' if I remember correctly."

Cate gasped.

"I had no choice. He bought me a commission, and I went where I was called. That was in 1811, when I was one-and-twenty." He took a moment to close his eyes, readying himself for what he was about to say and for the memories he was about to dredge up. He opened them. "I was a part of the Light Division. Infantry. In April of 1812, we went to Badajoz, Spain, to seize the city from the French."

He took a breath, almost feeling the anticipation he had that day flooding through his veins. "We breached the city's wall in one area but, amid the rubble and fighting, became confused. We became mixed with the Fourth Division."

His heartbeat sped up as images of wounded and dead soldiers flooded his mind and the sounds of gunfire and shouting came from all directions. His hands began to tremble. He clutched the wine glass tighter and grasped the armrest of his seat with the other. "It was chaos. None of us knew which way was forward and which was back." Blood had pooled in the stones beneath his boots as his comrades had fallen, one by one.

"We tried to keep moving forward, but they kept tossing grenades, and the volleys only continued. One of the officers fell after a bullet pierced his leg. I tried to help him stand, and that was when a Frenchman appeared before me."

He inhaled deeply, attempting to steady his breath. "The man lunged at me with his bayonet, aiming for my face. I tried to move away, though you can see the first scar where it struck." He traced the line from his eyebrow to his chin. "He had me backed up against a wall. I attempted to reach for my sword—for I'd dropped it when helping my friend—and he gave me the other scar." He traced the line from his cheek to the corner of his jaw.

His wife's mouth was open in an O, her hands pressed flat against the table. "And then what happened?"

Loftus took a final sip of wine, then pushed the glass away from him. It would do him no good to drink the rest. He shrugged. "And then he stabbed me."

"He—" Her eyes examined him from the top of his head to his abdomen, for she couldn't see his legs beneath the table.

Loftus nodded. "Yes. In the side. He killed my friend, and I fell unconscious." He gauged her response carefully, the wide eyes and tense posture. "Is this too much for you, Cate?" Most women would have already stopped him from relating the bloody details...and at the dinner table, no less. What had he been thinking? Gilbert would hit him upside the head.

She straightened, her expression also smoothing out. "Indeed, no. I would learn all I can about you. But if I may ask... why did the soldier not finish you off?"

"I suppose the man thought me dead. I was likely close to it. I was found after the battle—when the bodies were being stacked up. My comrades realized I was still alive, and I was eventually nursed back to health and sent back into the thick of it, continuing on in the fight until Napoleon's defeat in 1815." He exhaled heavily, his shoulders losing some of their tension.

Inside his mind, the battle still raged—but he'd wanted to share with his wife what he'd gone through. She deserved to know. If only she had the power to help take it away. Would she even wish to have that job?

CHAPTER 14

*C*atherine stared at her husband, her mouth slack. "But you were stabbed! Shouldn't you have been sent home, having done your duty?" She pressed herself back into her seat, eyes wide. "You could've worsened by staying. How did you even survive that? Was not your father concerned you would die and he'd lose his heir?"

Loftus shook his head. "The wound managed to miss everything important, by God's good grace. At one point, the doctor feared infection, but that never came to pass. I can only thank the Lord in heaven for my having lived. As for my superiors sending me home—they would never unless I'd lost a limb or eye. They needed every soldier they had, and at the end of that battle, they'd lost many. Badajoz was won, but the cost was very dear."

Her husband was a hero. Catherine stared at him with new eyes. "Your family must have been very proud."

He put his arm on the table, his expression solemn. "I received very few letters from my father when I was away. I do not think he was concerned with my welfare. Why should he have been with a spare at home?"

The room fell silent for a few moments. Catherine's heart broke at the subtle pain in his voice. He was doing a good job of hiding it, but for someone like her who had dealt with a similar situation, she was rather skilled at identifying emotions.

She placed her hand on the soft fabric of his coat. "Parents can be cruel, can they not? *People* can be cruel. Some care only for their own affairs and seek only how to improve their own images, never thinking of who they might hurt as they do so."

"I was never enough for him." A frown pulled on Loftus's lips. "I tried to be. I imagined the look of pride on his face when I'd return. His letters didn't say much but, surely, when he'd seen what a military man I'd become, he'd be very pleased."

"And was he?" She cocked her head, fearing the answer.

He straightened his shoulders. "On the day of my arrival, my father wasn't even home. Dining at a friend's house when he'd known of my homecoming for weeks. When he finally did come home, he looked at me as a father who did not know his son. Said it would've been better had I died on the Peninsula than come back looking like this."

Anger mixed in Catherine's stomach. How dare his father say that to him? How dare any father say that to his son? She pushed back her chair and rose, coming around to stand near to Loftus. He'd stood when she had, eyes wide with a hint of wariness in them.

She placed her hands on his arms, his muscles tensing beneath them, and tilted her chin up to look into his face. "What he said is inexcusable and incorrect. No father should speak thusly to his child."

His stare was vacant. "Sometimes I'm not sure my mother does not feel the same way. Perhaps they are right."

Catherine lifted one hand to his shoulder, gripping it tight. "They are not. Why would the blade have missed every important organ if you were meant to die? Why would infection fail to set in if you weren't meant to return home? God has saved you for a reason."

He pressed his hand against hers where it grasped his shoulder, his warm palm encasing her fingers. The empty look began to disappear from his eyes, and they filled with something new. Determination, perhaps?

"You're right. He has." He brought her hand to his lip and kissed her fingertips, his breath warm against them. What a new sensation to feel his rougher skin against hers. She certainly didn't know a man of his station without smooth hands, for they never lifted a finger except when playing cards or drinking—or wagging them in parliament.

A warmth blanketed her at the proximity of this man and the conversation they'd just had. He'd shared a piece of his heart with her. He'd put it on a tray and served it to her like the servants had delivered the dishes of food, and he'd waited to see what she did with it. He hadn't known if she'd find the flavor distasteful or not, but he'd served it, anyway.

His head was tilted down to look at her, and her hand tingled from the soft kiss he'd bestowed upon it. She wanted to gift *him* with something too.

Taking a step forward, she stood on the tips of her toes and pressed a kiss to his scarred cheek, closing her eyes to savor the moment. His intake of breath was noticeable, but he didn't step back or move away—just remained still.

After a second had passed, Catherine leaned back once more and opened her eyes, a rush of heat within her and a flare of warmth across her cheeks. Loftus's eyes were closed. He looked peaceful, as though he had fallen asleep on his feet. The clock in the hall rang the hour, and his eyelids opened slowly, revealing dazed irises and pupils.

"If—at any time—you feel the inclination to do that again, you need not hesitate." His voice came out soft. "I assure you, it is most welcome."

She giggled and nodded. "I shall take that into account in the future. For the present—" She yawned, covering her mouth with her hand. "I am rather tired and shall return to my chambers, I believe. Are you tending the plants tomorrow? If so, I should very much like to join you after speaking of the menu with Mrs. Stonehill. By the by, do you enjoy eating fish?"

Loftus's eyebrows raised. "You would like to join me?"

"I would, indeed. And what of the fish?"

He scratched the back of his head. "Erm—yes. I do enjoy eating fish. Are there any plants you would like to see tomorrow in particular?"

"No. Only the ones you are tending and harvesting from currently. I would like to be useful if I can be." She lifted her lips in a smile and bobbed a curtsy. She picked up her skirts and swished out of the dining room with a parting wink, savoring his expression of delighted astonishment. She would enjoy finding more ways to put that look on his face.

CHAPTER 15

*L*oftus paced back and forth in the conservatory, weaving around potted plants and the hanging ones where they intercepted his path. His wife was set to meet him in a quarter of an hour, and he hadn't accomplished anything since he'd set foot in the room half an hour earlier.

Whenever he grabbed a watering can from beside the door, the image of her gleaming eyes popped into his head, and he forgot what he was doing completely. When he attempted to examine the growth of his *Marum Syriacum* seedlings, he only thought of the warmth of her lips on his cheek and the feelings that had evoked within him. She had smelled so sweet with her head covered in flowers.

He squinted as he walked through the same slant of light for the fourteenth time, the sun shining a particularly bright beam through one of the conservatory's windows. It was getting warm.

He removed his coat and unbuttoned the cuffs of his shirt, rolling up his sleeves.

Plants. That was what he needed to be thinking about. He moved to the window to check the seedlings there, all of them growing well in their spot amidst the sun. He had multiple pots of seedlings here—some of them exotic—and the plants would serve the village well once they reached their full potential.

He was measuring how tall his *Polygala senega* had grown when he heard the door of the conservatory open. He wrote down the measurement in his notebook before lifting his eyes to the front of the room where he knew she'd be.

Though she'd been occupying his thoughts, he somehow wasn't prepared for the vision of loveliness before him. She wore a jonquil-colored day dress with a fichu tucked in the neckline. Her hair was pulled up in pins—without the turban of flowers this time—and she appeared as cheery as the slant of light he'd been walking through. And looking at her did not require squinting. Indeed, he wished to keep his eyes wide open to view every inch of her beauty.

"Good afternoon!" She stepped forward with a great smile, closing the door behind her. "How are they faring? Have I missed anything important?"

He returned her smile with one of his own, though it felt almost foreign on his lips. "You haven't. They are faring well. All is as it should be." He moved to a wooden cabinet at the side of the room and opened it, looking inside for an extra pair of gloves. "I'm very glad to have your company." He peered at her from behind the door and gave a self-deprecating laugh. "The plants do not respond to my questions or comments."

Cate's lips twisted. "Very rude of them."

He gave an exaggerated sigh. "You understand, then."

Finding the gloves he was looking for, he closed the cabinet and handed them to her. "You'll want to put these on before we start. Some of the plants we'll be touching are a bit prickly and can even sting." He shrugged. "We mustn't blame them—it is how they were born. Each is different from the next."

Cate traded her white gloves for the working gloves and followed Loftus's lead, listening to his instructions as he told her which plants were good for what and how to harvest the parts of each.

They moved from pot to pot, Loftus writing measurements and other observations in his notebook while Cate watered them near the soil. At each plant they stopped at, she asked him of the benefits of the plant and what illnesses it proved a remedy to. Loftus tried to give her short answers so as not to overwhelm her with a trove of information. He had no wish to scare her off...not when her presence brought more solace and delight than the entire conservatory full of plants. And that was a rather frightening notion.

~

One sunny afternoon in mid-May a few weeks after her wedding, Catherine strode down the corridor toward the conservatory with a merry hum on her lips. The carpeted floor muffled her footsteps as she turned down the hall.

Spending time with Loftus each day had allowed her to become more comfortable in his presence. They didn't always speak very much, but since she'd begun helping him with his work, she'd learned the names and purposes of most of the plants, and, more importantly, more about her husband.

For instance, he didn't have a favorite plant, for "there are too many to choose from," and he drank several cups of tea a day. He favored scones over any other teatime victual and enjoyed polishing her spectacles for her when they became smudged.

Catherine smiled to herself. He'd become a close friend.

She, in turn, had told him of her London life and her childhood growing up as a merchant's daughter. She hadn't yet told him of the details of her engagement with Lord Balfour, but perhaps in a few weeks or so, she might. She swallowed as her throat grew tight at the thought. She'd only do so if she were comfortable enough.

She arrived at the double doors to the conservatory and opened one, stepping in. Her husband crouched behind a pot of hollyhocks—what he'd call *Malva hortensis*—with a furrowed brow, scribbling in his notebook with his pencil. With that concentrated expression on his face, she could look at him all day. There wasn't a doubt in her mind he could do anything he set his mind on doing.

He looked up and his lips quirked. "Wife. There you are. I was beginning to wonder if you'd come."

Catherine rolled her eyes and moved down the center path. She smiled. "You know I would not miss our hours together, husband. They are what I most look forward to each day."

He pressed a hand to his cheek, his eyes gleaming. "More words like that, my dear, and you shall set me to the blush."

She took the final steps toward him and shoved his shoulder, nearly tipping him over with a chuckle on her lips. "I should like to see that."

He righted himself and laughed. "Perhaps one day you will. The more scandalous a phrase that comes out of your mouth, the more likely it is to happen." His eyebrows waggled in an exaggerated fashion.

"Is that so?" Amusement colored her tone. "I shall have to come up with something very scandalous, then, and say it when you are least expecting it."

Loftus grinned. "I await the words with pleasure." He stood and brushed the dust from his pantaloons. "Now, we must begin preparing the *Prunella vulgaris*. It is in bloom."

He led her over to a pot of vibrant purple flowers, their blossoms growing about eight inches from the soil on club-like spikes. Their leaves were smooth on the edges and pointed at the end—the color of their stems a light green. Cate attempted to commit the Latin name to memory.

"What is it normally called?" She tipped her head to the side.

He propped his hands on his hips. "Self-heal. The flowers and leaves are used to help inward and outward wounds and ruptures, bruises, sore throat, the spitting up of blood, etc."

She raised her eyebrows. "Impressive. How shall we harvest it?"

Loftus went to the cabinet and offered her gloves as well as a pair of snips. "We'll be cutting off the tops and pinching most of the leaves off of the stems." He moved over to a nearby wooden table and rested his hand on it. "We'll set what we've collected on here to dry. Once they have, we can put them in a bag and deliver them to the apothecary, but that shan't be for a day or two, I think."

Catherine nodded, her gaze darting from her husband to the flowers. Anticipation built within. This would be a fun task. "Let us begin, then."

Loftus moved the pot of Self-heal to the table, and both of them began snipping away at the blossoms, the flower heads falling as though it was the French Revolution all over again. It was an easy thing to do, and the movements were the same. Lift, cut, set down. Pinch, pull, put to the side. One didn't have to focus very hard, which made it ideal for talking.

Without looking up, she spoke. "How was your evening?" *How was your evening?* What in heaven's name had enticed her to pick *that* as the thing to ask him? Goodness gracious, she'd been with him for most of it! She didn't look at him. Couldn't.

"Last evening? I retired almost immediately after you did. If you're wondering how I slept, then the answer is...fine..."

She raised an eyebrow and darted a look at him. "Your tone and your hesitation do not convince me."

He heaved a sigh. "There are moments that my time spent in the Peninsula come back to haunt me. I have nightmares on occasion." He snipped a flower and placed it in the growing pile.

Her husband had nightmares? "This is the first I am hearing of this." She longed for him to grow more comfortable sharing intimate details of his life with her.

He grunted. "It is not seen as very masculine for a man to be reminded of his fears—to have fears at all. What wife wishes to comfort her husband in the dead of the night? Should not it be the other way around?"

She pinched a leaf a bit more aggressively than she ought to have. "You *did* comfort me when I had a nightmare."

"Not well." He muttered the words.

She pushed her spectacles up the bridge of her nose. "Oh, pish. Your presence is more a balm than you know. Will not you let me be the same for you?"

He set down his snips, his eyes earnest. "I feel as though I am at a disadvantage. You know what causes my nightmares, yet I still do not know the cause of yours."

She bit her lip. Could she give a vague answer? Her heart was already beating faster at the mere thought of telling Loftus about Lord Balfour and all he'd put her through. She set her snips down and gripped her hands together in front of her, her palms sweating. "Your nightmares are caused by the war. Mine are caused by a man."

She brushed her hands over the flowers, spreading them out to dry. Loftus did the same with the leaves, his eyes full of questions she wasn't sure she was ready to answer.

"A man?" His voice was a murmur.

She nodded in response, her gaze cast to the floor. He reached for her hand and slowly walked her to the nearby stone bench. They both sat down. She took a deep breath, examining her emotions. The memories weren't so bad when Loftus's hand covered her own. Perhaps Catherine had been wrong earlier. Perhaps she *was* ready to reveal her past to him.

"Who?"

The question was so simple, yet she had to force the name from her mouth. "Lord Kenneth Balfour," she whispered. She closed her eyes as the memories came tumbling back—memories she'd long tried to forget.

"The name sounds familiar."

She nodded, swallowing. "I am not surprised. His name is often heard in society. His initials are seen in the gossip pages nearly every day."

"And who is he to you?" His thumb traced over her knuckles.

She took a shuddering breath. "He was my betrothed."

Fear took a hold of her. Would Loftus wonder if it was Catherine's fault he had left? Would he wonder how far her reputation had been stained? What would happen when he found out how stained she truly was? Though her virtue was intact, she had come very close to losing it, and the toll of his words and abuse was a blot of ink on a white page, indeed.

～

*L*oftus's gaze snapped to Cate as his stomach dropped. Her betrothed? He'd known, of course, that she'd been betrothed before, but for her betrothed to be the person causing her nightmares left him reeling. He'd expected an attacker or a childhood trauma or something of the sort, but this man was alive and well—certainly not on a hangman's noose—and living amongst high society without a care. And, if Loftus remembered correctly, it'd been this very lord that had canceled their engagement—not Cate. Therefore, he'd gotten away from the situation appearing as though *he* was the one who'd been wronged.

What could he say? Clearly, whatever Cate had gone through had been complex. She didn't need him prodding her with questions. What she needed was some silent encouragement. He gripped her hand tighter as her face reddened and her eyes squeezed shut. He ached to see her in such turmoil.

She opened her mouth once more, seeming to choke on the words she spoke. "My father arranged the betrothal between Lord Balfour and myself. I never wished for an arranged betrothal but hoped it might go well." She scoffed. "How naive I was then."

She pressed her shoulder against his. He was happy to be her support as she continued her story.

"My parents told me I had to behave—as they always do—and I tried my best. I truly did. I played the proper London lady in his presence." She scowled. "But it wasn't enough." Her breaths became heavier. "Any time he deemed my behavior beneath what it should be in his eyes, he began to insult me—shout at me—call me terrible things. When I dared to do something I wanted instead of what *he* wished me to do, I received the same treatment. He said he could find a new betrothed at the snap of his fingers."

His blood began to boil and his jaw clenched as he thought of what the man had put Cate through. If he ever ran into him, Lord Balfour could be sure that Loftus wouldn't forget his military training.

She spoke on. "I did not wish to shame my family. Surely, he would get better once we were married. He couldn't be worse than what I was already receiving at home from my parents. The Lord knows they treated me no better. So I remained."

She inhaled deeply and shut her eyes tight. A few seconds passed before words fell from her lips again. "That was when the beatings began."

Loftus's blood turned to ice in his veins. The *what?*

～

The image of Lord Balfour's open palm flying toward her face appeared in her mind, followed by the phantom sting of pain on her cheek. She could almost feel his fingers digging into her shoulders as he violently shook her, his breath hot on her face. More than once, he'd thrown her to the ground like a child throwing a doll in a tantrum.

She opened her eyes, her pulse thrumming in her ears. Loftus's eyes were hard as he stared at the ground. His grip on her hand tightened, serving to remind her that he was her protector now—her husband, the man who could be her confidante. She could tell him anything.

She licked her dry lips. "Instead of only the shouting and insulting, he became violent. H-he would hit me if I said something to one of his friends that he didn't like." Her hands began to tremble. "O-once, we attended a card party, and—and I'm not very good at whist, you see—and we lost a game. When he had a moment alone after, he slapped me." She bit her lip. "I had to cover the bruise with powder."

Loftus swore under his breath, shaking his head. "And this jackanapes called off the betrothal? It's fortunate you weren't stuck with him, but for *him to* have been the one to protest..."

Catherine nodded, her stomach roiling at the idea of telling the next part of the story. "Yes. Lord Balfour was the one to call off our engagement. He claimed it was because of my behavior. My parents took this to mean my unladylike behavior, but I know the real reason." A bitter taste formed in her mouth.

Her husband furrowed his brow. "And what is that?"

Bile crept up her throat as heat came to the back of her neck and face. She swallowed, her breathing uneven. Loftus placed his other hand under hers so that both of his enveloped her fingers. She blinked, willing her eyes not to close for too long lest she see memories she didn't wish to.

"He called on me one afternoon. My father was out meeting

a business partner, and my mother was shopping. Tetley, our butler, let him in, and Lord Balfour visited me in the drawing room with Susan as chaperone. All was well enough...until..."

Loftus's shoulder tensed against hers as she leaned against it.

"One of the maids happened to be sick that day, so Susan ended up having to leave for a moment to get the tea things." Catherine's vision blurred. "H-he threw himself on me. He pressed his mouth to mine, and I suffocated as his hands grabbed at my clothes..." She sniffed, her voice raising. "I tried to scream, b-but I couldn't, and I could hardly move—" She let out a sob, ducking her head into the crook of Loftus's neck and crushing her spectacles against her face. Her shoulders shook.

Immediately, his arms were around her—one arm wrapped around her back and the other caressing her hair.

"S-Susan came in b-before anything—before he—" Her voice was muffled against his cravat. "And he became angry. He told me it wouldn't matter if we w-were together before we were w-wed since our marriage was to happen soon, anyway, but I refused. I would not relent. I had Tetley throw him out. *That,* I believe, is why he ended our betrothal."

Loftus continued to hold her close, and she breathed in his scent, the earthy fragrance calming to her nerves.

"That is why my nights are plagued by him. He has done much to damage me, Loftus."

Her husband stroked her back. "I am sorry you had to go through that, Cate. No one should have to deal with abuse at the hands of their partner. I only thank God you are away from him now."

"As do I. But now we are even. I have shared my story, and now we each may comfort each other at night." She leaned away from his embrace, emotionally drained but grateful for his support. "Let us speak of other things now. The day is young, and we've more harvesting to do. I am done with the past."

CHAPTER 16

*T*he next day, Catherine pulled pink thread through her embroidery and sank the needle into the middle of what was to become a flower, humming. Several French knots in yellow thread already dotted the bottom of the fabric and were waiting for pink petals like this one, and she was happy to oblige. The afternoon was bright, and the drawing room windows let in the perfect amount of light for her activity. The gold-cushioned chair she sat on was incredibly comfortable, and a few windows were open to let in the early-summer air. Pure bliss.

Footsteps outside the door preceded Bromley's entrance. "You have callers, my lady. Are you at home?"

She pricked her finger, dropping her embroidery hoop into her lap. "Did you say callers, Bromley?" She raised her eyebrows. No one had called on her since her arrival to Black-fern Manor. Indeed, she'd often wondered if news of the earl's marriage had spread at all.

Bromley clasped his hands behind his back. "Indeed, my lady. A Mrs. and Miss Haredon."

"Do send them in, please, Bromley." Catherine put her embroidery away. "Oh, and please have tea sent up."

"Right away, my lady." He clicked his heels and went on his way.

Anticipation grew in Catherine's stomach as she waited for her callers to enter the room. Their quiet chatter came from the hallway and then they were escorted in. Catherine stood, a wide smile on her face. Would this be the making of new friends?

"Good afternoon! I understand you are Mrs. Haredon and Miss Haredon?"

The women bobbed curtsies, and the older woman, a brunette with greying hair and a maroon gown, nodded. "Indeed. We are your neighbors on the south side." She gestured to the younger woman with lighter brown hair and a peach gown. "This is my Cecilia."

Miss Haredon stepped forward, curiosity in her eyes. "You are the earl's new wife?"

Catherine bowed her head and gestured to the chairs before them. "I am. It is a pleasure to meet you. Please, have a seat."

They sat, and the women looked at her expectantly, as though waiting for her to do something. Had she forgotten an important societal rule?

She settled her skirts around her legs and widened her smile. "Er—tea will be up in a moment."

Mrs. Haredon leaned forward, her voice hushed. "So how is it?"

Catherine pushed her glasses farther up her nose. "Pardon me?"

"Being married to the earl. How is it?" The woman's eyes were wide.

Catherine's eyebrows lifted. "Well—"

"We feel positively terrible for you." Miss Haredon reached

over and placed her hand on Catherine's. "It must be so difficult living here."

Confusion wrapped around Catherine's brain. What were these women speaking of? She scratched at her cheek. "I enjoy living here and being married. Why would it be difficult?"

At that moment, a maid came in with the tea tray and set it on the table. Catherine poured for her guests and helped herself to a bite of a biscuit as her companions shared glances. What had she missed?

Mrs. Haredon sipped her tea and set the cup and saucer down on the table. "Your husband...do not his scars...bother you?"

Miss Haredon sniffed and picked up a cucumber sandwich. "They're hideous, Mama. Of course, they bother her."

Catherine's stomach dropped. She set down her cup and saucer with a rattle as outrage flared within her. "I'll thank you not to speak of my husband in such a way again."

Miss Haredon's eyes widened. "But they are! I'm surprised you didn't marry Lord Berkley, but then, I suppose he doesn't come with the estate."

Catherine clenched her skirts in her fists, her jaw tightening. "I do not share your opinion. Truly, I believe his scars to be most beautiful. They also serve as a reminder of what he has done to keep us safe and to keep our country secure, Miss Haredon."

Miss Haredon scoffed. "Beautiful? You are doing it a bit too brown, my lady."

Catherine stood. "Indeed, I am not, but it matters not if you understand." She eyed Mrs. Haredon, who quickly put her half-finished scone down and nudged her daughter with her elbow. Both stood. Catherine pasted on a false smile. "I believe this meeting to be over. If you cannot come without disparaging my husband, then do not come again."

She called for Bromley, who popped his head in almost immediately. "Yes, my lady?"

"Please show these women out."

As soon as they were out the door, she slumped back into her chair and glanced at the clock on the mantel. It had been seven minutes since they'd arrived. She sighed. What a waste of tea. She shrugged. More scones for herself.

She plucked one from the tray and scooped a dollop of clotted cream and jam on top of it, mulling over what they'd said. Was her husband's appearance the reason for her lack of callers in the weeks after their marriage?

She furrowed her eyebrows. Surely, that couldn't be. There were only two scars on his face. Would society really be driven away by such a thing? She shook her head, but the more she thought about it, the more she realized the answer. Yes.

The only reason these women had come today was for gossip—they hadn't even wished to know about Catherine, herself. Society cared for beauty only, and Loftus didn't fit their standard.

Catherine huffed. If these were the type of callers she was to get, then she would be content without any at all.

$\sim$

*D*ays later, Catherine sought out her husband around midmorning. It was earlier than usual for him to begin tending to the plants, but she peeked into the conservatory in the hope of seeing his handsome face.

She opened the doors, but all was quiet within. He wasn't there. Frowning, she closed the doors and turned around, going back the way she'd come. Where else might he be?

Deciding his study was the next best option, she began to walk there, the portraits on the walls staring down at her. She passed a few servants in the hallways, greeting them as she went, and when she finally reached Loftus's study door, she knocked twice.

His familiar voice bid her to enter from the opposite side, sending a flicker of excitement down her spine. She opened the door and stepped inside.

Loftus sat in a large leather chair behind a stately desk made of some sort of dark wood—the top polished and shining. Beside him was a stack of foolscap, and to his right was an inkwell and pen knife. A quill was poised in his hand as he looked up at Catherine's entrance. A gleam came into his eyes. "This is a surprise, indeed. You've never visited me in my study before."

She stepped into the room and closed the door behind her, a smile lifting her lips. "I've had no need to, I suppose."

He set down his quill and raised an eyebrow. "And you've a need to now?" He lifted a hand to pause any response. "Do not misunderstand me—I am more than happy with your presence here."

Catherine tilted her head. "I was thinking about the Self-Heal and wondering if it was dry by now. You mentioned that after it was, we might deliver it to the apothecary." She moved toward his desk and glanced at the foolscap there. "I have been wanting to visit the village but have not yet had the chance to..." Catherine raised her gaze to his in a silent plea.

Loftus sat back in his chair, eyes wide. "You wish to deliver it yourself? I was going to have a servant do so."

Catherine nodded. "I would be more than happy to. I'll take Susan with me, of course. It's not too far a distance, is it?"

Her husband brought a hand to his chin. "Perhaps a bit far to go on foot, but you may take the carriage, certainly. Are you sure you wish to do such a menial task? If the villagers see you doing so, your name might be bandied about." He assessed her with a wary expression.

Catherine shrugged. "It wouldn't be the first time. I don't

give two figs for others' opinions if they aren't close to me." Her cheeks warmed. "Although, I would not wish to bring down your good name." She would feel terrible if her antics made the townspeople speak worse of Loftus and their family.

Her husband frowned and grabbed her hand in his own. "Do not think of such things. You are a boon to my name—not a detriment. I'm sure the Self-Heal is dry by now. Indeed, I'm fairly finished with my work here. Let us collect it, and we'll ready you to go."

He stood and placed a few pieces of foolscap on top of one another, setting them on the others. He held out his arm and escorted her toward the conservatory.

She eyed him as they walked. "You could come with me, you know."

He grimaced. "The village is not a place I enjoy. Not anymore."

They collected the flowers and leaves in the conservatory and bagged them in a linen sack. Loftus had Bromley call for the carriage to be brought around, and in less than a quarter of an hour, she sat with Susan in the equipage, moving at a steady pace down the country lane.

As soon as the village came into view, Catherine's curiosity was piqued. She'd only seen the Hogshead Inn, and that had been at night. Now she was able to see the village in sunlight, with the people bustling between shops and on the streets. They passed a milliner and modiste, a bakery, a book-shop, a penny university for the scholars to drink coffee, and all sorts of shops as the coachman drove toward the apothecary.

The people on the street met Catherine's gaze through the window. Ladies in twos and threes glanced at each other and whispered behind their hands whilst gentlemen tipped their hats and joked with their companions. Catherine kept her eyes on all of them for as long as she could. What were they saying?

Were they speaking of her? Of Loftus? Of something else entirely?

As a child, companions of hers had wished to fly or breathe under water for as long as they wanted. She, on the other hand, had always wished to read other people's thoughts. It would be easy to know how to think of someone if one knew how they thought of others, including herself. But then, she would learn things she did not want to know.

The carriage rolled to a stop in front of a small building—a sign above the building declaring *Mr. Grine's Apothecary*—and the footman lowered the steps, then assisted Catherine and Susan down. They walked into the shop, Catherine with the bag in hand, and were greeted from behind the counter by a sturdy man with muscular arms and grey hair.

"Good day. What may I help ye with?" He hooked his fingers in the pockets of his apron, his spectacles perched on the tip of his long nose.

Catherine stepped toward him. "I presume you are Mr. Grine? I'm Lady Hardwicke. My—"

The man's bushy eyebrows raised. "Ye're the earl's new wife, eh? I admit, I was mighty s'prised to hear he'd married. How is he?"

She cleared her throat. "He's well. The reason I'm here is that my husband and I recently harvested the leaves and flowers from some Self-Heal, and I came to deliver it to you."

He leaned over the counter to look at the bag in her hand. "Ah. That's fine of ye, I say. I'm running low on it. Seen lots of bruises lately and scrapes on the lads. Now it's summer, they're gettin' into all sorts of trouble."

Catherine's lips quirked up. "I imagine they are." She handed the bag to him, and he paid her. She dropped the few coins into her reticule, appraising the many jars of herbs that lined the walls and the bottles on the shelves. "You have a nice business here, Mr. Grine. A very neat array of items."

The man ducked his chin, a red hue dusting his cheeks. "Thank ye, my lady. I do my best. It's easy when there ain't no competition around and yer husband supplies me with the herbs that I can't get so easy." He rubbed his chin. "That reminds me—would you tell him I'm low on Butcher's Broom?"

"Butcher's Broom. I will. Good day!" Catherine left the shop, hopping back into the carriage. She tried to commit the name to memory so she wouldn't forget before she got back to the manor.

She'd been hoping to stroll around the village for a little while, but all of the eyes on her made her uneasy. Perhaps everyone knew already who she was.

Her stomach rumbled. The scents coming from the bakery were delicious, but the idea of going in and hearing whispers with her name included made her wary. Was she simply over-thinking? She leaned her head back against the squabs. She didn't care. She'd eat at home. She wasn't prepared to face more of what she'd faced when Mrs. and Miss Haredon had called the other day.

As the village passed away to acres of farmland, a man burst from the door of a small white house with a bloody rag in hand, appearing frantic. He tossed it on the ground and reentered the home.

Catherine wasted no time in knocking her fist against the carriage roof, her pulse soaring. "Pull over, James!"

The coachman did as he was bid, and before the footman could help her out, Catherine was on the ground and running toward the home, her skirts clutched in her hands. Cries of pain could be heard as she neared and she pounded on the chipped door.

Moments later, the same harried-looking man threw it open, blood on his hands and waistcoat, his eyes wide. "Who are you?"

"What has happened? Perhaps I can help." To take time to

explain further seemed foolish. The blood was coming from someone, and perhaps Catherine could be useful.

A hard look came into the man's eyes. "I can't afford to pay. My wife needs my help." He began to close the door, but she lodged her foot in the entrance.

"My assistance costs nothing. What has happened?"

Two seconds passed before he grunted and tossed the door back, stepping away to let her in. The cries still came from somewhere in the home.

The man rushed toward the corner of the room and entered another, sitting beside a woman lying on the bed who must be his wife. He pressed a clean rag to his wife's arm. He looked over his shoulder, panic in his eyes. "She fell and sliced it open on the corner of the slate over there. It won't stop bleedin'."

While Catherine didn't know why the woman was continuing to bleed, if she didn't stop, it could spell death. She needed help.

Sketches of plants scattered Catherine's mind, their names beneath them in Latin and English. There were several species that could help.

"You stay there." Catherine hurried outside, scanning the ground for a plant Loftus had shown her in one of his books. It was so common he didn't even grow it in the conservatory, and its appearance was distinct.

God had led her here, surely. Would Catherine be able to do her part and find what she needed?

Please, let me find it. Please, God. Please.

She took a few more steps forward, and then—yarrow. A beam of light shined on the patch of light green as though God himself commanded it to do so.

She raced forward and plucked the plant—flowers, leaves, and all. Darting back to the house, she pulled the leaves and flowers apart as small as she could within her hands and raced to the woman's side. "Here."

The man's forehead wrinkled as he squinted at her open palm. "What is that supposed to do?"

"Trust me, it will help your wife." She pulled her lips tight and gave him her most earnest expression.

With a wary look, he stepped aside, pulling the nearly soaked-through rag from his wife's arm.

Not wasting a moment, Catherine pressed the crushed plant onto the wound, her hands becoming wet with blood. The woman groaned. Catherine's heart ached. "I'm sorry, miss, but the pressure is necessary."

The woman grimaced. "I can bear it as long as it will help me."

The man got a new rag and pressed it over the wound once more, the yarrow beneath. He eyed Catherine, skepticism in his gaze. "Ye say this'll work?"

Catherine nodded. "The plant I put on your wife's wound should act as a coagulant." At the man's confused expression, she clarified. "It will make her blood thicken so it stops flowing from the wound and we can bandage it."

They stood in silence, waiting for the results. Her heart raced. Had she done the right thing? Would the woman stop bleeding, after all?

Less than a minute later, the man lifted the rag from his wife's arm to witness that the yarrow had done its job. The woman was no longer bleeding. Catherine exhaled a breath of relief.

The man leaned back against the wall and lifted his arm to his forehead, wiping away the sweat there. "Praise God. I do not know how to thank ye, miss."

The corner of Catherine's mouth raised as she silently thanked the Lord. "Before you do, let us bandage the wound up. Have you any scraps of cloth?"

In quick order, they had the woman's arm covered with fabric bandages, and Catherine stood near the door to leave.

She hadn't any idea why she'd been so moved to interfere in the first place—after all, it was none of her business what occurred in another's home—but how satisfying to be of service to the couple.

The man met her at the door, something round and covered in a white cloth in his hands. "I realize I don't even know yer name, miss. Mine's Timpet. Timpet Boath."

Catherine smiled. "It's nice to meet you, Mr. Boath. I am Lady Hardwicke."

His jaw slackened. "Ye mean to say that ye are the Earl of Hardwicke's—"

"Wife. Yes." She nodded. Would this man speak poorly of Loftus like the others?

He shifted the object to one of his hands and rubbed his jaw with the other, a perplexed expression on his face. "How did ye learn about the plant?"

Her smile had faded a bit, but it widened now. "My husband taught me, actually. We have a large conservatory, and he loves to study herbs and medicinal plants. Many of the herbs at the apothecary come from our home, you'll find."

He furrowed his eyebrows. "I hope ye don't mind my frankness, my lady, but in the village, they speak of him as some sort of monster. I wasn't sure what to think." He tilted his head. "But he don't deserve it, I reckon—not if ye're so happy with him."

"I am, indeed. He's a wonderful man." She spoke with sincerity.

Mr. Boath handed her the object. "It's not much, but it's with our thanks to ye, my lady." He looked over his shoulder toward his wife, who had risen and now stood near the kitchen, tending to something there. "We'll certainly do our best to spread the word that the earl is not as everyone thinks."

Her heart lightened. "Thank you, Mr. Boath. If you or your wife ever need anything, please send word to Blackfern Manor."

Once she returned to the carriage, she unwrapped the item he'd given her. A small cream-colored wheel of cheese appeared from beneath the layers of fabric. A grin took over her face. Perhaps she'd have Cook make toasted cheese on bread for dinner.

Arriving back at the manor, Catherine handed the cheese to Susan to carry to the kitchen whilst Catherine entered the foyer. That was when she heard it. The voice she'd hoped not to hear for at least a few more weeks. The dowager's voice.

CHAPTER 17

*C*atherine followed the grating sound toward the drawing room, her lips pulling farther downward with every step she took. Why had her mother-in-law decided to come home now, when everything was going perfectly? Catherine sighed inwardly. She had a bad feeling the dowager would only serve to complicate matters between Loftus and herself.

As she neared the drawing room, she inhaled a deep breath and straightened her shoulders, pushing the door open. "Good afternoon, Mother." She'd definitely never called the woman "mother" before, but now was as good a time as any to begin. Perhaps they might start over and get to know one another— not that they had truly ever gotten to know one another in the first place.

The dowager ceased speaking, her eyebrows lifting almost to her greying hairline. Both Loftus and Gilbert were in the room, and they each stood at Catherine's entrance.

"Daughter." The woman spat out the word as though she'd been choking on it and someone had forced it out of her. Her pale lips thinned as she looked Catherine up and down, her eyes widening as they stopped on something. "My heavens!"

"Cate, are you well?" Loftus rushed forward to grasp her arms as Gilbert swore under his breath.

What were they speaking of? Catherine looked down to where Loftus focused—on a bright red blood stain on her gown. "Oh, dear."

Concern etched into every line of her husband's face. "What has happened? Are you hurt?" His hands moved over her arms as he checked her dress for other stains.

She shook her head rapidly. "It is not my blood. I am uninjured."

Loftus sighed with relief, his shoulders visibly lowering. He gestured to her abdomen where the stain was. "How did this happen, then?"

She bit her lip as an anxious heat swept her. She waited for the anger to flash over his face. She had embarrassed him in front of his family. Lord Balfour would have taken her to the hallway to give her a slap or two by now.

Her hands began to tremble, and she grasped her skirts. "I-I helped a villager in need. His wife had cut open her arm and n-needed assistance."

"You're quite pale." His eyebrows furrowed, and he lifted a hand toward her face.

She flinched away, closing her eyes. Would he hit her in front of his family? Loftus hadn't yet acted toward her with aggression, but she hadn't yet done anything to upset him, either—until now.

At his sharp intake of breath, she slowly opened her eyes. An incredulous stare was on his face, his hand frozen halfway to her cheek. He dropped it and swallowed.

"Oh, do stop fussing over her, Loftus. She'll just go to her chamber and change." The dowager, having apparently missed the interaction, flicked her hand as she gave a huff from the settee.

When her husband stepped back, Catherine fled from the room, her cheeks aflame as though she'd stayed out much too long in the sun. Had she misjudged what he'd been about to do? Was he saving his shouting for a time when they'd be alone? Had her flinching earned her an extra slap later on?

$\sim$

*L*oftus resumed his seat on the cushioned chair next to the settee, feeling as though he'd just been trampled by a horse. Had Cate really believed he was about to hit her? She'd certainly flinched as though she thought so. The very idea made him feel physically ill.

"The state of her dress!" His mother scoffed. "Sometimes I question the wisdom of you having married her, son. If this is how she's to act, then she will not do our family name well."

Gilbert sat straighter in his chair. "I do not believe she noticed the mark, Mother."

"How could she not?" Their mother's tone had grown shrill. "It was a huge red circle like the bullseye on a target." She lifted her teacup and saucer from the table and took a sip. "Mark my words, she'll bring our name into the gossip papers."

Loftus stiffened. "That is ridiculous. I am proud of Cate for helping the farmer's wife." He moved to go after her, but his mother's words as she plucked a biscuit from the tray stopped him.

"It does not do for a husband to follow his wife about like a lovesick calf." Her lips pulled down. "You can tell from the girl's expression when you drew near her and with how quickly she fled the room that she doesn't return your admiration. You may as well keep it to yourself." She took a bite of her pastry.

138

Gilbert said nothing, only looking out the window with his chin propped on his fist.

Loftus's heart sank. Could his mother be right? He'd begun to think that—perhaps—Cate harbored some romantic feelings for him. And that this marriage of convenience might turn out to be more than just convenient. Had he been completely wrong?

Cate had indeed flinched away from his hand. He'd never tried to touch her face before. Maybe it wasn't that she was afraid of him hitting her but that she was opposed to his touch. Opposed to *him*. The thought was almost too much to bear.

He shook his head. Nothing had changed since the day they married. He was still the same scarred man he'd been then. Why had he expected her to find affection in her heart for him?

~

*C*atherine took dinner in her room that night, though she didn't eat much, holding her stomach as she waited for bootfalls to sound down the hallway toward her husband's chamber. She could hardly hold anything down with anxiety roiling in her stomach as it was. Ever since she'd left Loftus with his family in the drawing room, she'd been here—locked away and hiding with a racing pulse and heart that was beating much too quickly.

He would come. Everything she'd been taught—all of her experiences with the opposite sex—told her he would. Why could not she have minded her own business? Why could things not carry on as they had been?

When footsteps approached down the corridor, Catherine closed her eyes. It was the familiar tread of Loftus—not too heavy nor incredibly light. He had a soldier's gait, something like a march, and he always picked up his feet. He probably wouldn't drag them even if he faced the gallows.

She pulled her knees to her chest and wrapped her arms around them in a tight hold. She held her breath.

Thump, thump, thump, thump. The steps neared her door. *Thump, thump, thump.* And moved past it.

She opened her eyes, breathing in once more as the footsteps continued a bit farther down the hall. Then came the creak of a door and two bumps from the room next to her, and all was quiet.

Clearly, she'd not been mistaken—the person in the hall had been her husband. Why, then, hadn't he knocked on her door? Was he planning on entering through the private passage?

Catherine tilted her head to the side but heard nothing more from his room. She frowned, and her grip on her knees loosened. Did not he wish to shout at her? Admonish her for how she'd humiliated him?

She waited a half an hour, but still, he did not come.

Finally, she rang for Susan and prepared for bed, her abdomen a bundle of unease. Would he take his anger out on his valet? Verne definitely did not deserve it. She'd known a few servants in her own home that would have bruises some days. Her father had a temper and wouldn't hesitate to strike someone he deemed inferior. Tomorrow, she would assess Verne for injuries.

Susan finished brushing out Catherine's tresses, and she got into bed, pulling the coverlet over her shoulder as she turned on her side.

"G'night, my lady." Susan crept out the door and pulled it closed, leaving the room dark except for the lone candle burning at Catherine's bedside.

She watched the flame dance for a minute, wishing she might feel so peaceful, before she heaved a breath and blew it out, shutting her eyes. Today was the day she had broken the

peace between Loftus and herself, and now she would deal
with the consequences.

CHAPTER 18

The next day, Catherine entered the conservatory with hesitant steps. Would she still be able to help her husband tend to the plants?

He looked up at her entrance but looked away just as quickly. "Good afternoon." He nodded, measuring the ivy.

Catherine's shoulders eased at his seeming disinterest. She'd passed Verne in the hall that morning and hadn't seen any visible bruises on the man, so perhaps Loftus hadn't taken his anger out on him, after all. Indeed, looking at her husband now, he didn't appear irritated in the slightest.

Catherine headed for the cabinet, grabbing her gloves when she got there and discarding her white ones. Loftus moved to another plant farther away, measuring it and writing the details in his notebook.

"I—" It was difficult to choke the words out. She took a breath before attempting it again. "I am sorry for yesterday."

Loftus turned his head toward her, a gleam of interest in his eyes. "What do you mean?"

Catherine wrung her hands in front of her. "I mean, I

embarrassed you in front of your family. I hope you'll forgive me for doing such a foolish thing. I had no idea—"

"Do not apologize." Though he put a stop to her words, there appeared to be a hint of disappointment in his eyes. "I was not embarrassed—only concerned for your well-being."

"But your mother—"

"All is well." Loftus lifted his hand. "Do not think of it any longer."

She stepped over to join him at the seedlings he crouched beside, scribbling in his notebook, the sun washing them through the windows. He acted as though yesterday's incident had been nothing when it had taken up the entirety of her evening—even her dreams and morning. He wasn't behaving like any man she was acquainted with.

She pursed her lips, forcing herself to bring up the topic. "You didn't shout at me yesterday."

His pencil stopped moving. He looked over his shoulder at her and shielded his eyes from the sun. "I haven't ever shouted at you."

She clasped her hands behind her back. "You never had a reason to before. You did yesterday, but you still didn't."

He brushed the dirt from his trousers and stood, a perplexed expression on his face. "Did you want me to?"

She shook her head. "No! No, no, certainly not." She tilted her head. "But why didn't you? Lord Balfour always shouted when I embarrassed him or did something wrong. So does my father."

Loftus's eyes softened. "I am not that cad of a lord, nor am I your father—and you did not embarrass me. Even if you had, I would not shout. A gentleman does not raise his voice at a woman."

Catherine murmured, "Nor is he meant to raise his hand to one, either, I suppose."

Loftus's face hardened. "Never." His tone brooked no argument. He ran a hand through his hair. "You have been through very much, Cate, but most men are neither like your father nor Lord Balfour. I'd like to hope that most in society would treat you with respect."

She bit her lip, moving her arms to cross over her chest. Would they? They certainly hadn't thus far.

He straightened his shoulders. "I cannot always say what others will do, of course, or how they will behave, but I can promise you that I will always treat you with the respect you deserve. I will never raise my voice, and I will never raise my hand to you. I understand your experiences have led you to believe that you will be treated this way from most of my sex, but I think you'll find that your father and Lord Balfour are the exceptions and not the rule."

Catherine looked away from her husband's piercing blue eyes and gazed out the window. Could it be true? What if she'd gotten it all wrong, and it wasn't simply in a man's nature to yell, but specifically in those two men's natures? What if men in general weren't more likely than women to raise their hands to their servants, but those two men were?

She turned and blinked at him. "Thank you."

They stared at each other for a moment before he cleared his throat and lifted his pencil to his notebook again. "You need not thank me—it is only what a good husband does." He moved toward the Black Hellebore. "What are your plans for today?"

Catherine smiled slightly. "After this, I was hoping to take tea and then go for a walk in the garden or along the forest edge. Maybe even a ride." She stepped beside him, nudging his arm with her shoulder. "Would you care to join me for any one of those things?"

He tilted his head, his pencil slowing against the notebook. "Erm..."

She raised her eyebrows, a spark in her stomach at the anticipation of his answer.

He scratched his jaw and shifted on his feet. "I'm rather busy today with Mother's abrupt arrival. It's thrown everything off balance—"

Catherine reached out and placed a hand on his arm, turning him to face her. She widened her eyes. "I didn't get to see you at dinner last night." She didn't mention it was her own fault that that had been the case. "Just come and have some tea with me after we tend the plants. We'll take a little walk, and maybe we'll see some new plant species or find some creature I haven't seen before." She pushed her lips forward in a hopeful manner, not letting go of the dark fabric of his coat.

His gaze darted out the window and then back to her. He swallowed, and she could swear a pink hue crossed his cheeks. "I suppose I could...move some things around in my schedule." Before she could clap her hands, he lifted a finger. "But we mustn't be out for too long. I have a meeting with my steward that I can't miss."

Catherine's lips quirked up. "I will not keep you. Now, let us finish this work so we might have more time." She picked up the watering can at the side of the room and began to move from plant to plant, a merry tune on her lips. Gone was her anxiety, and in its place was a much better emotion—excitement.

～

*A*s Loftus lifted a bite of scone to his mouth and listened to his brother capture his wife's attention, he tried not to roll his eyes. This had not been what he was expecting when she'd said they could have tea together. Of course, he didn't believe it was what *she'd* been expecting, either, for Gilbert had, oddly enough, been the one to bring in the tea tray—claiming he'd run into the maid just outside the door to the room.

"...and then we raced to the top of the hill, and it was a very close thing." He paused to take a sip of his tea. "Trafferth is faster than Lord Beecham's mount, however, and we came out in the lead. 'Twas a good day, that."

Catherine nodded, her eyes wide. "That sounds very entertaining. Once my parents send over my horse from London, we shall have to have a little race." She smiled. "He's quite the agile creature."

Gilbert's eyebrows lifted, and he leaned forward in his seat. "I did not know you had a mount, Catherine."

Loftus tilted his head, a jab of awareness poking him. Neither had he. He cleared his throat. "What is his name?" He lifted his teacup to his lips and took a sip, trying not to grimace. Cate, surprised at his brother's arrival, had forgotten to put any sweetener in Loftus's tea—instead adding double the amount to her own cup without looking. Did she notice how sweet the liquid was now as she drank it? Loftus certainly wasn't going to say anything—he was grateful she had invited him to tea at all.

No odd expression crossed his wife's face as the tea passed her lips. She set the cup and saucer down, her eyes getting a faraway look. "His name is Woodbine. He's a grey stallion with the most wonderful coat you've ever seen. It looks like the color of the morning fog. I do hope my parents will send him soon." She bit her lip. "They've no use for him in London, and I cannot believe he's getting the exercise he needs."

Loftus rubbed his chin. Why *hadn't* her parents sent the horse yet? He'd write to them. If Cate wanted her horse, then he'd make sure she'd have it as soon as possible. He finished his cup of tea and set it down.

Immediately, Gilbert spoke up. "You appear rather tired over there, brother. Another cup of tea might do you well."

Cate bent toward the teapot, but Loftus waved a hand. "No

more for me, thank you. I'm not tired, as you say, though I do have a few things on my mind."

"An Englishman saying no to tea?" His brother scoffed. "Practically treasonous. Come, brother, you might even convince your wife to put an extra spoonful of sugar in it. Then you'll certainly have no reason to sink so low in your chair."

"No, thank you." Loftus gave his brother a blank expression, his tone dry. "I suppose they'll have to hang me."

Cate leaned back in her chair, her lips twisted to the side in amusement. "Perish the thought! I, for one, will be glad to have another cup. Another for yourself, Gilbert?"

He handed her his cup. "Please."

Cate poured again whilst Loftus grabbed a cucumber sandwich from the tray and finished it in three bites.

The rest of the tea passed as slowly as molasses dripping from a jar. Would his brother never let them escape? Finally, however, he left the room with a cheeky grin. At last, Loftus could be alone with his wife.

~

*C*atherine strolled the pebbled garden path, her hand wrapped around her husband's arm. The sky was grey but bright, and she raised her face toward where she believed the sun to be, closing her eyes for a moment. Taking a deep breath in, she inhaled the lovely scent of the blooming flowers, the peonies and lilacs filling the air with their delicate fragrances.

When she opened her eyes to find Loftus staring at her, her heart quickened and a heat the sky hadn't provided flushed her face.

She ducked her chin and gestured to the organized sections around them. "Was this your doing—the garden? Which is your favorite flower?"

When he looked away, she almost wished to pull his gaze back onto her. It heated her as well as any summer's day. "Some of it was my mother and her mother, but yes. I have added onto it. As for my favorite flower, there are too many to choose from. I couldn't name just one."

They moved down the main path and branched onto a smaller one that wove between beds of foxgloves and tulips. Catherine lifted a finger to her lips. "What have you added and what was already here?"

He escorted her past a bubbling fountain where a few birds took baths at the top basin, though they flew away when they neared. Catherine wiped the back of her neck. It did seem to be getting rather warm. If only she could take a quick bath in the fountain, as well.

"My grandmother added these bushes you see here to afford whoever was in the garden a bit of privacy. My mother added the rose bushes, for she is very fond of them. She also added the—" He turned to look at her, and words stopped flowing from his mouth.

Catherine raised an eyebrow. "Is everything all right?"

Concern laced his expression. "I could ask the same of you, Cate." He took a step forward and reached for her hand. "Your face is as red as the tulips we just passed. Do you feel well?"

Embarrassment worked its way through her body, battling the tingling that came from his gripping her hand. She attempted to give him a reassuring smile. "I'm well—just a bit warm."

He placed her hand on his arm and began to walk again. "Let us stroll in the shade, then."

He strode across the lawn and pulled her into the forest line, Catherine becoming dizzy from the quick movement.

He tilted his head toward her, his earthy scent flooding her senses. "Better?"

She nodded. It was a bit better in the shade.

They had walked for a moment in companionable silence when the birds suddenly seemed too loud and the crunching beneath their feet began to grate at her ears. The beginnings of a megrim were beating their way through her skull. Why now? Had the brightness of the day been too much for her? The sun wasn't even out.

She tried not to think about it. She desperately wanted this time with Loftus. Now that his mother was here, there'd be less time alone with him. She didn't want to wait however many weeks until the woman left for London again until she could talk openly with him.

She inwardly groaned. Even the thought of dealing with the dowager made Catherine's stomach ache and twist itself into knots.

Loftus stopped and crouched to examine a plant, pinching the leaf between his forefinger and thumb. She tried to look down at it, but she couldn't focus. She squinted and took off her glasses, polished them, and replaced them on the bridge of her nose. The edges of the plant crisped into straight lines.

"What is it?" She bent at the waist to get a better look.

He hummed. "*Hypericum perforatum.* Also known as St. John's Wort."

Catherine straightened and propped her hands on her hips. "I've heard of it before. It has some medicinal properties, does it not? Why don't you grow it in the conservatory?"

Loftus stood as well, brushing his hands together. "It's quite abundant around here. There's no need for me to do so." He shrugged.

How strong his shoulders looked. And his arms... For a minute, Catherine wished to wrap her own arms around them —to lean her head into his chest.

That was, until she saw the dark hooded figure staring at them from fifty feet away and her heart leapt into her throat. Her mouth went dry and her limbs rigid.

She blinked, but when she opened her eyes again, the figure was still there. Her pulse thrummed in her ears like flies buzzing about. Alarm made the hair on her arms and back of her neck stand on end. It couldn't be.

"Cate?" Loftus raised a brow. When she didn't speak, he turned to follow her gaze. "What are you looking at?"

"The man." She whispered the words, barely loud enough for her own ears to hear. She wasn't sure if the figure was indeed a man or woman, but she *did* know one person who hadn't been pleased with her when she'd left London. Her hands began to tremble as fear skittered up her spine. It wasn't, was it? Why would he be here? She'd left London behind. She'd married another.

Loftus looked all around. "I don't see anyone. Where?"

The figure hadn't moved. Catherine wanted to shout at Loftus. How couldn't he be seeing what she was? It was as clear as day, the dark of the cloak standing out against the foliage. *He's right there!* She was a stone. Her tongue would not move, nor would her mouth open.

Her vision blurred as Loftus stepped toward her and grabbed her hands. She tried to point in the area where she'd seen the figure, but when she blinked, it was gone. Her breaths came heavier. The danger they were in had only increased. The man had the element of surprise now.

Speak, Catherine. Speak!

She choked the words out—a croak on her lips. "We have to go."

"Who, Cate? Who did you see?" Loftus's lips pulled down, his tone holding an edge of panic.

"Him. *Him.* We *have* to go." She tried to tug on Loftus, but he wasn't moving.

Loftus only furrowed his eyebrows. "Cate..."

Everything was loud. Her heart, the birds, the squirrels scurrying in the trees—everything. Her head ached as though an army drummer was beating against it with all his might, and she felt as though she was going to cast up her accounts at any minute. She shifted her gaze to the forest line, the air heaving in and out of her lungs. No sign of the figure.

"We have to go!"

Why wasn't Loftus moving?

"We have to go! He's out there!" The world felt like it was crumbling around her. Why couldn't her past leave her alone? *He'd* been the one to break off their engagement, not her.

She choked on a sob and pulled free as the sky darkened, shadows all around her. "He'll hurt me! He'll hurt *us!*" She picked up her skirts and tried to race back toward the garden but tripped on a tree root, falling to her knees.

Loftus called out from behind her, but she barely heard him past the beating of her heart. Everything was blurred now. Nausea overwhelmed her, and her stomach relieved itself of its contents, yet the minute it ceased, she was on her feet again and running toward the back door of the manor.

She had to get inside before the cloaked figure could reach her. Lord Balfour would stop at nothing, it seemed, to see her unhappy.

Arriving at the back door, she looked over her shoulder to see Loftus running after her. She couldn't explain to him right now. She needed to hide. She darted down the corridor with a bitter taste in her mouth, her head pounding with every step she took.

The halls were darker than usual, everything around her a blur of colors and lines and shapes. Her chest expanded and deflated every second with air, though she couldn't seem to get enough of it.

Crash! She sprawled across the carpeted floor along with a suit of armor, pain lancing her leg as the heavy metal torso fell on it. There was no time to stop. She must hide somewhere, but where? Where wouldn't Lord Balfour find her?

She pulled her leg out from under the armor, forcing her feet to move once more.

"My lady?" The butler's shape came into view before her. "My lady!" He moved toward her, but she skirted around him.

The secret hallways. That was where she should go.

Then everything went black.

CHAPTER 19

$\mathcal{L}$oftus raced into the manor, his heart beating out of his chest. What had come over his wife? What exactly had she seen in the woods? Who was *the man*? Did he need to call a doctor? His blood flowed triple-time through his veins as a crash sounded up ahead in the corridor.

His booted feet took him as fast as they could down the hall to a fallen suit of armor, the helmet rolled to the side and gauntlets detached. His wife was nowhere to be seen, so he leapt over it and continued toward Bromley's voice.

"My lady!" Bromley's mouth was wide open as Cate staggered around him, running headfirst into the papered wall with a sickening crack. She fell back, collapsing in a heap on the floor.

Loftus's throat constricted. Bromley immediately dropped to his knees at her side, and in a moment, Loftus was in the same position, cradling her head in his hands. Her face was still flushed, and her cheeks were warm beneath his fingers.

His mouth was dry, but he forced himself to swallow. "Have someone fetch the doctor."

Bromley nodded and scurried from the hall, leaving Loftus alone with his wife.

What had happened? One minute, she was well, and the next, she was ill and running away. He leaned down and brushed a kiss to her forehead. Was it the stress of his mother's arrival? And who had she seen in the forest—perhaps a poacher in the woods?

He lifted her in his arms and moved down the corridor. He had just begun up the stairs when his mother's voice sounded from behind him. "A man and wife should not show so much affection when others are around."

He bit the inside of his cheek and looked over his shoulder. "Cate is unconscious, Mother. I am bringing her to her chamber." He continued up the stairs, but now he would have no peace, for his mother followed. Her slippers were quiet on the steps behind him, though her voice was not.

"Unconscious?" She tutted. "Had too much to drink, has she? I knew marrying into a merchant's family would do us no good."

Loftus adjusted his hold on Cate as he reached the top of the staircase and increased his pace down the corridor in an attempt to lose his mother, her comments like needles digging under his skin. "Most definitely not. She was feeling unwell outside and..." He cleared his throat. "Fainted."

"Indeed? Shall I fetch my smelling salts?" Disappointment laced her tone as Loftus pushed his wife's chamber door open with his boot.

"Thank you, Mother, but that will be unnecessary. I've sent someone to fetch the doctor." He placed Cate on the bed with all the care he could and rang the bell for her maid, his mother still standing at the door. He raised an eyebrow. "Did you wish to ask me something?"

Her lips thinned, grey curls waving in the breeze she

created with her fan. "No, indeed. I do wonder, however, how childbearing will go if her constitution is so weak." With that, the woman left, her vibrant skirts swishing as she turned on her heel and disappeared from view.

Loftus huffed. His mother never was one to keep her opinions to herself, but it wasn't the time to worry about that.

Susan came in almost immediately and gasped at the sight of Cate in bed, a purple bruise already forming on her forehead. Her hand flew to cover her mouth. "What's happened?"

Loftus explained as well as he could, and they tried to make Cate comfortable as they waited for the doctor to arrive. He pulled a chair next to her bed and seated himself in it as Susan took one in the corner, her hands twisting in her lap.

Five minutes after Loftus had brought Cate to her chamber, she opened her eyes. Her chest began to rise and fall as quickly as it had earlier, and she grasped the coverlet. "Where am I?" Her voice was shrill.

Loftus pressed his hand over hers on the bed, which caused her to jump. Her gaze darted to his. "Loftus?" Her hand trembled under his.

He tried to make his voice as soothing as possible. "Do not fret, darling. We are in your chambers."

Cate struggled to sit up, but Loftus placed a light hand on her shoulder, silently urging her to remain lying down. "You should rest, my dear. Your body has been through much stress today. The doctor will be here soon."

She shook her head. "I cannot rest. I have to hide, or *he* will find me." She licked her lips, attempting to swing her legs off the bed.

Right. This did appear to be the crux of the matter. It was the reason she'd fled in the first place. Loftus shared a concerned glance with Susan before turning back to his wife and cradling her hand in his. "Who?"

Her eyes became glossy with tears, and as she blinked, a few traced almost invisible patterns down her cheeks. "The man I saw outside. I was trying to tell you. Lord Balfour."

His head moved back, his shoulders straightening. "You saw Lord Balfour in the forest?" What would the man be doing on the estate?

She bit her lip. "I saw a cloaked figure. I do not know who it was, but who else could it be? He is the only one I know who wishes me harm."

The tension around Loftus's chest eased, and he exhaled. "I do, of course, believe you when you say you saw a cloaked figure, but—perhaps it was a poacher. Our land holds much game, and many hunters may not be able to resist trespassing—"

"It wasn't a poacher." Her tone was adamant. "It was him. I *know* it was him."

A knock on the door sounded, and when Susan opened it, the doctor entered. He pushed his spectacles high up on his nose. "I presume this is the patient?"

Loftus stood to greet the man, looking over his shoulder at Cate. Where were *her* spectacles? "Thank you for coming, Dr. Fench. My wife has hit her head and also is feeling ill."

Dr. Fench placed his black leather bag on the side table, eyeing Cate with a raised brow. "Indeed." He moved closer to her bedside and held up a finger. "Follow my finger with your eyes, my lady." He brought his finger up and down and left and right, then hummed.

Loftus scratched the back of his neck and propped one of his hands on his hip, helplessness settling around him. "She complained of being too warm earlier."

The doctor leaned forward and placed a hand on her forehead. "Warm, but no fever."

What else had occurred? "She was stumbling around a lot."

Dr. Fench gave him a blank look. "Is your wife given to drinking?"

A bubble of irritation grew in Loftus's stomach. "No." His tone was cool. "She only drinks at dinner and only one glass then. When we were outside, she vomited."

"And is there a possibility of pregnancy?"

Loftus stared at the man, his mouth going dry. "No." There certainly was no chance of that. In the future, yes, but not...

The image of his wife and Gilbert standing so close to each other in the woods came to mind. Her silken hair had hung down in waves, and her dress had been covered in dirt. Could they have...?

He swallowed and shook his head once more, banishing that thought from his mind. He'd already chosen to believe his wife and brother. He could trust them. "No, there is not a possibility of pregnancy."

Dr. Fench pulled a watch from his waistcoat pocket and flicked it open. He grabbed Cate's wrist and stared at the watch, his lips thin. "Her pulse is a bit fast, but not significantly so." He closed his watch case with a click and stuffed it back into his pocket, looking down at Cate. "What symptoms did you feel before you vomited, my lady?"

She squeezed her eyes shut, her eyelids wrinkling. "I'm still feeling unwell. My stomach aches, and the nausea has not yet left completely. I have a terrible megrim, and something strange is happening with my vision."

The doctor grunted. "You've gotten too much sun, I believe, which is the cause of your megrim and your aches. The megrim is the cause of your impaired vision. It should leave as soon as your megrim goes." He pulled a vial of laudanum from his bag and set it on the table. "Take this for your pain."

Cate covered her eyes and nodded.

Loftus stepped forward. "Thank you, Dr. Fench. Your quick attendance is also appreciated."

The man gave a small smile. "It is not often that a man gets to meet the earl's new wife. I will come back in a few days to see how she fares. Good day." With those words, he was out the door and being escorted down the hall by Bromley.

Loftus ran a hand down his jaw and moved to the chair he'd vacated upon Dr. Fench's arrival. "Please have tea brought up for the countess, Susan. Peppermint, please, for it will help with her nausea." She stood, and he spoke again. "If we don't have any dried, have some collected from the garden."

The maid nodded and scurried off.

Loftus took his wife's hand. She startled and lifted the opposite hand from her eyes but relaxed when her eyes flicked to his.

"He's out there, Loftus." She bit her lip, her voice a raspy murmur. "I know what I saw."

He pressed a kiss against her knuckles, inhaling her clover perfume. "I will protect you. He can't hurt you here."

Her eyes were wide. "Promise?"

He nodded, pressing her soft hand against his cheek. "Promise."

Not twenty minutes later, Loftus sent servants and stable-hands out to search the surrounding lands. Maybe they'd come up with something or find a clue as to who had been traipsing around Blackfern without his knowledge. Even Giles bounded amongst the men, his tail wagging and gangly puppy legs scurrying in every direction as his nose pressed to the ground.

Evening had fallen by the time everyone returned, and to Loftus's dismay, nothing had been found. There were no foot-steps, pieces of fabric, broken branches—it was as though the person had never been there at all.

How was he supposed to protect his wife if this person covered their tracks so well? He even spoke to the gardener to see if the man had caught sight of the figure, to no avail. The servant had been tending to the bushes at the front of the house when the incident occurred, so he hadn't seen a thing.

Would this cloaked figure appear again, or was it truly just a poacher? And if the figure showed themselves again, would he be able to keep Cate safe?

CHAPTER 20

Catherine's teacup rattled against her saucer as she set it down on the tray in front of her. Her mouth slackened, and cold fingers seemed to wrap around her lungs, squeezing the air out. "Nothing?" Her voice was but a murmur.

Her husband's head dropped as he moved closer to her side, pushing the hair from her face. "I'm afraid not." He sighed. "The servants were out for hours, but nothing could be found."

Catherine's megrim was more of a dull ache now with the help of the laudanum, and her nausea had almost gone away due to the peppermint tea Loftus had had sent up. She was on her fourth cup now, for it was delicious and washed the bitter taste of bile from her mouth. Yet a few hours of rest and tea hadn't allowed her to forget her anxiety nor what the figure's appearance could mean for her future at Blackfern Manor.

Loftus's hand stroked her cheek, bringing her back to the present. "Whoever you saw is no longer here, and if they were hiding in the forest when we were searching, then they are aware we know of their presence. They wouldn't dare come back now."

Catherine leaned into his touch and nodded. "I hope that's

true." She kissed the center of his palm, drawing her eyebrows down. "I'm sorry for how I behaved, earlier. I-I wasn't feeling myself. I—"

Loftus placed his other hand on her other cheek and looked down into her eyes. "You were simply afraid, darling. You do not have to apologize for that. I am only glad you are better now." He bent his head down and placed his lips to her forehead in a tender kiss, lingering for a few moments with his warm breath upon her.

She wished to melt back against her pillows as his lips evoked feelings she'd never felt before.

He pulled away, and she instantly felt his absence. She opened her eyes to see his small smile. He brushed his thumb over her cheek and dropped his hand from her face. "Get some more rest, my dear. I'm sure you need it." He looked to the corner of the room, and his lips quirked. "Susan, of course, is here, and I'm right next door if you need me."

Susan's eyes were averted, her head nearly buried in her knitting.

Catherine would've laughed if she were feeling better. "Thank you." She tried to put all of her gratitude into her voice.

With a nod, he turned and stepped out of the room, closing the door behind him with a quiet click. Her covers were nearly all the way up to her chin to cover her nightgown, but she pulled them up farther, anyway, as her husband left the room. It seemed a bit colder without his presence.

"I'm done with my tea, Susan. Thank you."

The maid put down her knitting and picked up the tray. "Is there anything else ye need, my lady?"

Nothing Susan could help with, unfortunately. Not unless the woman could explain what love was or how to escape a violent man. Catherine put a hand to her mouth to stifle a yawn. "No, thank you. I think I'll rest as my husband suggested." She scooted down the mattress and shifted against her pillows, settling against them as Susan left the room.

A soft glow flickered from the candles—one on the side table and one on the dressing table. Both danced as though they were attempting to outdo the other. She'd been more paranoid earlier in the day but was almost peaceful now, knowing that Loftus—her protector and the man who had come to her rescue at the inn—was only a few steps away.

Did she love him? She held an affection for him—that was certain. Could she even love a man after what she'd been through? After all Lord Balfour had done to her?

Her eyes began to grow heavy from the effects of the laudanum Susan had mixed in her tea. When they closed, the last thing she thought of was Loftus and the feel of his lips on her forehead.

CHAPTER 21

When Catherine awoke the next day, sunlight streamed through the curtains in too-bright beams. She squinted and reached for her spectacles from the side table, only to realize that they weren't there. That's right—she'd lost them yesterday in the chaos. Loftus had mentioned the servants hadn't found anything, so they were, apparently, gone forever.

As much as Catherine disliked being without her spectacles, she quite enjoyed the idea of some sort of woodland creature having found them and put them on. A red squirrel would look rather dashing with her spectacles on its nose.

A commotion came at the door, and Catherine pulled her coverlet up, shrinking beneath it.

"Ye're finally awake! I'll have to tell his lordship." Susan's voice preceded her entering the room, the foggy woman moving from one hazy area to another. As much as Catherine tried to squint and rub her eyes, they were no good without her spectacles.

She heaved a sigh. "I'm sorry to say that I cannot see a thing, Susan. Not clearly, anyway. I suppose I'll have to get new spectacles, for they fell off of my face yesterday. How late have I slept? What time is it?"

Susan hummed. "A quarter after two, my lady."

"A quarter after—" She flung her coverlet off of her legs. "I must help tend the plants."

As soon as she stepped on the floor, the ground shifted beneath her, and her head spun, the throbbing of yesterday coming back with a vengeance. She placed a hand to her forehead. "Oh, dear."

"My lady!" Susan was at her side in a moment, directing her back to the edge of the bed. "We might dress ye today, but I don't believe ye're strong enough to be going anywhere, let alone tending plants."

Catherine nodded, the painful roiling in her stomach starting up again as though scolding her for moving. She attempted to swallow past the dryness of her mouth. "Perhaps we start with a cup of tea and a scone, and go from there."

Susan was at the door before Catherine could even finish the words. "I'll be right back, my lady. Don't ye worry."

A few moments later, a knock came at her door.

"Come in." She still sat on the edge of the bed. The door opened, but that was not Susan's shape...

~

*A*t his wife's call, Loftus opened the door and stepped inside. His mouth went dry. Her eyes widened, and her lips formed an O.

"Oh—I..." Heat rushed to his face, and he turned to face the wall, the image of her in only her nightgown burned into his mind. His heart stuttered, and his palms were suddenly damp. He'd never seen a woman in a state of undress before—the white fabric of her chemise brushing against her calves and the neck of it just skimming her collarbone. She was a vision with her shining hair falling out of a braid along her shoulder and her cheeks flushed from sleep.

"Loftus! I-I wasn't expecting you—not that your presence is unwelcome—but Susan just left, and I thought..." A rustling of bedcovers mixed with her higher-than-usual voice.

"I do apologize, my dear. Susan informed me you were awake, and I hadn't the foggiest idea you'd be—" His throat almost seemed to close as he pictured her again. He closed his eyes and shook his head. "Forgive me."

The sounds coming from behind him quieted, and Cate's voice sounded again, softer this time. "You may turn around now."

He spun, his wife now sitting up in the large bed with her covers drawn up to her shoulders. Her arms were atop the coverlet, bare aside from the small capped sleeves of her chemise. The sun bathed her creamy skin in a hue of gold, making her appear almost otherworldly.

He sat in the chair beside her bed—the same he'd occupied the day before—and raised his lips into a smile. "How are you feeling?"

Cate laid her head back against the dark headboard and met his gaze, her eyes bright though her voice was a bit raspy. "Better than yesterday. I attempted to stand upon waking, but it appears this illness is not fully done with me yet."

Loftus's heart tugged. "Did the tea diminish the nausea? And is the laudanum helping with the pain? If not, I have a store of powders and tinctures that might be of assistance." He furrowed his eyebrows.

She reached out, her hand warm through his gloves. "The tea helped immensely—and it was delicious. I do believe I might begin drinking it even when I'm not ill." She grinned. "Susan has been ensuring I take the laudanum, and it has been counteracting the pain, although I do not like how tired it makes me."

She pursed her lips, drawing his attention to them. They were pale pink in color, like a peony. He'd dared to kiss her forehead the night before, but would he ever dare to kiss those lips or taste their sweetness?

A conflict brewed within him. His mother had said his affection for his wife was one-sided—that Cate did not feel the same, but was that the truth? Was he deceiving himself when he thought he saw a glimmer of admiration in her hazel eyes? Was he telling himself a lie when he believed her kiss on his hand might be more than that of mere friendship? He reached into his mind and pulled out the question at the center. Could a woman—any woman—truly love him with his visible and invisible scars? And, if she did, would it be the love of a friend, or the romantic love he so wished for?

"Loftus?"

His eyes refocused on Cate's face, one of her delicate eyebrows raised. He nearly cursed under his breath for his inattention. "Sorry, I was—erm—thinking about the *Coriandrum sativum* seedlings. What was it you were saying?"

She blinked. "Oh, yes, those are coming along very nicely, I believe. I was wondering if there are any herbs you have that I might take for the aches in my head and stomach—instead of laudanum, I mean. Preferably an herb that doesn't make me drowsy."

Loftus ran a hand over his jaw. Certainly, he must have something. "I'm sure of it." He squeezed her hand. "There are many plants used for pain relief."

Susan bustled into the room with a tray for Cate, a lone scone and pot of tea on it. "I thought ye'd be here, my lord." Susan placed the tray on Cate's lap and hummed to herself, moving across the room to sit in her chair.

Loftus pierced Cate with a quizzical look. "This is all you're having?"

Cate shrugged. "I don't think I'll be able to stomach any

more at the moment." She halved her scone and held one piece out to him. "Are you hungry?"

He shook his head, his eyes widening. "I would not presume to take a woman's breakfast from her, especially as paltry as it is. Please, enjoy yourself." He stood. "I'll look for something to relieve your pain and come back with it soon."

Cate swallowed a bite of scone and licked her smiling lips. "Thank you very much, husband mine. When I am up and about once again, I shall buy you a gift for treating me so well."

Loftus returned her smile. She didn't need to give him a gift or any such thing, for being married to her was the greatest gift God had ever given him.

A little while later, he sat in his study, poring over herbal books and tomes about botany relating to medicine. He flicked through the pages, careful not to rip the thin edges. *Verbascum densiflorum* wouldn't help ease the pains she was experiencing, nor would *Malva neglecta*. He chuckled as he came across *Lepidium sativum* in one of the books. Cate definitely had no need of *that* herb's help—she had all of her hair, and as far as he knew, didn't have scurvy.

He sat back in his chair and closed the book. Well, there was a quicker solution than to make his back ache by leaning over more volumes. The answer wasn't in the conservatory, but he did know where to find it. Though it would take him a bit longer to arrive back at Cate's side than he'd imagined. She'd be safe in the house under the watchful eye of Susan.

～

Once Catherine had broken her fast, she felt more energized. With Susan's help, she even managed to dress into one of her easier-to-get-into gowns—a pale green day dress with a cream ribbon tied around the waist that made her feel as though she wasn't ill nor forced to lay abed and drink copious amounts of tea. Perhaps Loftus would even think she looked pretty and comment on her change of attire when he came back with whatever plant he was bringing her. Her heart lightened at the thought.

She'd just settled on top of her coverlet with a book in hand when a knock sounded at the door. She set the book aside, her heartbeat quickening. *Hesperides* would have to wait—especially given that her husband was at the other side of that door. She clasped her hands in her lap and leaned against the headboard, attempting to look pleasing.

He stepped into the room. It was not Loftus. "Catherine! How sorry I am to hear you are feeling unwell." Gilbert. He was dressed very finely in an expensive-looking red waistcoat and black jacket, his expression one of worry.

Her smile dimmed, though she was still appreciative of his presence. She sat up straighter. "Thank you. Dr. Fench said I got too much sun yesterday."

Gilbert tutted, his pomaded hair making no movement as he took the chair beside her bed. She was almost glad he sat so near, for now she could see him more clearly. He straightened his lapels. "'Tis a pity. I was hoping to ask you if you wished to go for a walk, thinking the fresh air might do you well."

Catherine twisted her mouth to the side and spoke in an apologetic tone. "I'm afraid I'm not yet well enough, but we may go as soon as I am."

Gilbert didn't seem to mind. He slapped a hand on his knee, one side of his mouth turning up. "We shall settle for chatting, then." He tilted his head. "What's this I hear about a stranger on the property? My brother mentioned something of it at dinner last evening, but he was rather vague."

Anxiety shot through Catherine at the memory. She cleared her throat. "When Loftus and I were out yesterday...taking a walk, we—well, I—saw a cloaked figure in the forest only a short distance away. The person was staring at us."

A frown crossed Gilbert's face. "Odd, indeed. And my brother did not see this person?"

Catherine shook her head. "The man disappeared rather soon after I saw him, and then I became ill and your brother's attention was on me."

Gilbert leaned forward, and she could smell his scent of citrus and nutmeg—quite different from Loftus' scent, but not unpleasing. "What makes you believe this figure was a man?"

Catherine quailed. She was not about to tell Gilbert about her past with Lord Balfour. He was a friend, yes, her new brother, yes, but she wouldn't. She *couldn't*.

She attempted a calm facade and shrugged her shoulders. "The figure was tall like a man and broad, as well."

Gilbert settled back into his chair. "They're likely harmless, whoever they are. They won't get inside the house, of course."

Alarm pulsed through Catherine. She hadn't thought too much about *that*. What if he tried to break in? What if he succeeded?

Gilbert's gaze caught on the book beside her on the bed. "What are you reading?"

She handed it to him, and he slid his hand over the leather cover, inspecting the spine. "Poems, eh? Sit back, then. I'll read them to you."

He crossed one leg over the other and flipped open the book, clearing his throat as he began on a random page.

> *"Sadly I walk't within the field,*
> *To see what comfort it wo'd yield,*
> *And as I went my private way,*
> *An olive-branch before me lay.*
> *And seeing it, I made a stay,*
> *And took it up and view'd it; then*
> *Kissing the omen, said amen!"*

Gilbert stopped in his reading, his mouth twisted into a frown and his brows lowered. "Loftus would enjoy this one, no doubt, with its mentions of plants like the olive and what-not, but I cannot finish it. It's simply too boring. I've never claimed to be a pious man."

Catherine stifled a huff and tried to keep her expression impassive. She'd been rather enjoying the poem. She'd have to search it out once he left in order to finish it.

He turned a few more pages in the book before his eyes lit. "This one looks interesting."

> *"In man ambition is the common'st thing;*
> *Each one by nature loves to be a king."*

Catherine shifted atop the coverlet, observing the intrigue on Gilbert's face. "Do you have great ambitions, Gilbert?" She placed a hand on her stomach as a stabbing pain jabbed her there. She breathed in through her nostrils, and it faded somewhat.

He flicked his eyes up to her and leaned back lazily. "Me? I suppose I have the same ambitions as any other young gentleman my age." He began to tick off each on his fingers. "To win at cards or make money via speculation, to have a pretty wife on my arm or a mistress at my side, to be admired where I go—whether that be the club or a soirée. I take pleasure in what all young men take pleasure in." He shrugged. "I've been taught how to run an estate, just as my brother has, of course." He dropped his hand. "Being a second son means I must earn my living." He wrinkled his nose. "I am not yet ready to step into that. Loftus provides me with a healthy pocket of coin on a monthly basis, so I needn't pick up my book of sermons yet."

A bubble of surprise formed in Catherine's chest. "You've plans to become a clergyman? Did not you just say that you aren't particularly pious?"

He flipped a few more pages, his eyes on the book instead of her. "Indeed. I thought it'd be easier than joining the navy or becoming a barrister." He waved a hand. "It doesn't bear thinking about, for I shan't have to actually replace our vicar for some time yet."

"What sort of vicar shall you be?" Catherine's hands were balled up in her coverlet as she asked him, her tone one of hope.

Gilbert closed the book and placed it back beside her. "One that keeps my congregation awake—of that, you can be assured." The corner of his mouth tilted up. "No sleeping young bucks on my watch. Should I see a pair of closed eyes among my flock, they'll be designated trees in the next year's Easter musicale."

She tilted her head forward, a wry smile on her face. "Not fig trees, I hope?"

A confused expression crossed his face for a moment, indicating that her quip about biblical fig trees—specifically ones out of season—was not understood. Gilbert recovered in quick time. "All sorts of trees, my dear. Figs, olives, what have you. They shall have no speaking parts at all and shall be made to stand in front of the congregation in their branches and leaves."

A laugh escaped her, and she covered her mouth just as a knock sounded at the door. Before Susan could get it, it opened and Loftus was at the other side, a few small branches in his hand.

Catherine smiled and was about to greet him when Gilbert grabbed her hand. He grinned in Loftus's direction. "Brother, come in! I've just been keeping your poor wife company while she's ill. Herrick's poems do have a use, it seems."

A muscle in Loftus's jaw twitched as he stepped farther into the room, his smile nowhere to be found. "I'm glad to hear it."

Catherine glanced between the brothers and fought the desire to furrow her eyebrows. What was happening? Was

Susan seeing this? She shot her a look, and her maid shrugged, seemingly also uncertain of what was occurring. Why was Gilbert holding her hand? She tried to extricate it from his grip, but he was holding firm. She almost wished to explain to Loftus that nothing untoward had happened in his absence. Her lips parted. "Gilbert was telling me—"

"I was about to tell dear Catherine how lovely she looks—even when feeling as she is." Gilbert swept her with an admiring gaze. "That color suits you very well."

She blushed, ducking her head. "Why...thank you."

Loftus remained where he was, his lips set into a thin line. "How nice of you to look after her, brother. I can take it from here."

Gilbert reluctantly released her hand. "Only if you're sure."

"Positive." Her husband's voice was low and serious. It brooked no argument.

Gilbert slapped his knees, a hint of satisfaction in his eyes. "Well, I suppose I must leave, then. I shall visit you again tomorrow, dear Catherine, if you aren't yet able to move about." With that, he skirted around his brother and left the room, humming quietly to himself.

Catherine met her husband's steady gaze without faltering and offered a tentative smile. "How good it is to see you. Have you managed to find what you're looking for?"

He didn't return her smile, though he lifted the branches in his hand to show her, an almost anxious expression on his face. "I have. I had nothing in the conservatory that could help you the way I wanted and nothing dried on hand, so I had to venture out on horse to find it."

"And what is it that will help with this pain? I will admit, my aches have not yet ceased."

"They are branches from a willow tree. Drinking a tea made from its bark helps to relieve pain. I'll only need to shave a bit of the bark from them and brew a pot for you. Keep in mind—

it will be rather bitter." The corners of his lips turned down. "I'll dry the rest of the bark so I have more in store for later. You need only a small amount of bark per pot of tea."

She wanted him to come closer, but he remained in the same spot he'd been in when Gilbert had left the room. Had she done something wrong? "Thank you, Loftus."

He dropped the hand with the branches back to his side and nodded, his icy eyes piercing her for a few moments. What was he hoping to find?

CHAPTER 22

*L*oftus let out a heavy breath as he took his handful of branches to the kitchen, his boots like millstones on the uneven stairs. A terrible ache filled his chest, mingling with an unpleasant heat in his abdomen—a mix of irritation and pain.

Had his brother been in Cate's company for the entire time Loftus had been gone? If that was so, then Gilbert had been with her for more than an hour—*in her bedchamber.*

That was Loftus's chair. Cate was Loftus' *wife.*

The image of Gilbert grabbing Cate's hand flashed into Loftus's mind as if being seared there. He'd called her *dear Catherine* or some such drivel—not that she wasn't dear, but it certainly wasn't Gilbert's place to say so. Loftus gritted his teeth. Nor was it his brother's place to comment on Cate's appearance with such a look of admiration on his face.

Perhaps this was more than mere irritation.

He entered the kitchen, much to the surprise of Cook and the scullery maids. She lifted her hand to her cheek, imprinting flour there as he strode in. "My lord, we weren't expectin' ye down here today!"

"My apologies." He tried to appear contrite as he moved to a table in the corner that was always kept clear for his use. "I'm preparing a tea for my wife." Did Cate even wish to be his wife? His heart pounded dolefully in his chest as Cook went back to kneading a lump of dough and the scullery maids resumed chopping vegetables.

He set the branches upon the table and grabbed a knife, then ran it down the length of the first one. The bark peeled easily, coming away in long strips of green and brown.

Gilbert had been reading her *poems*. That was a husband's job. They'd not been alone, of course—Susan had been there—but...

He stifled a sigh. There was no denying his brother was better-looking than Loftus was. Gilbert never had nightmares of war, for he'd never seen battle. He probably didn't have nightmares at all. What had he to fear, truly?

Loftus set aside the now-naked branch and began on the second one. He imagined Cate's laughter. He'd heard it just before entering the room. His brother always seemed to evoke her laughter. Had Loftus ever managed to do the same?

He searched through the fog that embroiled his brain, hoping to find an answer there. He thought he had, but couldn't be sure.

Would she be happier with Gilbert as her husband? The very idea of them—of his brother and Cate—

He grunted as the knife slipped from the bark and sliced the side of his finger, giving him a shallow cut resembling something he'd get from moving foolscap around too swiftly. Nevertheless, blood came beading from it.

He muttered an oath under his breath and set the knife and branch down, then pulled his handkerchief from his pocket. He pressed it to his finger.

Perhaps his wife would be happier without his attention. After all, she'd admitted as much to him—she had never wished to be in an arranged marriage. It had been her parents' idea, and she'd been forced into it.

Everyone else seemed to believe he would never make a love match, so why should he even try? He'd just step back and let her live as she wished. He'd close his heart, and he wouldn't get hurt.

He grunted. He'd still be buying her a new pair of spectacles.

CHAPTER 23

*C*atherine scrunched her nose, trying not to sneeze at the overpowering scent of ambergris and rose perfume that filled the carriage. The dowager sat across from her. How could she stand that infernal scent?

It had been three days since the beginning of Catherine's illness, and the symptoms were finally gone with the help of Loftus's willow bark tea and much resting in her chamber where the sun could not reach past her closed drapes. Gilbert had suggested she take the air and visit the village modiste to see about having new gowns made. After all, now that she was an earl's wife, she'd do well to look the part. Catherine didn't want to embarrass him with her out-of-fashion dresses. The dowager had insisted on coming and helping Catherine, for the woman wouldn't have "my daughter-in-law dress like a dowd."

Loftus had been oddly quiet on the matter. In fact, he'd been oddly quiet about all manner of things since he'd come back from fetching the willow branches those days ago. Her lips pursed. What was troubling him? Two days ago, he'd handed her a box with a new pair of spectacles and hadn't said a word about it. She wasn't even sure he'd realized she'd been without them. She hadn't really seen him since then. Catherine had asked Gilbert about it, but he'd made some quip about Loftus's plants not growing tall enough and laughed it off.

"Do try to smile. Your lips do not look well in such a frown." The dowager's voice cut through the air as sharp as any knife, pulling Catherine from her thoughts.

Catherine's eyes met the woman's steely ones. She was the pot calling the kettle black—that was for sure. Even now, her thin lips were pulled into a tight line, wrinkles at the edges. Not a friendly face at all. Even so, Catherine forced her lips upward and leaned farther back into the crimson squab.

The carriage began to rumble over the cobblestones of the village. The dowager turned her turbaned head to face out the window, so Catherine did the same. Mr. Grine's Apothecary rolled by with its vibrantly colored bottles in the windows, and the buildings grew closer together, their storefronts more inviting and the boardwalks more crowded.

Within minutes, they were entering the modiste's shop. Fabrics of all colors and textures, from peach bombazine to blue cotton in a paisley pattern, assaulted Catherine's eyes. Lace hung from wooden hooks on the walls, almost too delicate to touch. Ribbons in different widths and embroidery thread sat on a counter nearby as though someone had just placed them there and forgotten to pick them back up.

A pale-skinned, dark-haired woman appeared from behind a row of fabrics, her arms outstretched and a wide grin on her face. A few small wrinkles lined her eyes.

"*Bonne journée*, my lady. Who is it you have brought me?" She grabbed the dowager's hand and turned her green eyes to Catherine, looking her over with a keen gaze.

Catherine fought not to squirm.

The dowager dropped the woman's hand and gestured to

Catherine with a sigh. "This is my son's wife, Lady Hardwicke." She shot a frown at Catherine. "Catherine, meet Madame Lisette."

Madame Lisette grabbed Catherine's hands just as she had the dowager's, her smile widening. "Ah, *une comtesse! Très bien.* And what are you ladies looking for today?"

Catherine opened her mouth, but the dowager spoke first, waving a hand in the air as she did so. "She'll need at least seven new day dresses, seven gowns for the evening..." She put a gloved finger to her cheek and tapped it. "One new ball gown. It's not as though Loftus is invited to any of those, but we must be prepared..."

Catherine gritted her teeth. That last comment was unnecessary.

The dowager nodded. "Yes, I suppose that's all."

If Madame Lisette's smile got any wider, her mouth would rip at the seams.

The woman instantly got to work, bringing Catherine to the back and shoving her behind a curtain. The measuring tape was threaded around all of her limbs, and her measurements were written down in a little leather notebook. As Madame Lisette rushed around with the tape held aloft, it seemed as though they made up a sad party of two guests with one streaming ribbon to decorate, the dowager looking on in disdain at their festivities.

When the measuring was done and Catherine redressed, she was pulled over to the fabrics.

"Which do you like?" Madame Lisette threw her hand toward a long line of fabrics. "I think the *rose* would suit you well. Perhaps a light *violette.* It would suit your brown hair very nicely, *non?*"

Catherine was about to agree—then the dowager cleared her throat. "I normally believe you correct, Lisette, but I disagree this time. Catherine should wear something more like this." The woman pointed at a beige color, her eyes serious.

Catherine shared a look with Madame Lisette, who appeared as confused as she was. Were Catherine to wear that color, she'd look...sickly. Sallow. Ill. Loftus would think her illness had returned. She would *not* be wearing that color.

Catherine moved forward. "I don't think it would suit me. What about this one?" She pointed to a dark-blue satin. "It's beautiful."

The dowager's face turned an angry shade of purple as words hissed from her mouth. "That? You'll look like a trollop."

Catherine took a step back, a bit intimidated by the woman's ferocity. How could blue satin make her look like a trollop? If the cut of the dress was modest, then there would be no issue. Indeed, Catherine could almost swear she'd seen the dowager in this very color!

Madame Lisette stepped in between them, a look of caution on her face. "Perhaps we look at the cottons for now, *oui*?"

They nodded their heads and followed her to another section of the shop where she pointed out more fabric.

With Catherine eventually settling on a few fabrics she loved and a few she'd like to toss into the fireplace, they left the store, and Catherine was able to take a full breath again without the awful taste of molded roses on her tongue. Thank heavens for Madame Lisette. If it hadn't been for her, they'd likely still be in that store right now arguing. She was *not* wearing beige...or grey so long as Loftus was alive. That color was for the bleakness of half mourning and decidedly not for a newlywed.

A great sigh heaved from behind her, and as Catherine turned, a look of resignation appeared on the dowager's face along with—was that...regret? She took a step closer to Catherine and held out her hand, her shoulders drooping.

Catherine reluctantly placed her hand in her mother-in-law's, unsure as to what was happening. Was this apoplexy? Everyone always talked about it but never really explained what it was.

The dowager squeezed her hand and sighed again. "I'm sorry if I'm being difficult, Catherine."

Catherine's eyes widened of their own accord. She was *apologizing*? The *dowager*?

"I've always wished for a daughter, you know, but I've only been blessed with boys. That is the way of things sometimes. But then, when Loftus told me he'd be marrying you—well, I was so excited. I would finally be able to do all of the things with you that I never got to do with my sons. I'm sorry, Catherine, for I am new at this and do not know how to be a mother to a daughter."

Catherine blinked at her, lips parted. "Oh. I...I see."

An exasperated laugh escaped her mother-in-law. "My sons were forever running around and getting into one thing or another. I always had to put my foot down. I suppose I don't know how to do anything else."

Guilt squeezed at Catherine's insides. She hadn't been treating this woman fairly. All this time, Catherine had believed that the dowager hated her, but that hadn't truly been the case at all. This marriage had just muddled Catherine's judgement, and her anxieties had blinded her to the woman's true kind nature. How quick to judge she had been.

Catherine squeezed her hand back. "I'm so sorry...Mama." The word felt odd on her lips, but it probably would for some time. "I was unaware you felt this way. All this time, I believed you'd disliked me, so I attempted to stay away from you."

The dowager smiled—an actual smile, and Catherine's heart warmed. The gesture made her mother-in-law look rather pretty. "My dear, let us not dither about the past. I wish to know you and to learn more about your life. Now that I'm back from London, we'll be spending more time together, of course."

"I would like that very much." Catherine's stomach grumbled, and the dowager chuckled.

"I'm hungry as well. Let us stop to get tea at one of these shops. Many of them are actually rather good."

A quarter of an hour later, they were ensconced in the corner of a tea shop, their small wooden table adjacent to one of the large windows at the front. The serving maid had just deposited a steaming pot of tea between them, along with all of the additional necessities—sugar bowl, milk pot, and lemon wedges. The girl set a plate of currant biscuits before them, the circular treats dotted liberally with the purple and red berries.

The dowager began to pour, her eyes meeting Catherine's. "Oh, dear, could you please order us some lemon cakes? I'm afraid I forgot to when the girl came over." She tilted the teapot up and looked over her shoulder at the counter where the girl was wiping it down. "She's just over there, and I'd hate to wait for her to come back."

Catherine pushed back her chair. "Of course. I'll be right back."

She made her way past tables with chatting patrons and smiled at the girl. "Might we have some lemon cake, please? Two slices will do fine." After the server agreed, Catherine headed back to their little cozy corner with its abundance of light and ample view of pedestrians on the street outside.

When she sat back down, her tea was exactly the color she wished it to be. The dowager twisted a rather large ring on her finger, her eyebrows raised. There was an uncertain look on her face. "That is the way you like your tea, yes? Milk and sugar?"

Catherine dipped her head. "Indeed. How did you know?"

The dowager continued to twist the ring, looking somewhat abashed. "I must admit, I've been paying attention when we've taken tea altogether."

Catherine's chest expanded with warmth. She lifted the cup to her lips and took a sip. It was evident the shop used different leaves than Catherine was used to, for she'd never tasted a brew like this before, but—besides being a bit more bitter than normal—it was as she usually had it.

She smiled at the dowager. "It's perfect."

The tension in the woman's shoulder's eased. "Is it? Wonderful."

The serving girl arrived with a plate of the lemon cake and set it on the table. As the dowager reached for a slice, the large green stone of her ring, set into an oval mount, caught the light. All around the stone, intricate designs and curves were etched into the gold band.

"What a beautiful ring." Catherine stared more at the stone on top. It didn't look quite like an emerald...

The dowager glanced at it before picking up her teacup and saucer. "Thank you. It's jade, from the East Indies. My mother gave it to me."

Catherine moved her slice of lemon cake to her plate. "Well, she had very good taste in jewelry."

The dowager's smile was subdued as she set her teacup down and placed her hands on her lap where Catherine could no longer see them. "What are your parents like?"

The next half an hour was spent in pleasant conversation, with Catherine getting to know more about the dowager and revealing more about herself. The dowager's parents, from the stories she told, were quite indulgent with all of their daughters —the dowager being the youngest of three. She grew up quite differently from Catherine, whose parents had not indulged her and who—though she'd grown up in the same wealthy environment—had not experienced the same love and kindness her mother-in-law described.

After finishing their repast, they paid and left the tea shop, Catherine's hunger for food and answers sated. They were walking back to the carriage, which had been left only a little way from the shop, when a familiar face down the street caught her notice. She frowned.

What was Gilbert doing at the apothecary? Had Loftus sent him there for some reason? That seemed unlikely. Indeed, didn't Gilbert spend most of his time at the neighboring estates? She had to find out why he was in the village.

CHAPTER 24

*C*atherine walked with the dowager to the carriage, and as the woman stepped in, made her excuses. "I forgot to pick up something from the apothecary. It will only take a moment."

Her mother-in-law moved to get back up. "Oh, well, I'll come with you."

"No!" The word came out a bit louder than necessary. Catherine lowered her voice and tried to calm her tone. If Gilbert was up to something, it would do no good to have the dowager complicate matters. Besides, if Catherine was to get to the bottom of this, she had to be stealthy— and the dowager was decidedly not. "No, there's no need, really. I'll only be a moment." She glanced at the footman and tried to smile. "I'll take Frederick with me—not that any harm will befall a married woman in plain daylight, anyway."

The dowager raised her eyebrows and leaned back into the red cushions. "If you're sure..."

Catherine nodded. "I'll see you in a minute." She gestured for Frederick to follow her and rushed down the street.

Hopefully, Gilbert hadn't moved on from the shop yet. Why

would he be there? Was he ill? Was Loftus? Surely, if Loftus was ill, he'd be treating himself or explaining to Mrs. Stonehill how to treat him. Something niggled at the back of her mind that there was more to the matter than mere illness. This place was where Loftus did his business—a business that Gilbert wasn't involved in. Was she looking for problems where there weren't any? She had to find out.

She stepped around couples arm in arm and groups of shoppers, some of them giving her irritated glances, and strode toward the apothecary with Frederick only feet behind her.

The oak door creaked as she entered, leaving Frederick outside. Thankfully, it didn't interrupt Gilbert from his hushed conversation. She stepped inside and closed the door behind her as softly as she could, straining her ears to catch a bit of what was being discussed. A long line of products on a shelf hid her from view.

She caught only a few words—"plants," "danger," and "isn't right." Her curiosity flared. There was only one way of getting answers...by asking questions.

She walked past the shelf and propped her hands on her hips. "I didn't expect to see you here, Gilbert."

He nearly jumped from his spot where he leaned over the counter, his face reddening to a rusty shade as he turned toward her. "Catherine! How...lovely to see you." He glanced between her and Mr. Grine, whose brows were drawn almost into a knot over his eyes.

The latter man greeted her with a nod. "Good to see you, my lady."

She smiled at him. "You as well, Mr. Grine." She took a step toward her brother-in-law. "What brings you here, Gilbert? Are you feeling unwell? You know as well as I that Loftus could help you with many ailments, for we have the herbs at Blackfern."

Gilbert pulled at his cravat. "I am perfectly healthy, my dear.

You needn't worry about me." He cleared his throat, his Adam's apple bobbing. "This visit was more of a...personal...nature." He looked over his shoulder at Mr. Grine. "Isn't that right, Grine?"

The apothecary grabbed a large marble mortar and pestle and began pounding some sort of seed into dust. He frowned at Gilbert, the large muscles in his arms moving with the turning motion. "Aye. And it needn't happen again."

Gilbert laughed. "Yes, well, we all make mistakes. We'll see if this one's yours or mine." He offered his arm to Catherine. "May I escort you out?"

She shook her head, unease growing roots within her. His words were spoken as if in jest, but the words themselves were...eerie. Was there danger in the village Mr. Grine should be watching out for? And what kind of mistake had been made?

Mr. Grine continued to grind the seeds. He didn't seem to take Gilbert's warning seriously—so perhaps neither should she. This was Gilbert—he was a jester. He must be exaggerating something. He *did* tend toward the dramatic.

"No, thank you. I have to get something here."

Gilbert dropped his arm, his smile lessening. "A shame. I'll see you at dinner, then."

As soon as he left, she perused the shelves for something to buy. She'd already spent too much time here. The dowager was likely wondering where she'd been.

Dalby's Carminative, Godfrey's Cordial, Charles Linead's Balm of Gilead, Steers' Opodeldoc...

What to choose?

She'd rather go with an actual medicine than something some quack concocted, so she asked Mr. Grine for a small bag of fever powder.

She was back down the street in a trice. Frederick opened the door to the carriage and let the steps down, then assisted

Catherine inside. The dowager blinked open her eyes and raised her head from where she'd rested it against the squabs, her arms crossed over her chest. "Oh, are you back already? I'm afraid I must've fallen asleep." She raised a hand to cover a yawn.

Catherine inwardly rejoiced at the dowager's slumber and lack of scolding. "Yes, I am. I only needed to retrieve this powder." She settled into the seat across from her mother-in-law and gave her a smile, setting the cloth bag down beside her.

The dowager smacked the roof of the carriage, and her eyes began to droop closed again. Catherine pulled the red curtain back from the window and surveyed the street as they moved out of the village, which was much busier now than it had been when they'd arrived.

A woman dressed in a pretty pink gown entered the book shop, the door closing behind her. Catherine made a mental note to visit there the next time she traveled to the village. Maybe Loftus would join her too.

As they reached the end of the block, her heart stopped.

There *he* was, a cloak about his shoulders but the hood drawn away from his face, leaning against the corner of a building. He met her gaze as the carriage rumbled by, a knowing smile lifting one corner of his lips. Her body tensed, a wave of nausea knocking into her like an ocean wave as her fears were confirmed. A scream burst from her throat.

The dowager's eyes popped open, and she lurched forward in her seat, reaching out toward Catherine. "My heavens! What is it, dear?"

Catherine dragged the window curtain shut and pushed herself as far into the opposite corner of the carriage as she could, her booted feet scraping against the floor. She gasped with every breath. "He was out there! In the village!" Her voice was piercing, even to her own ears. She closed her eyes, hoping that might take away the churning in her stomach.

The dowager moved over to Catherine's side of the carriage, sitting beside her and wrapping an arm about her shoulder, placing the other hand on Catherine's. "Who, dear? Who did you see?"

Catherine shook her hand, slowly at first but more quickly as her fears began to mount and hot tears spilled over her cheeks. "T-the same m-man I saw in the forest at Blackfern." She choked on a sob. "I-I just saw him." She pointed at the now-covered window

The dowager ran a wrinkled hand down Catherine's cheek. "Oh, dear, you're working yourself up. I'm sure it's nothing to worry about."

Catherine shoved her face into her hands in a violent manner. "You don't understand!" Her shout was muffled in her palms. "I know him! *I know him!*"

The dowager opened the uncovered window of the carriage. Catherine moved away from the opening, huddling into a ball on the seat as the woman called out to the driver and the horses quickened. "Faster! The countess is unwell!"

How had he found her? Catherine curled her body tighter, pressing her face into her knees. What did he want?

CHAPTER 25

*L*oftus was in the conservatory the afternoon his mother and wife had gone into the village, so he was afforded a very good view when the carriage came racing up the driveway, the horses pulling it as though lightning struck at their feet.

"What the devil..." He dropped his snips and pulled off his gloves, depositing them haphazardly as he ran from the room. What had happened? Had something gone wrong on their outing?

A feeling of unease stirred in his abdomen—one that wasn't easy to shake.

He got to the front doors of the manor just as Bromley was opening them, Cate being helped in by both the coachman and the footman. She looked on the verge of collapse, with her eyes half lidded and her skin flushed.

His stomach dropped. He raced forward and took the coachman's place, thanking the man for his assistance. Loftus's mother came in just after them, wringing her gloved hands. She followed as they led Cate toward the stairs, though Loftus wasn't sure his wife would have the strength to climb them in her state.

He glanced over his shoulder. "What happened, Mother?"

The dowager, for the first time in her life, looked flustered. Her eyes went wide. "I-I don't know. She claimed to have seen a man at the edge of the village. The same one she'd seen the other day. The one in the cloak."

Loftus exhaled a heavy sigh and pressed his fist against his thigh. Perhaps it wasn't a poacher, after all. He bent and lifted his wife into his arms, cradling her against him. Cate's hair tickled his chin.

"It's all right, darling." He tightened his arms around her, his voice a whisper. "You're safe now. I'll keep you safe. I'm sorry I wasn't there."

She sniffed into his chest as he reached the top of the stairs and made his way down the hall.

The minute he set her on her feet in her chamber, she covered her mouth and reached under her bed to cast up her accounts into the chamber pot stowed there. He grimaced. Poor dear. Kneeling beside her, he brushed his hand down her shoulder, trying to be a comforting presence as her heaving continued.

These were the same symptoms she'd experienced the other day when she'd gotten too much sun.

When her stomach relented, he took the pot by the handle and slowly tugged it away from her, pushing it to the side. He smoothed back the wisps of hair that had plastered against her forehead. Then he assisted her from the floor with as much care as possible and directed her to her bed, where he pulled off her kid boots and gloves.

"My dear, do you believe you were in the sun for too long again today?"

She scrunched her eyes but shook her head without a word.

He began to pluck the pins from her hair, one by one, causing her brilliant curls to fall like a ribbons.

"Your mother and I went to a tea shop." She croaked out the words, and he stopped in his movements, tilting his head toward her. "Something there must have upset my stomach. They have a blend of leaves I've never tried—perhaps it's that."

He continued removing her hairpins, frowning. "Are you not experiencing the same symptoms you were before?"

She shook her head. "This sickness is different. I am not dizzy, nor do I have a megrim. My vision is clear as well."

Loftus nodded, pulling the last pin from her head. Perhaps she *had* merely eaten something that didn't sit right, then. "Dr. Fench has likely been called for already."

Cate closed her eyes. "He may very well come, but it is not this illness that worries me, for it shall be gone in a matter of days." She opened her eyes, and they pierced him with their hazel depths. "*He* was there, Loftus. I saw him in the village. He didn't have his hood on this time, though he had the same cloak. Lord Balfour was there." She shuddered.

If she'd seen him—seen his face as she'd claimed to—then there was no denying it. The man was here to cause trouble.

Gilbert appeared in the doorway, his countenance a mask of concern. Without pause, he strode into the room and knelt at the edge of the bed, grasping Cate's hands. "What happened? Are you ill again?"

Suddenly, Loftus felt as though he was an unknown onlooker—a stranger in his own home watching some happily married couple deal with the aftermath of a troublesome afternoon. Loftus breathed in through his mouth and exhaled through his nostrils. He'd promised himself he'd let her alone —keep his own heart safe from what was sure to be a crushing letdown. Cate would never pick him if she was given the choice.

Nevertheless, he couldn't help the stab of jealousy at the sight of his brother touching Cate with such familiarity.

She relayed to Gilbert what she'd already told Loftus, and the man's gaze never strayed from hers. Seriously, had his brother finally fallen in love? Gilbert had always sworn himself to be a bachelor through and through. He'd never seemed to enjoy the idea of becoming attached to another person.

At the end of Cate's retelling, Gilbert stood. "Why are you so sure this man will cause you harm? Why are you so sure he is here for that purpose? My dear, he might seem ominous, yes, but I'm sure he's harmless."

Interesting. Loftus straightened his shoulders. Cate had never told Gilbert about Lord Balfour, it seemed.

Cate's mouth twisted into a scowl, her eyes pained. "He and I share a troubled past, and that is all I will divulge."

Gilbert's eyes widened. "He isn't from around here? I'm surprised I didn't take note of him in the village."

Cate shook her head.

Loftus crossed his arms over his chest and lifted his chin. "What were *you* doing in the village? Aren't you meant to be at Lord Stanhope's at this time of day?" Loftus pulled his pocket watch from his waistcoat and flicked it open. Indeed. It was odd that his brother should be home at the moment—much less, in town earlier.

Gilbert stuck his hands in his pockets, shuffling his boots on the blue carpeting. "Ol' chap canceled. Said his sister needed him to escort her to something or other—can't remember what just now."

Loftus tilted his head. "Is that so? Didn't his sister make her come-out this year? I thought she was currently in London, attending the soirees, balls, and the like." A tension formed within him—a stone in his midsection getting larger and larger. His brother was hiding something.

Gilbert lifted a hand to the back of his neck, scratching there for a moment. His cheeks grew ruddy, and he gave a lopsided smile. "Did I say sister? I meant mother."

Loftus grunted. "Well, how did you enjoy your time in the village, then? Far better than my wife, I presume. What shops did you visit?"

Gilbert held his hands up, a light chuckle coming from him. He glanced at Cate, then turned his attention back to Loftus. "My, brother, what an interrogation. If you *must* know, I visited the tavern, went to the tailor for new waistcoats, and even popped in on the milliner." He stuck a hand into his pocket, then extended his fist toward Cate.

Her lashes fluttered as she looked up at him. "Why, what is this?"

Opening his palm, he revealed a peach-colored silk ribbon. Gilbert grinned. "For you, my lady." He handed it to her, and she let it fall into her fingers, appreciation gleaming in her eyes.

Loftus's hands curled into fists at his sides. His jaw clenched. He wished to be elsewhere so he might not witness what was essentially his brother courting his wife, but he was not—not for one second—about to leave her alone in her bedchamber with Gilbert.

Footsteps sounded down the hall, and Dr. Fench appeared beside Mother in the doorframe, his black bag in hand. "Lady Hardwicke is ill again, is she?"

He asked for the room to be cleared, which meant Gilbert had to go. At this, a small smile tugged at Loftus's lips. His brother and mother waited in the hall. Once the chamber door was closed, Dr. Fench began his examination—Cate explaining her ideas of the cause of her illness.

Loftus leaned against the chamber wall, his arms crossed over his chest as the doctor performed the same tests he had the last time—plus a few extras. The bleary look on his wife's face made concern slither into Loftus's heart. Was this more than an affliction from something she'd eaten? But then, she *did* say the symptoms were different this time. Perhaps it was a coincidence. He bit the inside of his cheek. Whatever it was, hopefully, she would feel back to her normal and healthy self soon.

Ten minutes passed before the doctor began to place his tools back into his bag. By then, Cate was lying on her coverlet, her eyes half closed and her hands on her stomach.

Loftus stood away from the wall, catching the man's attention. "What are your thoughts?"

Dr. Fench glanced at Cate and shook his head. "I agree with your wife. This sickness seems different from the last. It's not as complex, and it happened after she ate at the tea shop with your mother. Something there must have set her humors off balance."

Edmund rubbed a hand along his jaw. "Would not my mother also be ill? They ate the same things."

Dr. Fench sighed. "Humors are curious things. There are many reasons why they may or may not become imbalanced. If the blood was cooler to begin with or not, if the room had enough air, et cetera. Your mother may simply have a better constitution."

Loftus straightened his shoulders. "What would you recommend, then?"

The doctor closed his bag and scooped it up from the side table, a small bottle in his other hand. "Laudanum for pain. Time for the rest."

Dr. Fench handed the bottle to Loftus, and as soon as the man left, Cate croaked from the bed. "I don't want that." Her brow furrowed. "Please."

Gilbert and Mother entered, their gazes flitting between Loftus and Cate.

Mother spoke first. "What did the doctor have to say?"

Strange that she should be so interested in Cate's illness. She certainly hadn't been interested in the last. Perhaps she was worried for her own health because she'd eaten the same things Cate had.

Loftus set the laudanum aside. "She's ill from the food at the tea shop." His tone became wry. "Thank you very much for sickening my bride, Mother." She huffed and he continued. "Anyway, it doesn't appear to be very serious. She's more affected by the subsequent appearance of..."—Loftus struggled to find the right word for Lord Balfour without giving up Cate's secret—"her acquaintance."

Susan scurried into the room, her arms full with a tea tray that smelled of mint. She kept her eyes down as she wove around the family members in the chamber and placed the tray on Cate's bedside table. "I thought ye'd like the tea his lordship recommends for the nausea, since I heard ye weren't doing well. Took me a mite longer to make it since we had none dried. I had to get some fresh from the garden. I came as fast as I could." She wrung her hands in front of her. "Didn't want to interrupt Dr. Fench neither."

A weak smile broke across Cate's face as she pushed herself up against the pillows, and she reached out to pat Susan's hand. "Thank you, Susan. That was very thoughtful."

As quick as she'd come, the maid left the room—being sure to grab the full chamber pot on the way out.

Loftus hated seeing Cate in such a state. Had her constitution always been so poor? She'd never mentioned being sickly before. Had it started when she'd arrived here? What did it mean if it had?

CHAPTER 26

*W*hen Catherine awoke the next day, her stomach gave a lurch and she was on her knees in a matter of moments, her chamber pot cradled in her arms. She couldn't breathe as liquid filled her throat and she coughed up the contents of her stomach—mostly tea.

When the roiling within her stopped, she groaned and set the pot down, throwing an arm over her forehead. All night, her stomach had been like this—aching one minute and churning the next like the seas beneath a ship sailing along the Cape of Good Hope. Not that she'd ever journeyed there.

"My lady!" Susan's voice pierced the darkness of the chamber. Approaching footsteps preceded a sword of light stabbing Catherine in the eye.

She groaned once more.

"Well, ye can't be in the dark all day long. It's a quarter to three, my lady." Susan tutted.

Where was all of the time going? If she kept sleeping for so long, the illness consuming all of her hours, she'd soon be dead —in a cycle of constant sleep.

Susan lifted the chamber pot from the floor and left the

room, coming back five minutes later with it clean. "Have ye any desire to eat anything? Some broth'll likely do ye good. Or toast, maybe? I'll bring ye up some tea, at least."

Catherine wrinkled her nose. Toast sounded too...dry—and her mouth was already dry. Would her stomach even take solid food at the moment? She climbed back onto her bed, pulling her arms and legs up. "Broth, please. Tea would also be pleasant."

In short order, Susan brought all Catherine had asked for. She darned stockings in the corner of the room whilst Catherine spooned hot broth into her mouth and sipped at the peppermint tea, her strength momentarily renewed by the nourishment.

The dowager came to visit an hour later. By then, the tray was long gone and Catherine was watching the flickering shadows of tree branches dance along the walls. She'd already studied the tapestries with their colorful depictions of events and people and listened to the creaking of footsteps in Loftus's room as he changed clothing for a ride. She had no desire to read, at the moment. Such an exciting day.

"Oh, you poor dear." Her mother-in-law moved to her bedside and placed a wrinkled hand on her cheek. "I feel so terrible that you're unwell. I wonder if you would not be so ill if we hadn't gone to that tea shop." She placed her hand to her own neck. "This is my fault."

Catherine's eyes widened, and she tried to push herself up against the headboard. "Never think so, Mama. This is no fault of yours. The doctor said it might be as simple as a matter of constitution." She shrugged. "I'm still acclimating to the cooler Cumbrian air—that is all."

The dowager seated herself in the chair beside the bed, the deep lines in her face softening. "Oh...well, if that is what the good doctor says, then perhaps I need not judge myself too harshly. I *am* worried about you, however, my dear." She eyed

Susan, her lips thinning. "Fetch us tea. Poor Catherine must be half starved."

Catherine tried to protest, but once Susan stepped out of the room with a chagrined expression, the dowager continued where she'd left off. "After all, my dear, you had quite a fright in the carriage. You gave *me* quite a fright with how you reacted to that...man."

Catherine swallowed, gripping the coverlet tighter. The idea that he might be staying in the village was enough to make bile rise again in her throat. She did not want to talk about Lord Balfour, but if she was to allay the dowager's fears or reassure her in some way, she needed to explain.

She took a breath. "I am sorry for my outburst." She ducked her chin. "Such was my shock at seeing him again that I could not control it. This man I saw—the one I'd seen in the forest—is not a good man. Indeed, he is not someone I ever wish to reacquaint myself with. He has caused me much grief in the time I have known him, and the idea that he has sought me out frightens me greatly."

The dowager nodded, her eyes gleaming with hesitation. "I see. And this man... What do you fear from him?"

Catherine's heart began to pound. Lord Balfour's smug smile burned into the back of her mind. He knew exactly where Catherine was, and with whom.

"He must not wish for my happiness." Her voice quavered as she spoke. "He does not like that I am married, for I once was meant to be married to him. He seeks to take what I have, and that is all he's ever wanted since he met me." She swallowed. "He'll harm me." She squeezed her eyes shut, shaking her head. Her voice lowered into a frantic whisper. "No. He'll kill me."

The door thumped open. Catherine gasped, her eyes popping open. She nearly jumped out of her skin, but it was only Susan entering with the tea tray.

"Sorry, my lady. Didn't mean to startle ye." Susan set the

tray down on the bedside table and moved back to her chair in the corner.

The dowager poured, her face set in grim lines. "You have much weight on your shoulders." She spooned sugar into Catherine's cup and poured milk into it, handing it to her. "Loftus never mentioned that you were once betrothed."

Catherine's face burned as she held onto her saucer. "It was only for a short amount of time."

"And yet it was to this terrible man?" Her mother-in-law finished preparing her own cup.

Catherine nodded and pushed her spectacles up her nose. "My parents arranged it."

The dowager's mouth turned down. "How awful."

Catherine took a small sip of her tea for fortitude, the dowager's understanding bolstering her. Perhaps she could share more with this woman.

She set the teacup aside as her hands began to tremble. "His name is Lord Balfour. He is a...violent man. He would strike me if I failed to do what he wished. He eventually ended our engagement in London." She swallowed past a lump of emotion in her throat. "That was around the time I left. My parents had no sympathy for me."

The dowager took another sip from her teacup before placing it and the saucer down. She tutted. "What a sorrowful story." She pierced Catherine with a stare. "If only it were true."

CHAPTER 27

*C*atherine's shoulders tensed. Surely, she hadn't heard the dowager correctly. "What?"

"Your story—it would be very moving if any of it were true." The woman put a finger to her lips. "Well, Lord Balfour is a real man, of course, but it's laughable to accuse *him* of ever raising his hand to a woman."

It seemed for a moment as though Catherine's head had detached from her neck and was floating away from her body, the dowager's words becoming quieter as the distance grew between her head and the room. All of a sudden, it crashed back down into the space between her shoulders, and Catherine began breathing again.

She blinked. "Mama—I'm telling the truth. I—"

"You are doing no such thing." The dowager dismissed Susan from the room with a wave of her hand. "When you saw the cloaked figure in the garden and Loftus sent out the servants to find the trespasser, they found nothing. No one. Then you see the same person—Lord Balfour—in the village, and when I look out the window, what do I see? Nothing." She leaned forward, her lips held tight in a frown. "You threw yourself into the corner of the carriage over nothing more than an empty street."

Catherine's eyes burned. Her jaw clenched. "I saw him. *He was there.* How could you not have seen him standing right against that building with the white sign—"

The dowager scoffed. "I saw that very building with my own eyes, girl, and there was no man there—certainly not Lord Balfour. Indeed, no one was even walking past there the moment you screamed. No man, woman, or child."

Catherine bit the inside of her cheek. "He must've slipped away before you saw him."

A pinched expression came over the dowager's face. "Likely story. Even if that *were* the case, why would a gentleman follow a ruined woman up to Cumbria? *He's* the one who broke off the engagement—not you." She folded her hands in her lap.

Catherine gasped. "Ruined?" How could her mother-in-law assume that of her?

The woman went on as though Catherine hadn't spoken. "You claim that he is violent, but I have never heard anyone speak of him thusly. I have met him a few times myself, and he always acts with propriety. Furthermore, you say your parents arranged the match. You should have been pleased indeed for such a feat. It is not often a merchant's daughter"—the dowager's nose wrinkled—"might have the chance to marry a peer."

Catherine glared at the woman who presumed to know the whole of the story. "You do not know him. He acts much differently behind closed doors. And my parents—"

Her mother-in-law leaned back in her chair, a smug smile on her lips. "Your parents. Do you know, I met your parents on my latest trip to London?"

Catherine's eyes must've widened, for the dowager nodded. "I know, it is strange for the widow of a duke and a merchant to run into one another, and yet, we did. They told me a great deal about you."

Her knowing tone sent a spiral of ice through Catherine's lungs, freezing the air within them. What had they said? Surely, nothing that Loftus didn't already know—Catherine had told him everything.

"You, my dear, are quite the thorn amongst roses." The dowager rested her cheek in her gloved hand and feigned surprise. "It was rather shocking to learn that the woman my son had married had not only been jilted by her betrothed but was also known throughout London drawing rooms for being strange and unladylike." She pursed her lips. "I even met a young man—a Lord Fortescue or some such—who was more than eager to tell me of his encounter with the woman. According to him, Miss Blynn was 'outrageously forthright and not at all a model of good breeding.'"

That cad had spoken of Catherine to the dowager? Catherine scowled. To think she'd even considered him handsome.

Catherine crossed her arms over her chest, her heart racing. But she kept her voice cool as she spoke. "I do not know why you choose not to believe me when I say Lord Balfour is a bad man. I will admit to being a bit unusual, but my father is the one who arranged the betrothal with your son. If you are angry about that, then take it up with him. Loftus knew I had been jilted before he signed the marital contract."

"Believe me—"

"As for seeing Lord Balfour in the village and the forest, I am telling the truth. I have seen him both times. He simply must have slipped away before you saw him."

"Lies!" The dowager spat the word, her face mottled red.

Catherine's heart spasmed as the invisible knife the dowager threw entered her chest and made its mark. Where was the kind woman from earlier that day? Hurt poured from the place she'd been hit.

Catherine swallowed. "Outside of the modiste, you said you

wanted to get to know me. You said you wished to treat me as your daughter."

A cruel laugh escaped the woman's throat. "And you believed it too. I've known from the beginning that all you'd do is cause trouble for this family. Ruin our good name. Loftus—the daft man—has made a mistake by bringing you here. All you do is lie and seek to ruin us. Once I tell him the truth, there'll be no escaping for you."

Catherine wanted to throw something. She'd been used terribly and deceived by someone she'd begun to trust. Coupled with the nausea in her stomach, this day was really turning out to be unpleasant.

"Loftus won't believe you." Catherine met the dowager's gaze, lifting her chin. "He'll see that I've been telling the truth all along."

"Perhaps *you* believe you are. And you're quite convincing. I would believe you myself if I didn't know otherwise." A light came into the dowager's eyes that made Catherine's stomach tighten with unease. "Your parents said you'd always acted oddly. Never have you wished to follow the rules. You accuse people of things they haven't done, and now you're seeing things that aren't there." She smiled wickedly. "You're mad."

Catherine inhaled sharply. She tried not to show her fear. She knew for a fact that she wasn't mad, but the very accusation was dangerous. A woman could be sent to a madhouse on accusation alone. "I have all my faculties about me, I assure you." Her pulse raced and her arms tingled. Where was her husband? She needed saving and wasn't well enough to do it herself right now.

The dowager stood, much to Catherine's relief, and looked down her nose at her, that foreboding smile still on her face. "We'll see how long they remain."

With those parting words, she spun and left the room, a flurry of silk and menace.

CHAPTER 28

*G*ilbert choked on his tea two evenings later when Catherine told him what his mother had said. "She threatened you with the asylum?" He sputtered, setting his teacup down.

The sun was setting outside, and Catherine was almost feeling back to her usual self. Tomorrow, she'd probably be well enough to tend plants with Loftus and finally get to the bottom of why it seemed as though he was ignoring her. Well, he wasn't *completely* ignoring her—he had sent a servant with flowers up to her room. That was nice. Otherwise, however, she hadn't really seen head nor hind of him. Not for long.

Dinner was in an hour, but Gilbert had gotten ready early in order to have a cup of tea with Catherine—which was very thoughtful on his part. If only her husband had done the same.

Catherine nodded. "And she seemed to imply that it would be only a matter of time before I would be taken there."

Gilbert's jaw slackened. "My mother's a bit overbearing, but to think she'd speak to you in such a way..." He rubbed a hand over his face. "My brother would never allow you to go there, Catherine. He'd sooner die."

Catherine poured herself another cup of tea, adding an excess of sugar. That was always guaranteed to raise her spirits. She stirred it in and took a sip. Very sweet—perfect.

She raised her eyes to Gilbert. "It is worrisome, even so."

He pulled at his cravat and brought his cup to his lips. "You must trust us, Catherine. We will keep you safe."

Catherine allowed herself to relax a little. It was reassuring to know that even when Loftus was inconsistent, his brother could be relied upon.

~

*L*oftus was seated at the head of the dinner table, picking at the fish placed before him. The room was silent, neither his mother nor his brother speaking a word. The candelabra at the middle of their place settings gleamed down upon the china procured by his father during one of his trips to the Continent.

He took a sip of wine and let the cool liquid slide down his throat. How was his wife doing up in her chamber? He'd visited her this morning, but only for a moment. Seeing her was too painful when he remembered that she loved his brother. Well—he assumed she did, anyway. He didn't know for sure. Gilbert had been visiting Cate every day of her illness, however, including making a visit an hour ago. If there wasn't affection on her side, there was on his.

His mother straightened her shoulders, catching Loftus's attention. "I wasn't going to tell you this yet. Indeed, I was going to wait, but I find I can no longer keep this information to myself."

Loftus's eyes widened. He set his fork down.

His mother continued, though reluctantly, as if pained. "When in London, I gathered a great deal of information from a few acquaintances, and have subsequently come to the conclusion that your wife, Catherine...is mad."

A choking sensation began in Loftus's chest, then moved up to his throat before he erupted in laughter. He'd never heard anything more ridiculous. Certainly, his wife was a bit eccentric, but she definitely wasn't mad.

His mother's eyebrows pulled into a scowl. "What is so humorous?"

He struggled to speak between his still-uneven breath. "I-it's just—"

A haunting scream stabbed through the evening's relative quiet, chilling Loftus's blood. *Cate.*

He threw back his chair with such force that it tumbled to the floor with a crash. He was through the door and in the hall in a moment, then running up the stairs two at a time with his heart in his throat. Gilbert called out from below, but whatever he said went unheard past the torrent of blood rushing in his ears. He needed to find his wife. Now.

The hallways and corridors seemed too long as he raced down them—their endless turns unnecessary. Why must her room be so far away? The back of his neck prickled. Had Lord Balfour finally decided to act on his unnamed threat?

As soon as Loftus reached the door to Cate's bedchamber, he barged in, scanning the room. The bed was empty. She wasn't here.

"My lord!" Susan's panicked voice called.

The door that connected his and Cate's rooms was ajar. He jogged over to it and opened it wider.

Susan knelt on the rug beside Cate, who was on her back with closed eyes.

He nearly swore under his breath as he strode toward his wife's prone form and fell to his knees at her side. "What's happened?" His voice was rough.

Tears flowed down Susan's cheeks, and she wrung a handkerchief in her hands, shaking her head. "I don't know. She wished to get up to pace around her chamber for a bit and stretch her legs. She was feeling better after tea with yer brother. She said she heard a sound in yer chamber and thought it might be you."

The maid ducked her chin, lifting her wary eyes. "She wanted to ask ye why ye've been avoiding her." She swallowed. "I stayed here, for I didn't want to interrupt a private conversation, of course. A second later, she screamed, and I went to check on her. The wall was open, and she was on the floor as she is now."

Indeed, the door to the hidden corridor in the wall was open. Was someone in there, hiding, even now?

Loftus lifted Cate and laid her on his bed, then faced Susan. "Please watch over her."

Mrs. Stonehill peeked into the room through the adjoining doorway, her eyes wide with concern. "My lord, I heard a scream—"

"Have Bromley send for the doctor. Station footmen outside my bedchamber door. No one but Dr. Fench and Susan come in or out of this room tonight. Have Bromley send the rest of the footmen after me into this passage. They should take different directions. If any intruder is seen, have them apprehend him." Loftus lit a candelabra to take with him. "I'll be back."

As he stepped into the darkened corridor, the temperature dropped. He peered to the left and right. Which way would the intruder have gone?

Taking a left, he made haste through the narrow hall, searching for any indication of the man's presence. He stopped every once in a while to listen for any sounds of movement. He soon began to hear footsteps behind him and voices as footmen entered the corridor, taking different directions in the same maze he was in. They would smoke this fox out.

Fear pushed him to increase his pace. He wouldn't let this

man get away as he had the other times. Skirting around cobwebs, he focused on the ground, searching for any footsteps in the dust. The only set was the small slippered ones Cate had left the other day, along with puppy prints.

He turned a corner, nearly running into a footman.

The man's eyebrows raised. "Apologies, my lord." The servant spun around and turned down another hallway.

The search continued for another three-quarters of an hour until there was no more hidden corridor to traverse. Bromley met Loftus outside of his chamber with his lips pulled down. "The footmen found nothing, my lord."

Loftus pinched the bridge of his nose. "Nothing? No man's footprints? No sign of...an intruder?"

Bromley's displeasured look increased. "I'm afraid not, my lord."

Disappointment swelled in Loftus's stomach. He'd failed his wife. He'd let Lord Balfour get away. He rested his arm against the wall, leaning his forehead against it, and closed his eyes. Loftus had promised to protect her, and he'd been unsuccessful. He'd broken that promise.

"Thank you, Bromley." The words were a murmur. "You may go."

A few seconds after the man's footsteps could no longer be heard, the voice of Loftus's mother broke the silence. "No sign of the man, hm?"

Loftus opened his eyes and straightened. His mother stood five feet away, her hands clasped in front of her and a smug expression on her face. "I do seem to remember that you couldn't find the man in the forest either. Neither did you see him when your wife saw him." She tapped her chin. "And, do you know, I did not actually see the man on the street when your dear wife said he was there."

If she kept digging at him, she'd soon be dredging up his

anger. It was there, in the river of his stomach—somewhere between the rocks of insecurity and disappointment.

"What are you inferring?" His tone was cool as he stared at her.

She huffed. "This is what I get for having a son who studies *leaves.*" Her nose wrinkled in distaste. "I suppose I shall have to spell it out for you. The attacker is not real. There is no intruder. Your wife is simply mad."

Loftus scoffed, his ire rising. "This again?"

His mother spread her arms. "She is fit for an asylum. We, none of us, have ever seen this man, have we?"

His jaw clenched. "That doesn't mean she hasn't."

She shrugged. "You'll see. She'll be locked in an asylum before long."

He turned from her. *Over my dead body.*

Loftus moved past the footmen and entered his chamber. Dr. Fench was putting his instruments into his black bag. Thank God, Cate was awake, but her eyes were moving from one spot in the room to another, and she blinked frequently. She was mumbling, but he couldn't hear what she was saying.

"How is she?" The sight of his wife barely moving on the floor was not an image he was likely to get out of his mind for the foreseeable future.

When Dr. Fench turned to face him, his expression was serious. They moved to the side of the room to talk in private. "Not well. Truthfully, I'm not at all sure what has caused her illness in this case. Her symptoms are unlike any I've dealt with previously." He shook his head with a sigh. "She's flushed but does not have a fever. Her heartbeat is very slow. Her eyes are unfocused, and I do not believe she can see me well, even with her spectacles. She keeps speaking, but her words do not make sense. Perhaps she sustained some sort of head trauma when she fell. Time will tell."

"Water..." Cate rasped from the bed, and Susan was quick to

lift a glass to her lips. She drank the liquid as though she hadn't had a drop all day. Within seconds, the chamber pot was thrust into Cate's lap to catch her vomit as the same liquid reappeared.

The doctor peered over his shoulder and glanced back toward Loftus. "That proves worrisome, as well. Your wife has not been out in the sun lately? Has she been eating or drinking anything unusual?"

Loftus crossed his arms over his chest. "She's just been getting over her other illness, so all she's been doing is staying in her bedchamber and drinking tea and eating toast and broth for the last few days. Nothing odd at all." He rubbed his chin. "She can't possibly be getting too much sun, for she hasn't been outside."

The doctor hummed in thought and nodded. "I suggest you continue caring for her as you have been, for now. In the meantime, I'll check in with a few of my associates in London and see if they are familiar with this illness. I'll hope to visit with their answers—and a treatment—as soon as possible."

Loftus's chest tightened. That could take days—a week or even more. In that time, Cate could worsen. She could—

He swallowed. "Thank you, Dr. Fench."

The doctor, while trying to be helpful, would not be enough. Loftus would have to do what he could as a man—as a husband—to see that his wife survived whatever was afflicting her. He couldn't lose her. He'd do anything for her. She was the reason he woke up in the morning and was excited for the day. She was the reason he made up extra tasks to do in the conservatory. He couldn't count how many pages of his notebook were filled with scribbles now, solely because he couldn't keep his eyes off her but needed to look as though he was doing something important.

It didn't matter if she didn't love him, for he loved *her*.

CHAPTER 29

$\mathcal{L}$oftus awoke the next day, his eyes opening to peer up at his red bed canopy—only, it wasn't there. He blinked, awareness taking over. That's right. He'd slept in one of the guest chambers last evening, for his bed was now occupied by his ill wife.

He rubbed his palms over his eyes and flung the covers back, then swung his legs over the side of the bed. He had to see how she was doing.

With a ring of the bell in the corner of the room, his valet was there in moments, and Loftus was suitably dressed and ready for the day. Verne insisted on a quick shave, pestering him until he took a seat.

Before Verne could hold Loftus for another moment—protesting about his cravat or some other flaw on his person—Loftus pulled on his boots and hurried from the room, heading toward his wife's chamber. Did she fare any better today? His heart beat a fast rhythm as he knocked on the door.

It was pulled open by Susan, who held a finger to her lips and stepped back to let him enter. He took careful steps inside, his gaze drawn to the bed where Cate lay. There was still a flush on her cheeks that made her appear as though she'd gotten a burn from the sun or was afflicted with fever, though he knew that not to be the case.

Her eyes were closed, the coverlet drawn up to her chest. Her hands were laid across her stomach as though to ease some pain there.

"She's had a terrible night, I'm afraid." Susan's voice was a whisper. "The poor dear's been in between wakefulness and rest for many hours. Her stomach was hurting her earlier, so I made her some of that willow bark tea ye recommended when she was sick before. It's helped some, I think." She cleared her throat. "When she's managed to keep it down, that is."

Loftus nodded, his jaw tightening at the news. "Has her eyesight improved since last night? And is she still mumbling?"

Susan shook her head. "Her eyesight hasn't improved, I don't think. When she talks to me, she isn't looking at me. She's still speaking—murmuring. I don't know to whom. It's not to me."

Loftus ran his hand over his face as he mentally searched through his catalog of roots and herbs. What could he give her that might help?

The maid's eyes widened as she continued. "My mam used to tell me that when a person was close to death, they'd begin to see ghosts all around them. Souls stuck here on earth and destined to wander. Do you think she could be speaking to them?"

At the idea of Cate being so close to death, Loftus's muscles tensed. If he thought of her as so ill, the mountain he had to climb seemed insurmountable. He steeled himself, taking a deep breath and rolling his shoulders back and closing his eyes.

Please, Lord. Help me heal my wife through the creation You have so generously given to humankind and all creatures. Let her live and be well again. Give me the tools to scale to this peak and descend with her life intact.

When he reopened his eyes once more, he met Susan's gaze, a new sense of determination and hope within him. "I do not believe that anyone lingers on earth, Susan. When a person dies, they go to heaven, or they go to hell. They do not stay around."

Susan's eyebrows raised. "Who could she be talking to, then?"

That, he wasn't sure. Whoever they were, they weren't actually there. Loftus began to pace the room, the sounds of his boots muffled by the plush red carpet.

As much as he hated to admit that his mother was right about anything, she *was* correct when she'd said that no one—aside from Cate—had ever seen Lord Balfour or a cloaked figure on the property or elsewhere. Loftus definitely didn't share her view that his wife was mad, but hallucinations were something to consider.

He dragged a chair from near the fireplace and positioned it next to the bed. He grabbed a notebook from his bedside table and a pencil he'd left nearby before slumping into the seat. "Let me think about it."

Susan moved to the remaining chair near the fireplace, a basket of mending waiting beside it.

Loftus crossed one leg over the other, his mind whirring like the gears of a clock—one piece setting the other in motion until all were moving at the same time. Turning to a fresh page, he scribbled down the symptoms of Cate's illness.

Flush
Slow heartbeat
Vomiting
Impaired vision
Ache in the stomach
Possible visual hallucinations

Loftus lifted his head as a thought struck him. "Did you hear the same sound coming from my room that she claimed to hear last evening?"

Susan poked her needle into a stocking, her eyes earnest. "No, my lord."

Possible auditory hallucinations

He then thought of the other times she'd been ill and wrote the symptoms of those incidences in his messy scrawl. Many of the symptoms overlapped with each other, though not all. Could it be that it had been the same illness the entire time, coming and going in waves?

He set his pencil aside, thrusting his hand into his hair. What sickness worked in such a way? None he knew of acted in such an odd manner. And what illness caused such symptoms? Dr. Fench hadn't known—that much was for certain. Could it be tending the plants that was affecting her? Was her body averse to something, unbeknownst to her?

He set his notebook aside and stood, propping one hand on his hip. He'd watched her while she handled the plants on countless occasions. Never once had she failed to wear her gloves or acted in any way that should have put her health at risk.

This was so frustrating, he could nearly tear his hair from his head. If she perished, then what good was his love?

With a low groan, he moved to the corner of the room to pull the bell for tea. While that was being prepared, he would go and grab his botany books from his study. Surely, one of those would give him some insight into this problem.

In his study, he selected the tomes he needed from the bookshelf. He took a moment to rearrange a stack of correspondence and was on the move again.

Clutching the leather volumes in his arm, he returned to his chamber. Quietly, he pushed the door open. If Cate was to get better, the first thing she needed was rest. And yet Gilbert was inside, holding a tea tray. Susan stood next to him, whispering.

If he could stomp into the room right now without waking his wife, he would, but Cate came first. Loftus settled for raising an imperious eyebrow as his brother took notice of him.

Loftus set his books on his chair and crossed his arms in front of his chest. "What are you doing here?" His voice was hushed but as pointed as a knife.

Gilbert raised the tea tray in his hands, a lazy grin on his face. "I brought tea."

Loftus fought the urge to slap a hand to his forehead. "I can see that well enough. Where is the maid who was supposed to bring it?"

Gilbert's grin widened. "I told her I'd take it for her when I met her in the hall heading up here. I wanted to see Cate."

Jealousy lit in Loftus's abdomen. "So it's 'Cate' now, is it?"

"There's a certain ring to it, I must admit." Gilbert's mouth twisted to the side as he glanced at her lying in the bed. "She's quite the angel when she sleeps."

Loftus's fists clenched at his sides. "Set the tray down, brother."

Gilbert did so, though he took his time with it. "Shall we wake her so she may enjoy it?"

Loftus bit the inside of his cheek. "Tending to my wife is my job—not yours. The tea is not for her, but for me. She must continue to sleep, for now. She has gotten little of it these past hours."

Gilbert sighed dramatically. "What a shame. I had hoped to speak with her. Something about our visits energizes me more than a cup of coffee."

"You look as though you've already enjoyed one or two of

216

those this morning." Loftus narrowed his eyes. "Indeed, why are you awake at this hour? Shouldn't you be sleeping still?"

His brother shrugged, a small gleam in his eyes. "Worry for your wife's sake, of course. What else would have made me rise so early?"

"You think far too often of my wife." Loftus's voice was a low growl at this point. "I'll start to wonder if you have designs on her if you keep it up."

A low chuckle came from Gilbert's throat. "Who's to say that I do not? She's a thing from my dreams, brother." He tutted, turning his head to gaze at her. "Though, if such a piece of heaven were to fall, it would be a nightmare."

What did he mean by that? Before he could ask, his brother had left the room, his footsteps hardly audible as he moved down the hall.

A surge of anger pulsed through Loftus for the way Gilbert had spoken, his brother's smug expression flashing through his mind and increasing his ire exponentially.

He tempered his anger with a few deep breaths and rubbed his forehead, picking his books up from the chair next to Cate's bed and sitting on its comfortable cushion. Now was not the time to become distracted.

Susan moved over to the tea tray. "Would you like me to pour, my lord?"

He opened up his copy of *The British Herbal* and nodded. "Yes, please."

She did so, then set the pot down to reach for the bowl of sugar. Loftus's gaze flitted to her hand as it touched the spoon within. "No sugar in mine, today, thank you."

Susan reached instead for the milk pot, but Loftus's attention was stuck on the sugar. He narrowed his eyes. Something looked different about it.

Setting the book in his lap, he picked up the bowl, bringing it closer. Within the light brown of the sugar were small speckles of a darker brown. If one didn't pay attention, they wouldn't see them, but they were noticeable closer up.

Susan handed him the cup of tea, her eyebrows raised. "Is something amiss, my lord?"

His mouth pulled to the side in a frown. "There just might be."

When he said nothing further, she returned to her chair near the empty hearth. Loftus set his tea aside and took a pinch of sugar between his fingers, moving the substance back and forth. The grains fell back into the bowl, though the darker ones were a different texture—larger than the regular sugar and coarser.

He lifted the bowl to his nose and gave it a sniff. It was sweet, as he expected it would be, although there was a hint of another smell there. Something different. Something that wasn't sugar.

He set the bowl down and placed his book on the side table. "If my wife wakes up, do not allow her a cup of tea from this tray." His tone was fierce and Susan's eyes were wide as he gave the command. He pointed at the tray, his unease growing. "Actually, remove it from this room entirely, please, Susan. I'll not take any chances."

Loftus was belowstairs before his head could catch up with his feet, moving into the kitchen at a quick clip.

Cook brightened when he entered the warm space. "My lord! We haven't seen ye down here in an age."

He tried to smile but found his lips wouldn't cooperate. "I'm sorry for my absence, Mrs. Drayer. Please, might I see the sugar?"

She wiped her hands on her apron and raised an eyebrow. "The sugar? It's right o'er here." She led him into the larder and over to a small chest, patting it with a hand. "Mrs. Stonehill has the key."

He bit the inside of his cheek. Right.

One of the scullery maids was sent to fetch Mrs. Stonehill, and before long, she appeared, the jingling keys on her chatelaine announcing her arrival. She clasped her hands together when she saw Loftus and Mrs. Drayer. "I was told I'm needed?"

Mrs. Drayer nodded. "His lordship wishes to see the sugar."

"Indeed?" Mrs. Stonehill pulled the key from a ring at her waist and unlocked the chest without further ado.

Loftus lifted the lid and peered inside. In the main compartment were small cones of sugar, and smaller compartments to the side held sugar that had been ground into granules and powdered. At the bottom of the chest were also multiple pairs of sugar nippers and hammers.

Loftus eyed the granules in particular. If this was where the sugar for tea was coming from, did this sugar also have something mixed into it? He leaned down close to examine it, but as far as he could tell, this sugar hadn't been touched.

He closed the lid and nodded, signaling for Mrs. Stonehill to lock the chest once more. If *this* sugar was pure and the sugar above stairs was tainted, then something was occurring to make it so in between. A mental spider connected a piece of silk from one end of his brain to another, and realization hit him.

Cate was the only person abovestairs, aside from himself, who took sugar with her tea, and somebody was taking advantage of that fact.

Loftus shuddered, a chill raising the hair on his neck.

Someone was poisoning Cate.

CHAPTER 30

*L*oftus pored over the books later that day, his back beginning to ache with how long he'd remained sitting in the same position. He shifted his legs and sat forward a bit to give himself more room to stretch.

Every once in a while, he glanced over the edge of his book to view his wife, her chest rising and falling softly under the coverlet as she slumbered. She'd been awake for a few hours earlier and had encouraged him to take care of the plants in the conservatory—saying that Susan could watch her in the meantime.

He'd been reluctant to go, but it seemed his worry had been for naught. Susan had kept her safe whilst he'd been gone.

He rolled his shoulders and tilted his head back and forth, preparing to settle back in, when his eyes caught on something gleaming in the corner of the room. He squinted. It was the tea tray from earlier. Displeasure flowed through him.

"Susan, when I asked you to remove the tea tray from the room, I *did* mean it." Disappointment deepened his voice.

She looked up from her mending, her lips parted. "Oh, but I did, my lord! I took it back down to the kitchen."

He gestured toward the offending object. "Then what is that over there?"

She looked where he pointed and stood. "Oh, dear. I forgot to bring this one down. My apologies, my lord. Lord Berkley brought it up and had tea with her ladyship when you were in the conservatory."

A jolt of alarm shot through him. "Bring it here at once." Panic sharpened the command.

Susan scurried over to him, the tea tray in her hands.

Loftus inspected the sugar and let out a bitter exclamation. It had been altered in the same way the other sugar had been. He pushed a hand through his hair. "My wife had sugar in her tea?"

Susan blanched. "I-I believe so. I'm not entirely sure."

"How long was he here for?" Loftus's tone was hard.

"About an hour, I'd say. She became worse then, so he left her to rest."

"Devil take it!" He rubbed his hand down his jaw. "Take the tray to the kitchen. Dispose of the bowl of sugar. Find out exactly who brought the tea tray up before my brother intercepted it."

Susan nodded and rushed out the bedchamber door.

Not ten minutes later, she arrived back at the chamber, nearly out of breath. "The maid who brought the tea tray both times was Pansy, my lord."

He stood. "I'll see her in Mrs. Stonehill's office belowstairs. At once."

Pansy, as it turned out, was a petite girl of about fifteen years, with blond hair and a pale face—now mottled with red and streaked with tears. The wilting servant before him was either competition for the actresses on Drury Lane or completely innocent and incapable of causing harm to another person—including Cate. Most likely, the latter.

She sobbed, her shoulders shaking with her breaths. She

held a handkerchief to her nose and wiped it. He hadn't even said anything yet.

"Pansy..." He started with her name, unsure where to go from there with her crying as she was. 'Twould be of no help to upset her further.

She sniffled, swiping the tears from her eyes. Her mouth formed a sad frown. "I-I don't know why ye want t-to s-see me, m-my lord. M-me mam said if I did me job well, ye'd never ask to see me."

He sighed. "Indeed. I only wish to ask you a few questions. That is all. You've no need to fear for your job if you've done it well, as you say."

Her tears slowed, and she blinked up at him, lowering the handkerchief from her face. "What kind of questions?"

He clasped his hands behind his back. "Have you been... mixing anything into the sugar or milk before you bring up the tea tray to my wife? Perhaps even into the tea, itself?"

If she was the culprit, he couldn't expect her to answer this truthfully, but the confusion on her face appeared genuine.

She furrowed her eyebrows. "Me brothers used to put salt in me tea, but I'm much too old for tricks like that. I'd not try it on her ladyship. I don't think she'd find it funny if I replaced the sugar with salt or put vinegar in the milk."

Despite the serious situation, Loftus had to stifle the smile that threatened to raise his lips. He ducked his chin. "I do not believe she'd appreciate that, no. Have you seen anyone else mix anything into them before the tray is brought up? My wife doesn't appreciate the...childish tricks. She has grown out of such things, you understand."

Pansy nodded and squared her shoulders, giving Loftus a look that made her seem much older than her years. "I understand completely. I haven't seen anyone else do anythin' to the trays. When I bring them up, Lord Berkley is more than pleased to take them from me, and he always tells me he'll make sure not a biscuit is out of place." Her chin lifted.

Loftus's jaw tightened at the mention of his brother, but he kept his expression passive and nodded at the maid. "Thank you very much, Pansy. You may return to your duties."

As Pansy left the cramped housekeeper's office, Loftus leaned against the wall and brought his hand up to cover his eyes. He believed the girl. Which meant there was one person likely to have committed these crimes—Gilbert.

~

*T*he days were a blur as Loftus attended his wife, bringing her meals and tea up from the kitchen himself after having witnessed their preparation with his own eyes. He wasn't taking any chances when it came to her wellbeing.

Slowly, her condition was improving. In the beginning, she had slept for most of the day and night, unable to keep any sort of food or drink in her stomach. By the middle of the week, she was able to eat, and her vision was fully repaired.

Gilbert had continued his visits nearly every day, and while Cate was healing, Loftus ventured to guess that Gilbert wouldn't be anticipating this. Loftus checked the sugar bowl on every tea tray Gilbert brought, and all had the same substance within them. He always sent Susan to dispose of it and made sure the servants kept mum about Loftus bringing up Cate's tray so it wouldn't arouse his brother's suspicions. If Gilbert noticed a difference in Cate, he would be wary, which was why it was so important Loftus speak to her. Soon, it was mid-week. Thursday.

"Darling." He rested his hand on her arm as she brought her teacup to her lips, her dinner tray on her lap.

She turned her head to look at him, eyes tired. "Hm?"

He held his breath for a moment. How to explain it all to her? In the past days whilst she'd been resting between meals, he'd been scouring books. He'd finally found what he believed to be the thing brewing trouble for her. While many plants caused varying unpleasant effects when ingested, there were only so many that caused these specific symptoms. "I believe I know the cause of your illness."

She set her teacup and saucer down, her shoulders straightening. "You do? Not even the doctor seems aware. But then, you *are* very clever."

His face heated, and he brushed his thumb along her skin. "Your symptoms are...very unique, to say the least. There are not so many plants around that can cause them to occur."

She raised her eyebrows. "You believe a plant caused this? I haven't ingested any plants."

"Not knowingly." He looked at her pointedly, leaning back in his chair.

The light in the room dimmed as the sun continued its descent below the horizon.

Cate wrinkled her nose. "Whatever do you mean? Is someone poisoning me?"

Loftus heaved an exhale, his shoulders tense. "Yes. With *Mandragorum officinarum*. Specifically, the root."

Cate gasped. "Who would wish to do such a thing? What even *is* that?"

Loftus cleared his throat before explaining. "It's a plant called mandrake—very popular in Medieval times. Whoever has been poisoning you has been mixing it in with the sugar so you'd have it in your tea. The who is much more important than the what, however. I seem to have narrowed it down, but you aren't going to like the answer."

Her face went pale. "Tell me."

Loftus balanced his elbows on his knees. "My brother."

Cate's head moved back in disbelief. "No. Surely, not Gilbert."

Loftus nodded. "I questioned the maid who's been bringing your tea up, and I do not believe it to be her." He pushed a hand through his hair, pulling at it slightly. "Think about it—he's the one who's brought it to you on several occasions. He knows you take your tea with sugar."

She shook her head. "No. I cannot believe it to be him. It-it must be Lord Balfour."

Loftus's heart sank at the next piece of information he must relay to her. He grabbed her hand. Her skin was soft against his as he brushed a thumb over her knuckles. "My dear...I'm afraid that one symptom of mandrake poisoning is hallucinations. Every time you claimed to see Lord Balfour, you became quite ill shortly thereafter."

Cate's face became a mottled red, her eyes glossy with unshed tears. "What are you saying? That I... The whole time..." She blinked, and a tear dropped onto her cheek. "He was never there?"

Loftus brought his hand to her cheek and brushed the wetness away, his chest aching at the pain in her face. "Your mind told you he was," he said softly. "Everything in you was tricked by the poison."

She slumped against the pillows and threw her hand over her eyes. "I'm such a fool." Bitterness and despair filled her tone. "I've led everyone on a goose chase—especially you, searching for a man that was never here to begin with." She dropped her hand, and more tears began to fall. "All along, I'd believed he'd come back. Never had I questioned it. Not for a moment. What a burden I've been."

Loftus couldn't stand by any longer. He removed the dinner tray from her lap and set it on the side table, then sat on the edge of the bed and pulled her into his arms. She melted into his side, wrapping her arms around his shoulders as he wrapped his around her waist. She buried her face in his neck, her warm breath like the beating of butterfly wings against his skin.

He pressed his mouth to her head and kissed her soft hair that smelled like a field of sweet clover. "You could never be a burden." He brushed a kiss along her temple. "Do not think about the hallucinations, darling. I will not allow them to come again, now that I know the cause. Be glad that man is far away. He cannot hurt you. I would not let him, even if he were near."

Cate nestled farther into his arms, then looked up, concern in her eyes. "Then it is Gilbert who's poisoning me?"

Loftus immediately missed the warmth at his neck. "It is." He grazed her cheek with his fingertips. "You became ill in the garden after we had tea with him in the drawing room, remember? And the third time you became ill, he'd brought tea to your chamber before dinner." He frowned. "I'm still not sure how he managed the second time."

Cate's lips pursed. "I was out with your mother then. We had tea at that shop. Perhaps he could have bribed someone to mix the mandrake into the sugar?"

Loftus shook his head. "The tea shop uses white cones of sugar. You would've noticed the root mixed in, for it is brown and would have appeared odd in the sugar bowl."

Cate's lips parted, and she speared Loftus with a sharp glance. "Your mother prepared my tea that day. I didn't see her do so, for she asked me to order us some cakes."

Loftus's chest tightened. Perhaps his brother was not alone in his wrongdoing, after all.

"I'll have someone watching you, Cate. I'll arrange or Susan to be at your side—or Mrs. Stonehill or one of the maids." His lips thinned. "You'll be protected." He shifted on the bed. "In the meantime, you must act as though you are still ill whenever my mother or brother visit so you do not arouse suspicion in them. They must believe that you are still being poisoned. We cannot have them know that we have found out."

Cate nodded. "I will."

The rest of the week passed at a slow pace, with Loftus struggling to come up with a plan to prove his brother—and perhaps their mother—were poisoning his wife. He still found it difficult to believe that they could lower themselves to such actions. Be so cruel and uncaring. He struggled to untangle reality from what he wished reality was.

Every day, he studied his plants and thought about which ones he could use for his purposes when the time came to enact his plan—if he were to go with the one he had in mind. It was a bit...*precarious*...to say the least. His mind became lighter as he imagined his wife up in his chamber, her condition improving with every hour and every cup of poison-free tea and bowl of broth she ingested. She'd decided to stay, feeling safer there than in her own bedchamber, and he couldn't describe what bliss it was now that he was sleeping there, as well. Loftus loved hearing her breathing beside him at night, seeing the gentle rise and fall of her chest. Just knowing she was there was a balm to him. He hadn't had a single nightmare since she'd begun sleeping next to him. Of course, his affection for her now was such that he could no longer describe.

Gilbert appeared more and more agitated during his visits. Loftus could guess why. Not just because Loftus was always sitting at his wife's bedside. No. Gilbert's prey had suddenly ceased to worsen. The man certainly must be confused as to why the mandrake had stopped afflicting Cate. Loftus had been paying attention, and with the amount Gilbert had been mixing into the sugar bowl, a small elephant could've been felled by now.

Mother was also in a foul mood. She roamed the corridors with a scowl, snapping at servants left and right.

By the middle of the second week, Loftus was readying his

herbs, but Dr. Fench had been called to see Cate at Mother's insistence. Mother had not forgotten the asylum, of course. However, when the man declared Cate sane and vastly improved, Loftus feared the dowager might have apoplexy, such was the look of rage on her face—though she hid it from the good doctor.

The behavior of his mother and brother only convinced Loftus his suspicions were correct, impossible as they were to believe. One way or another, his family was about to be removed from his life. Would he be able to build a new one with Cate? A family like one he'd always dreamed of having?

CHAPTER 31

Two days after the doctor came, Loftus arrived at his chamber door and knocked on it for his visit with his wife. If he had his way, of course, he'd be spending every waking minute at her side, but as it was, he'd had an herbal mixture to concoct.

Susan opened it only slightly but upon seeing him, flung it wide. He stepped in, a grin upon his face at the sight of Cate looking so much better. Clearly, the herbal teas and broths he was having prepared for her were doing her well.

A healthy flush colored her cheeks—very different from the flush caused by the mandrake root—as she returned his smile from the bed. "Good evening." Her words were warm, her tone rich.

"How are you, darling?" He crossed the room to her side and placed a lingering kiss upon the back of her hand. Perhaps soon, he'd muster the courage to place one on her lips.

She squeezed his hand. "I almost feel like my regular self, I must say. The poison has almost left my body, I believe."

He sat down in his chair next to the bed, keeping hold of her hand. "Excellent news. I am very glad to hear it. The thought of losing you..." He flicked his gaze to the window across the room and swallowed. "'Tis no matter. I should discuss with you tomorrow's plan. I have instructed Bromley to send for the constable at eight in the evening. We'll be finished with dinner by then."

Cate raised a dark eyebrow. "So you plan to do something... during dinner?"

Loftus's shoulders straightened. "After. I shall add a mixture of herbs to the wine before he joins me in the library. These herbs are specifically used to make a person tired."

Cate nodded, prompting him to continue.

"I'll call you in—"

Her mouth opened. "Me?"

Loftus gave a sheepish smile. "Indeed. I'm afraid that if I'm to have the courage to do this, I'll need you at my side. Gilbert might feel more at ease with you there, as well." He swallowed. "Once he drinks it, he'll begin to feel the effects of the herbs and—in his befuddled state—I'm hopeful his tongue will be loosened. Before the herbs take their full effect and he's rendered unconscious, I'll attempt to direct him in conversation in such a way that he reveals his hand in your poisoning."

Cate bit her lip. "And from there, the constable will step in?"

Loftus nodded. "Exactly. Gilbert won't be able to put up much of a fight by then. The plants I plan to use are potent sedatives. They can even make a man appear dead when he's alive. I wouldn't be surprised if, right after he confesses, Gilbert falls to the floor in a heap."

Cate brought a hand to her mouth and covered her laughter. Loftus loved the sound of it.

Cate tilted her head. "What about your mother?"

Loftus's lips turned down. "She'll be easier. Once my brother confesses, she'll do the same. All we need to do is press her a little. She's more apt to make mistakes."

"It seems you have a big day tomorrow." Cate smiled.

Loftus shrugged. "I do. I still have to mix the herbs together." He sighed. "I suppose I should let you rest."

Cate yawned, as though agreeing with him. "Although I'd like to continue our conversation, my body thinks otherwise. I suppose I'll see you tomorrow, then."

Loftus kissed her hand. "Tomorrow. Finally, you'll be safe."

Cate's cheeks pinked. "We can start our life together. Again, that is."

His heart picked up its pace. Nothing sounded better than that. A life with this woman before him. Happiness, love, children...could all of those things truly be within his grasp?

CHAPTER 32

*L*oftus's nerves were surprisingly calm as he worked in the conservatory, measuring the herbs in preparation of grinding them into powders with his mortar and pestle. That evening, he would be pouring them into a glass of wine to give to Gilbert, but he needn't worry about his brother nor mother looking in on him in this place—neither had ever cared about his doings in this warm, windowed room. Even if they did, they likely wouldn't even be aware of what he was doing.

He put the root of *Valeriana officinalis* into the mortar along with *Lavandula* buds and the other herbs, grinding them together. With any luck, the *Lavandula* wouldn't be so fragrant as to alert Gilbert that something was off with his wine.

He poured the ground mixture into a vial and corked it, setting it aside to be mixed into the wine later. He heaved a sigh. The day wasn't going fast enough. He wanted this over with.

Dinner was a quiet affair, though Loftus didn't even taste what he forked into his mouth. Once the meal was over and his mother retired to her room, the tension in the room was palpable. Loftus leaned back against his chair, eyeing his brother. The time had come.

"Care to share a drink, brother? I was thinking we might open a bottle of wine from the cellar." He stood. "Come, join me in the library. The servants will fetch it."

Gilbert looked him over, wariness evident in his features. "What is the celebration?"

A smile grew on Loftus's face, his shoulders straightening. Gilbert had asked for his trust when he'd taken Cate into the woods the day after their marriage. Now, Loftus would make the man believe he'd given it. "Trust, brother. A celebration of trust."

Gilbert pushed his chair back and stood, a lazy grin forming on his face. His movements were languid. "Indeed, then let us go."

Loftus gestured for his brother to go before him, and as Gilbert moved through the doorway, Loftus nodded at the footman to his right. He'd already instructed the man to get the wine—a bottle he'd earlier opened and mixed the vial of powder into. The herbs had dissolved well. Loftus hadn't been able to tell the wine from any other except for how he'd marked the bottle with a small drop of wax on the underside.

He strode down the corridor after his brother and entered through the heavy carved doors of the library, his nose instantly hit with the scent of ink and linseed oil. Shelves upon shelves of books greeted him like old friends, and now they would be here to encourage him with the knowledge they had lent him as he did one of the most difficult things he had ever done—watch his brother fall and do nothing to prevent it.

Gilbert seated himself in an armchair in the middle of the room, and Loftus selected the settee opposite him, a short-legged table with carved feet between. As soon as the footmen entered with the tray of two wine glasses and the bottle, Loftus leaned forward. "I'll pour." Before the man left, Loftus stopped him. "Oh, and could you fetch my wife, please? I'm sure she'd enjoy stretching her legs."

Loftus uncorked the green bottle with a pleasing *pop* and filled first his brother's glass, then his own.

Gilbert's eyebrows furrowed. "Should not your wife stay in bed longer, what with her illness?"

Loftus picked up the cup and held it toward his brother, meeting his familiar blue gaze. "She has been feeling remarkably better the past few days. We are blessed that her illness is almost gone completely."

Gilbert raised his glass in Loftus's direction, a downward twitch in his lips. "To trust."

Loftus repeated the words and brought the wine to his lips, letting it rest there for a moment but not enter his mouth. He swallowed as though it had. Gilbert, to Loftus's dismay, never brought the drink to his mouth at all. Instead, he rolled the glass in his hand and set it back on the table.

"Will you not drink, brother?"

Gilbert looked up at Loftus's question and shrugged. "I fear I'm not in the mood for wine. Brandy is more the thing this evening."

Loftus's stomach tightened. Did that mean Gilbert had found out about Loftus's plan, or was he truly just pining after a different liquor? Either way, he'd have to change tactics.

Cate entered the room, smelling like a fresh spring day. The pale pink gown she wore accentuated her subtle curves, and her hair was drawn up in a knot at the back of her head with soft curls falling at her temples, the beautiful color of a wintering bramble.

Both Loftus and Gilbert stood at her entrance—Loftus setting his glass down and taking both of her hands in his. "My darling, how do you feel? It is so good to see you out of that chamber."

Her lips quirked up. "I feel very well, thank you, though it seems almost odd to be out of the room again." She flicked her gaze to Gilbert. "How are you gentlemen this evening? I do hope I'm not interrupting something." Her eyes gleamed with knowing as she met Loftus's.

He led her to the settee and shook his head. "I wouldn't have called you down if you were, my dear." He looked over his shoulder at the footman. "Frederick, bring us the brandy, please. Sherry for my wife. That is..." He tilted his head toward Cate and shared a meaningful look with her. "...unless you'd like some wine?"

She folded her hands in her lap. "I'd much prefer sherry, thank you."

Gilbert reclaimed his seat as Frederick left, answering her first question. "I cannot answer for Loftus, but I've been very well, my lady, albeit worried over you."

Cate relaxed into the embroidered pillow at her back. "How kind of you. I am so glad I am nearly back to my old self."

"Indeed." Gilbert's smile appeared forced. "Would you pardon me for a moment? I'll be back in only a minute."

Loftus nodded, and Gilbert left the room, presumably to go relieve himself into a chamber pot, or some such thing. Loftus needed to alter his plans, and it wasn't something he was looking forward to.

He turned to her, leaning close, his voice but a whisper. "He's not drinking the wine."

Her eyes widened. "What?"

"He claims he has no taste for it this evening. I do not know whether he suspects something is wrong or not, but he wishes for brandy instead, so I must change my plan."

Cate put her hand on his arm, her breath brushing his neck as she angled toward him. "What will you do?"

He swallowed, pausing for only a millisecond. His next words came out in a quick exhale. "I must drink the wine myself."

Her grip tightened. "No, Loftus! How could anything good possibly come of that?"

He lifted her chin with his finger so she looked into his eyes. "Good *will* come of it, for you will help me." Her lips trembled, and he continued speaking. "I will drink the wine. Once I fall unconscious, I will appear dead. You must act as though I am. Do you understand?"

Cate nodded, her mouth open slightly.

"Act as though I've suffered from some sudden affliction—something that has caused my life to end. An attack of the heart —anything will do. If he truly is the one who has been poisoning you all along, then..." He pressed a tightened fist against his thigh. "...perhaps my death—the idea of it—will cause him to reveal his part in your poisoning."

They were forced to separate as Frederick reentered the room with decanters of brandy and sherry and glasses on a tray. Gilbert arrived not long after, with Loftus sipping at his glass of adulterated wine, Gilbert at his brandy, and Cate at her glass of sherry.

"So you bought some gowns the other day, did you? Mother was telling me about it." Gilbert eyed Cate over his drink, a small smile on his lips.

She shifted in her seat and faced him more directly. "Indeed, though she wished for me to purchase some...interesting fabrics, I *will* say. I might very well blend in better with a bog than a ballroom."

Gilbert guffawed and Loftus stifled a laugh. "Indeed, dear sister. Our mother does wear some strange colors at times. I'm sure she meant nothing by it. Once, she insisted upon wearing—"

Loftus struggled to keep up with the conversation as it moved from fabrics and gowns to horses.

"He was the fastest horse I'd ever seen. I've never seen his match since." Gilbert swirled his glass, a faraway look in his eyes. "If only Faraday would've sold him."

Cate nodded. "Some owners are very attached to their animals. I wouldn't give up Giles for all the money in the world."

Gilbert raised an eyebrow. "Not even to become queen?"

Loftus's brain finally caught up with the conversation. He grinned, though he didn't feel so pleasant at the moment. "Why would she wish to be married to the king when she already has me?"

Cate placed her hand on his arm and gave him a soft look full of affection mixed with worry while Gilbert chuckled loudly, clearly thinking the statement quite humorous.

After a quarter of an hour passed and Loftus emptied his glass, the room began to spin at a slow pace, as though he witnessed the world turning on its axis. He blinked, struggling to keep his eyes open. His limbs began to feel heavy.

"Loftus?" Cate was looking at him with a raised brow.

He straightened his shoulders and nodded. Whatever she said next was muddled, sounding like a whisper from afar that had been dragged through the mud.

The low tone of his brother's voice flowed over the air, and he tried to pay attention. Loftus slid his gaze toward Gilbert— slowly and with painstaking effort. The man wore an odd expression—something that couldn't be read.

Cate's voice came at his side again, but his eyes were closing now. He couldn't keep them open any longer. Oblivion pulled him under.

CHAPTER 33

"*L*oftus? Are you feeling all right?" Catherine kept a steady eye on her husband. Yes, this was all a part of the plan, but she could not quell her unease, regardless. Her stomach tied itself in knots as his ice-blue eyes glassed over, resembling the top of a frosted pond in winter. He blinked a few times, not focusing on anything in particular—not that she could tell, anyway.

That was when his eyes rolled back and closed. Catherine gasped, her stomach dropping as her husband toppled forward. His body crashed against the table and sprawled onto the rug. The wine bottle tumbled from its upright position on the tray and fell onto the floor, leaking red liquid everywhere and mingling with the glass of the broken bottle of sherry. A scream erupted from her throat.

He'd landed on his back with his face as pale as the moon. Was he even breathing? He *had* said that the herbs were known to make a man appear dead, but...he truly looked dead.

Catherine fell on her knees next to him and shook his shoulders. "Loftus! Wake up!" She shot a glance toward Gilbert, who hadn't moved from his seat. He clutched his brandy, an indecipherable expression on his face. "Gilbert, call the doctor!"

She shook her husband again. "Loftus!" Tears stung the back of her eyes. It felt so real, this faked death. What if it was? She had to trust in God and in Loftus's skills with herbs—that he hadn't accidentally measured or mixed something incorrectly. Nevertheless, the tears fell down her cheeks.

She tilted her head toward Gilbert once more. "Gilbert! Why aren't you moving? We need a servant to fetch the doctor!"

He swirled his drink in his hand, examining the golden liquid as it moved around the glass. The corner of his lip ticked up, though for a moment, Catherine believed she'd imagined it. Surely, he'd have no reason to smile. Not unless he truly was the villain in all of this. A big part of her had not wanted to believe it.

Catherine leaned down and pressed her ear against Loftus's chest, listening for a heartbeat. She couldn't hear one. Not even something faint. She grabbed his wrist, pressing her fingers there. Nothing—no beat at all. Her own heart pounded, battling against her ribcage as her breaths heaved in and out.

She mashed her fingers against his neck until she was sure he'd have bruises, but no pulse could she detect. Had his plans gone awry? He'd done this for her, and now...he was dead. Not just under the pretense of it, but actually, truly, gone.

An ache began in her abdomen as her limbs froze. Her lungs seemed to be collapsing. The man she loved was no more, and she'd never even gotten to tell him how she felt about him.

A scream unlike anything that had ever come from her tore from her body—a sob and shriek and wail all mixed into one.

Her joints gave way, and she toppled onto him. She clawed at his waistcoat and jacket, pulling him nearer—as near as she could, her shoulders shaking with violent waves of grief.

Though the blood rushed through her ears and drowned

out nearly all other sounds, it was not long before the low rumble of chuckling reached her, increasing in volume the longer Loftus remained on the floor.

Catherine lifted her head, her hair falling into her face.

Gilbert was smiling. One of his legs was crossed over the other, and he leaned back in his chair as though he was sitting in his favorite club. "He's dead, then?"

She nodded, numbness taking over her body. If she broke now, Loftus would have died for nothing. She had to make Gilbert confess.

Burying the heaviest of her grief, she furrowed her eyebrows. "B-But he was your brother. How—"

Gilbert laughed again. This time, the sound was harsh. "Indeed, Catherine. I'm very moved. What a fortuitous day this has turned out to be." He took a sip of his brandy. "Truthfully, I'd always thought it would be by my own hand. That would have been far more satisfactory, but"—he shrugged—"I'll take what is given to me."

Outrage poured through her veins. She thought she'd known this man. This man had visited her every day under the guise of being a friend, and all along, he'd wished to kill Loftus.

"How can you say such things? This man is your brother! Your flesh and blood. He has always treated you well, has he not?"

Gilbert scoffed. "That man doesn't deserve the title of brother, and he certainly never deserved the title of earl." He downed the rest of his drink and stood. "Father always liked me better—everyone did. While Loftus was away with his ferns and ivies, I was the one focusing on the tasks that had to be accomplished."

Catherine sat back, her legs folded under her. "What do you mean?" She needed to keep him talking.

He began to pace back and forth in front of her, his eyes unfocused. "When Father sent him away to war, I was taught how to run the estate. I was taught how to keep the tenants happy. Everything was in my hands. Not his. Everything would have worked out perfectly had he died then. A war hero, some might claim—but I'd know better." He sneered. "You cannot make a soldier of a scientist. Or whatever he is."

She wiped her face. "I can imagine that was frustrating."

He sighed, coming to a stop behind his chair and gripping its back. "To think of the money I'd have had at my fingertips. The power. Every gambling hell would be open to me. Every mother would send their daughter my way."

Catherine raised an eyebrow. "But he came back."

A growl came from Gilbert's throat, and his knuckles whitened on the chair. "He came back." He began to pace once more. "He greeted me as his brother—as though nothing had changed. Everything had." A muscle in his jaw twitched. "When he returned, he took everything from me. Everything I'd been trained for, all of the time I'd spent with Father—all of it amounted to nothing, for the heir was back and ready to rule the moment our sire breathed his last."

Catherine did her best not to look at Loftus lest she lose her composure. It was almost harder to keep her attention on his snake of a brother.

A guffaw escaped him, and he threw an arm out in a gesture. "Father was horrified by Loftus's scars. Worst of all, Loftus went right back to his conservatory, more of a recluse than ever." He shook his head. "It's no surprise our dear papa died when he did. As for my brother, it was only a matter of time before he fell ill or some accident occurred. No one would care enough to look too closely. And then you came along. A product of a misstep of mine."

Catherine tilted her head. This was news to her.

He seemed to understand her confusion, as he continued his explanation. "You see, I became too bold. I suggested that if he were to relinquish the title, I would take over the estate.

After all, no woman would wish to marry him with his awful scars." A frown crossed his face. "He took that as a challenge, it seems, for not long after, *you* arrived with your maid and that blasted dog of yours."

Catherine raised her hands. "What does this have to do with me?"

"We cannot have more heirs enter the equation, now, can we? That would cut my place out. You are a very important piece, whether you want to be or not, dear Catherine." He licked his lips. "Perhaps you and I, under some other circumstances, would've made a pretty pair. Alas, you married my now-dead brother. What a pity. Your eyes really draw a man in." He clapped his hands. "But, I digress. Both you and my brother had to be stopped."

Catherine waved a hand between Loftus and herself. "Loftus and I—we never—we didn't—" Perhaps if she told him of it, Gilbert's interest might be reignited and she might be kept alive until the constable could come to save her.

Gilbert's eyes lit with interest. "Did you not? Then there's not a chance of anything in there." He looked pointedly at her stomach. "Regardless, my methods are necessary, for getting rid of a possible heir that might replace me is not the only reason for them."

This was the confession she'd been waiting for so painstakingly. Might as well let him confess to the rest, although the constable had surely heard enough by now to arrest him.

Catherine played dumb. "Your methods?"

Gilbert raised his eyebrows. "Indeed. Your illnesses are not at all an accident nor naturally occurring. Not in the way you might believe, anyway." His mouth quirked up into a satisfied smirk. "It is all the work of myself and a little help from Mother."

So the dowager *had* done something to her tea. Catherine put on a mask of confusion.

Gilbert resumed his seat, pouring himself another glass of brandy. "All it took was a little ground-up mandrake root in your sugar at teatime." He put the stopper back in the crystal decanter. "The sugar hides the bitterness perfectly, so you never noticed—and you're the only one in the family who takes sugar in their tea." He barked a laugh, flicking his gaze down to Loftus, who was still prone on the floor. "The plant is right beside the trail he rides every day, and he never even noticed it. I put it there myself."

He took a hefty sip of his drink, his eyes glimmering with mirth. "Meanwhile, you were screaming of a man watching you." He scoffed. "'Twas only the mandrake root taking effect on your mind. My mother and I certainly got a week's entertainment from it."

Catherine narrowed her eyes. "How did she give me the poison at the tea shop?"

He didn't hesitate to answer. "Her ring. She told me you even complimented it. I dried and crushed the flowers of the mandrake and put them into the ring, which has a small compartment in it."

Catherine shifted into a more comfortable position on the floor beside her husband and grabbed his cold hand, holding it tight for comfort. She swallowed before speaking again. "So besides making sure there weren't heirs, what was the point of poisoning me?"

A sinister smile pulled on the corner of Gilbert's mouth as he swirled the glass in his hand. He paused before he answered her. "You were supposed to be the first to die. The doctor knows of your illness. He knows that it's taken its toll on you. He also knows that Loftus was helping you with his own herbs and medicines."

The smile left his face. "When you saw me at the apothecary the other day, I was attempting to convince Mr. Grine to stop buying herbs from Loftus. I said it was only a matter of time before someone became ill because of them. I tried to convince Mr. Grine that Loftus was unwell in the mind and shouldn't be selling them, but Mr. Grine wouldn't listen. It would take more than my word to convince him."

He raised the glass to his lips. "I continued to poison you, for when you died, the village would finally be convinced, with the help of the doctor's testimony, that Loftus knew nothing about herbs—and no one would trust him again. Everyone would whisper about him—the man who killed his wife. It would destroy him."

Catherine couldn't take a breath. His plan was beyond cruel. Gilbert had planned to take everything from Loftus.

Gilbert set the glass down with a clink. "That's not the entirety of it, however. Getting rid of you wouldn't have made me earl, however much distress it would have caused my brother. After you died, I would begin to poison *him*. He'd begin to have hallucinations like you were having—with any luck, hallucinations of his dead wife. Perhaps they'd be caused by his grief, even." He shrugged. "In any case, he'd soon be deemed unfit to be earl and would be shipped off to some asylum. From there, it would have been easy enough to pay some doctor to make him die of 'natural causes.'" A grin came to his face. "But now, conveniently, we don't have to worry about that."

Catherine looked down at Loftus, new tears filling her eyes. Would she ever find love again? She ducked her chin, but Gilbert's snort brought her head back up again.

"Don't waste your tears over that worthless piece of baggage. Although, now that I've told you my story, you're just as worthless." Gilbert shrugged. "Then again you were a ruined woman. A spinster. Nothing to recommend you, anyway."

Catherine got to her feet, righteous rage filling her veins.

All her life, she'd been knocked down. She'd been judged and deemed insignificant. "Do not tell me who to cry over, and do *not* act as though you are capable of deeming whether something has worth or not."

Gilbert opened his mouth, but she raised her hand, speaking quickly.

"What worth does your life have? You spend it gambling and drinking and lazing around. Is that a life full of worth?" She clenched her fists at her side. "You say I have nothing to recommend me because I was a spinster and a ruined woman, but you're wrong. I have my honor and my dignity, as well as the love I hold in my heart for your brother, whilst you only have your pride, your cruelty, and your disdain."

Gilbert's lips parted, his eyes widening. "Say it isn't so, Catherine." A pitying smile formed on his face. "You cannot have loved him."

Catherine nearly quaked in her anger. "I do even now as his body rests near my feet. You also say that your brother is worthless, but he is twice the man you'll ever be, even if his heart has ceased to beat. Loftus only sought to better what was around him. He sought to *help* others." She pulled her chin up. "We all have worth in God's eyes, even if you can't see past your own inflated ego."

He scoffed. "There is no God. Why would my brother be dead if there was?"

Catherine's voice came out low as she stood her ground. "'To everything there is a season, and a time to every purpose under the heaven: a time to be born and a time to die; a time to plant and a time to pluck up that which is planted.'"

Gilbert slammed his drink down, his eyes blazing. "I find I'm growing rather tired of this conversation." He leapt from the chair and reached behind his back, pulling a pistol from his waistband. He trained it on her, and her eyes widened.

Catherine's blood chilled. With any luck, the bullet would strike something important and she'd be dead quickly, without much pain. At least she'd join her husband in the afterlife.

She fought against closing her eyes, instead staring at Gilbert. No....he should remember looking into her eyes as he took her life. Perhaps the memory would haunt him for the rest of his miserable existence.

Just as he pulled back the hammer, a shout from the side of the room grabbed his attention. A blur of black ran across the room and tackled Gilbert from the side. The constable? He'd certainly taken his time.

The two men scuffled on the floor, but the constable was quick to wrest the gun from Gilbert, sliding it across the floor and out of reach. Another man entered and helped the constable with tying up and securing Gilbert, whose face was red as he heaved and pushed against the constable.

"Who—what are you— You can't take me from here. I'm next in line to inherit! There'll be hell to pay for this, I tell you!"

Catherine gritted her teeth at the gall of that man.

The dowager appeared in the door the policemen had opened. Her face was pinched as she bustled into the room. "What's all this about? Unhand my son. This is an outrage!"

She didn't even seem to notice Loftus's body on the floor.

Gilbert's eyes widened. "Mother. Yes. This was *her* idea. All of it!" The dowager gasped and raised her gloved hands to her mouth, but Gilbert continued his frantic speech. "She planned the whole thing. 'Twas *she* who wished to poison Catherine and she who wished to kill Loftus, not I. She threatened me. Said she'd kill me, too, if I didn't go along with it."

Rage overtook the dowager's features, her wrinkles deepening like small abysses. A shriek erupted from her throat as she ran forward and lunged at Gilbert, who still struggled against the constable. A gasp escaped Catherine's throat, but it was for naught. The constable's assistant took hold of the dowager before she could sink her fingernails into him and secured her hands behind her back. He raised his hand in the air, a ring between his forefinger and thumb. "Think we found the ring, sir."

It was the same ring that the dowager had worn at tea.

The constable nodded. "We'll keep it for evidence. Grab the gun."

The dowager didn't seem to notice that the ring was no longer on her finger, so focused was she on her traitor of a son. Her mouth opened, and it looked as though she was about to breathe fire. "You terrible boy! To think I've been helping you, only for you to treat me so poorly in the end. How could I have birthed such misfortune?" There was the confession. It had come just as swiftly as Loftus said it would. The dowager sagged, and her eyelashes fluttered. "Someone, bring me smelling salts. Bromley? *Bromley!*"

Catherine slumped back onto the floor, careful to avoid the glass, and pulled Loftus's head onto her lap, the tears streaming down her face anew. She'd only just started this marriage and now it was at an end. She stroked his hair, running her fingers over the soft tresses he'd so often run his own fingers through. How had this marriage, once so full of promise, reached such an end?

CHAPTER 34

*H*alf an hour later, both Gilbert and the dowager had been taken away, leaving the manor in silence. The minute Bromley closed the door behind them, Catherine returned to Loftus's body in the library. It remained in the same position it had been in when she left it only minutes before, sending a spiral of disappointment through her stomach.

She lowered herself to her knees next to him and leaned against him, one hand over his chest. Why couldn't they have convinced Gilbert to confess in some other way? Why must it have cost Loftus his life?

The tears began to pool in her eyes and stream down her cheeks in little rivers. She pressed her cheek into his coat and smelled his earthy scent that always comforted her. Even through his shirt, his skin wasn't as cold as she expected it to be. Perhaps it took longer for a person's body to cool once they died than she'd thought.

She closed her eyes. She couldn't stay there all night. They'd have to move his body to the table for when visitors came. By now, of course, the servants all knew of his passing.

They knew what would have to be done, but she hadn't yet wanted to move him. He'd looked so strangely peaceful on the floor.

She adjusted her hand on his chest, only to feel something beneath her palm. Her eyes flicked open. She moved her hand again. There. She pressed her palm down.

Thud, thud.

It couldn't be. It couldn't. She checked again.

Thud, thud. Thud, thud. Thud, thud.

A gasp slipped past her lips, her eyes widening. She lifted her head and raised her hand to his mouth, feeling a small breath against it. The tears started again, but for a completely different reason.

"Bromley! Mrs. Stonehill! Verne!" She ran to the library door and shouted their names into the corridor.

Footsteps preceded their hasty arrival.

"He's alive!" She ran back into the room, not waiting for their mouths to close or gasps to escape. "I heard his heart beating and felt his breath. We must get him upstairs to his chamber at once. Bromley, Verne, will you be able to lift him? Someone call for the doctor!"

At their nods, she turned to Mrs. Stonehill. "Please inform the rest of the servants of this most blessed news."

The woman was off at once, and Catherine followed Bromley and Verne up to her husband's chamber, assuring that Loftus would be comfortable as they placed him on the bed.

"Thank you. I imagine he'd be a bit more comfortable in his night clothes, so perhaps you might change him into those. I'll step out of the room." Her cheeks went hot. "Please inform me when you're done."

Not long after, she was able to go back into the room. The coverlet had been pulled up to Loftus's chest, his arms atop it. A lone candle lit the room, the dark corners illuminated only by the moonlight from the windows.

The doctor came and went with word that her husband, although in a most unusual state of unconsciousness, would, without doubt, be awake by morning. The physician left Cate to tend Loftus, with instructions to feed him only broth upon his rousing.

Catherine yawned once he'd went his way. It was late, and what a long day it had been. Good thing she'd told Susan not to wait up for her this evening.

Kicking off her slippers, Catherine blew out the candle and crawled into Loftus's bed, the room so similar to her own that she didn't even trip as she made her way to the other side. She didn't bother getting out of her dress or stays or anything else, though she did pluck the pins from her hair. The Lord knew she'd never get a blink of sleep with those digging into her scalp.

Atop the coverlet, she scooted closer to her husband and wrapped her hands around his arm, snuggling into his side. The evening was warm, and she'd no use for blankets—this was all the warmth she needed.

She said her prayers, thanking God that her husband was alive, and closed her eyes. There was no place she'd rather be than beside the man she loved as sleep's oblivion claimed her.

CHAPTER 35

Did I die?

As Loftus's eyes blinked open and he gradually took in his surroundings, he couldn't help but come to the conclusion that he must have. He was in his bedchamber, the room aglow with white morning light, but that was not the only indication of heaven. At his side was the most beautiful woman he'd ever beheld—his wife—clinging to his arm as though if she let go, she'd drift into the open ocean. Her hair scattered across the pillow, surrounding her shoulders and shining like gold thread in the sun's rays. Her eyelashes fanned out in the same color, and little puffs of breath were escaping her pink lips as she slept.

How had this happened? Had his plan worked? Where was his brother? He wished for the answers to these questions, but more than that, he wished to let this peace continue for as long as it would, so he let his questions wait.

Relaxing against his pillow, he shifted a bit to better face Cate. How had he ever managed to marry a woman like her? She had such confidence in him, even when he, himself, did not. He lifted the arm not being held by her and tucked a piece of hair behind her ear, allowing his fingers to linger at the soft skin of her cheek.

As he pulled them away, her hazel eyes opened, appearing slightly fogged from sleep. The fog quickly dissipated, and she released his arm, tugging her hands away with a pink flush across her cheeks.

He smiled in reassurance and pushed himself up to a sitting position. He frowned. He was in his night clothes. Had she...?

Cate seemed to read his very thoughts, for she sat up as well, the pink gown she'd been wearing the evening before now wrinkled. Loftus pulled his eyes up from her shoulder, exposed from where one of her sleeves had shifted in slumber, his mouth going dry.

She didn't seem to notice. "Verne and Bromley changed your clothes. I...thought you'd be more comfortable in them. I hope you don't mind." She bit her lip.

Loftus shook his head, relief settling over him that his wife hadn't yet seen him naked. She would, of course, eventually, but he didn't wish for her to see him in such a state for the first time whilst he was *unconscious*. "Not at all."

Her eyes sparkled as a dove called from somewhere outside, its gentle coo like church bells, calling the flowers to raise their heads. They stared at each other for a moment, something building between them.

Cate reached out her open palm, her lily-white hand inviting on the coverlet. Loftus studied the lines of it, intertwining his fingers with hers.

A gentle tug at his hand indicated she wanted him nearer, so he obliged her and shifted closer, his hand never leaving hers. His heart began to beat faster as the distance between them lessened.

Cate leaned forward from her mound of pillows and placed his hand on her cheek. He cradled it like the smooth porcelain it resembled.

Her hand free again, she took his other one and pulled on it, forcing him to turn his body even more toward her. "I thought I'd lost you." She placed that hand on the delicate slope of her shoulder, the warmth there seeping into his skin.

Tiny shocks went through his fingertips at the mere touch of her skin against his. He ducked his chin. "When, darling? Last evening? You knew I'd be unconscious." Had she been worried something had gone wrong?

She leaned closer still, her eyes glossy. "I know, but...I thought I'd lost you. You mentioned before that men who'd taken these herbs had appeared dead, but to see it..." She exhaled. "It looked so real."

"Oh, darling." His heart squeezed at the pain lancing her voice and filling her expression. He brushed his thumb across her cheek.

"I never want to lose you again." She leaned into his touch, her tone becoming determined. "I simply won't let it happen."

A warmth spread throughout him at her words. "I'm right here, dearest."

She pressed one hand against his chest for support while the other, she raised toward his face. Could she feel how fast his heart was beating? He closed his eyes as her fingertips fluttered over his scars, tracing the lines that had marred his face for so long now.

Something burned inside him—a deep longing to be desired. To be wanted and loved. His lungs tightened as her breath whispered across his jaw.

She pressed her lips to where the scars intersected. "You are my treasure."

He inhaled a sharp breath, his eyes opening. He guided her face to look at him. "Do not say what you do not mean. I am...a scarred man." He shook his head, his shoulders tense. "I could not hope to be..." He sighed, feeling the pain settle deep into his bones. "I've been told time and again that they are unappealing. I'm...I...don't expect you to look past them, Cate. It would be too much to ask for."

A blaze lit in her eyes. "I love your scars."

Loftus opened his mouth to protest, but she shook her head.

"I love them. I do not love what caused them, nor the pain you've had to endure in your past or because of them, but I love them. They are a part of you, and they represent your bravery. Your heroism."

He sucked in a soft breath. Could she mean it?

Her eyes lost a bit of their fire as she continued. "When you smile, they pull to the side in the most adorable way. They make you appear quite roguish at times, even though you are anything but. When I first saw them, I thought they looked like the X on a treasure map—the one that marks where the treasure is." She ran her finger down them again and gave him a small smile. "It turns out, I was right."

Loftus's mouth went dry. He swallowed, his pulse racing. "What treasure have you found?" His voice was hoarse.

Cate hesitated, her face inches away. She licked her lips, drawing his attention to them. "Love. With you."

He couldn't remain still any longer. "May I kiss you?" It was nearly a plea.

When she nodded, his lips crashed against hers in a passionate kiss, his hand moving from her shoulder to the back of her neck. She tasted so sweet—like jam biscuits and honey —and her scent of clover and soap threatened to overwhelm him completely.

One of her hands clutched him close by his shirt while the other found its way into his hair, tangling up at the back of his head in a most pleasing manner. It was everything he desired. She fit perfectly in his arms. She was the soil to his roots and the leaves to his stem. Without her, he would never grow or live or thrive. Without her, he was just one piece, but never whole.

He pulled her tighter in his arms, attempting to convey that message through his kiss.

When they broke for air, his breathing was ragged. Cate's cheeks were as red as the roses in the garden outside, and her eyes were as bright as the stars.

Loftus rested his other hand on her cheek so both were holding her face, his fingers moving over her flushed skin. "I suppose I should tell you that I'm in love with you as well."

Cate placed her hands over his, pressing them. "Are you truly?" Her tone was breathless.

A low chuckle rumbled from his chest, and he nodded. "How couldn't I be? You're...you."

This time, she leaned up and pressed her lips to his in a tender kiss, achingly sweet and warm. . It was as though the petals of a flower had formed into lips and melded to his own, after being warmed by the sun.

He wrapped his arms around her waist and pulled her into his lap, placing small kisses all over her cheeks, chin, forehead, and nose. He would cherish this woman for all of his days.

She loved him. *She loved him.* He could hardly believe it. He'd never believed he'd find love, and yet he had, with the woman he'd married. She was his, and he was hers—just like Solomon and the Shulamite.

He placed her back on the mattress and leaned over her, trailing kisses along her jaw. He'd thought an heir to be a thing of the future, but now...

She squeezed his arm, and he lifted his head, looking into her eyes. Hesitation shone in them. He leaned back, taking her hand in his.

She closed her eyes for a moment, exhaling slowly. "I-I love you, but I-I'm not ready for...that. Not yet. Forgive me."

Loftus brought a hand to his wife's face, brushing away a strand of dark hair. Only tenderness flowed through him for his bride. "There is nothing to forgive, my darling," he murmured.

"I will wait as long as it takes until you are ready." He tilted his head, attempting to insert some laughter into the moment. "It's probably better that we wait until we're sure both you and I are well, anyway."

She shifted on her pillows and squeezed his hand, rewarding him with a smile. "Probably."

With a kiss to her hand, he stood from the edge of the bed and rustled around in the dressing room for a moment, coming out with a bundle of clothes. "Now, I'll get dressed in the guest room and leave you to rest some more. 'Twas a trying day yesterday, and I was asleep for the worst of it." He grinned. "I'll make sure to find Susan and send her to you." He kissed her forehead. "Sweet dreams, my love. I'll see you at the breakfast table, if you're awake by then."

As he left the room, he couldn't keep the smile from his face. The woman he loved, loved him, scars and all.

CHAPTER 36

*C*atherine attempted to go back to sleep after Loftus left the room, but no matter how hard she tried, she couldn't make her body rest—not after those kisses they'd shared.

Her heart still beat against her chest like a butterfly in a frenzy though he'd left nigh on half an hour ago, and she tossed and turned under the coverlet, her face heating at the thought of his lips on hers.

Why had she said she wasn't ready?

On her wedding night, the protest would've rang true. Then, she definitely hadn't been ready. Lord Balfour had made sure of that with his immoral advances and the way he'd attacked her. Visions of that night had haunted her—though since she'd married Loftus, they'd begun to go away.

Where Lord Balfour was violent and manipulative and cold, Loftus was gentle and kind and warm. Over the time they'd spent together, she'd gradually gotten used to being in his company and his touch. His affection required nothing in return, and he never asked anything of her that she didn't wish to give. She could trust him with her mind, her heart, and her body.

She closed her eyes and inhaled deeply, feeling all of the tension of the past year build up inside her. With one long exhale, she blew it away like the blowing out of a candle's flame. All that was left was the smoke of bad memories.

Catherine could let go of her anxiety and fears in this matter, for she'd seen who Loftus truly was. There was no more hiding. She wanted to *love*.

She got out of bed and went about her day, joining Loftus at the breakfast table. It was a far cozier occurrence with only the two of them there, and it was here that she explained all that had transpired the evening before, including his mother's involvement.

Loftus shook his head, taking a sip of tea. "Part of me is rather glad I was asleep while this all occurred, though I regret you had to deal with this all on your own. And to think that I was actually dead is, of course, terrible. Were it the other way around, I would have been beside myself. I do not know that I would have had the fortitude to continue with the persuasion."

Catherine shrugged. "I thought if I didn't, your death would have been for naught. I didn't want that to be the case."

He wrapped his arm around her shoulder from beside her and drew her close, pressing a kiss to her temple. She pushed her chair closer and nestled into his chest. This was exactly where she was meant to be.

After breakfast, a surprise came. Loftus and Catherine were tending to the plants in the conservatory when Bromley stepped in, a small smile on his face.

"Something's been delivered, my lord."

Loftus threw off his gloves and grinned. "Is it what I think it is?"

"It is, indeed." Bromley appeared very pleased.

Catherine looked between them, knitting her brow. What exactly had arrived?

Loftus turned to her and stepped forward, pulling her gloves from her fingers. "Come, my love."

With more questions arising in her mind, she followed him and Bromley out the back of the conservatory and through the gardens. Somewhere in the middle of the garden, Loftus stopped, his gaze brimming with mischief. "Close your eyes."

She raised an eyebrow but did as she was bid, holding onto his arm for balance and support as they moved from the stone path to grass underfoot. Never once did Loftus direct her into a bush or bed of flowers, and she loved the feel of his arm beneath her hand. And his scent. Did he make it himself? She'd truly never met a man who smelled as good. Like leaves and autumn with—was that hay? He'd never smelled like that before.

She sniffed the air. Definitely hay. And horse. Were they at the stables?

A whinny sounded nearby, and her heart picked up its pace. Was the surprise near here?

"Open your eyes," Loftus whispered in her ear, and she blinked against the daylight, her eyes adjusting to the sudden brightness. Before her was a horse. Not only a horse—*her* horse.

"Woodbine!" Cate rushed toward her grey stallion, his bridle being held by one of the stable hands.

Woodbine tossed his head in greeting as she threw her arms around his neck, pressing her cheek against his fine coat. Her heart nearly burst at being able to see her pet once more.

She let her arms drop and ran a hand down his muzzle, so soft and smooth. "I never thought I'd see you again."

Loftus appeared at her side, his hands clasped behind his back. "Your parents put up quite the fight when I requested they send him to Blackfern. They didn't want to spare the expense, I believe." He frowned. "Once I mentioned I'd cover the cost of sending him this way, they were eager to see him go."

Catherine bit the inside of her cheek, irritation welling within her. It was just like her parents to keep him for the sake of saving a penny. How did they not realize it likely cost them more to feed and house Woodbine than to send him here? Maybe they had resisted just to spite her. At least they hadn't sold him. That was a miracle in itself.

She turned a grateful expression on her husband. "Thank you, Loftus. This means more than I can say. I've been so worried that he's been mistreated there." She hooked her arms around her husband's neck and pressed a kiss to his lips. He wrapped his arms around her waist and pulled her closer.

If only they could remain this way forever...

"Ah!" A startled sound escaped her as Woodbine nudged his muzzle into her back and pushed her farther into Loftus, sending her husband chuckling.

She turned to the horse with her hands propped on her hips. "I suppose you wish to go for a ride, huh?" She grinned. "Give us five minutes."

At the stable hand's beet-red face and her husband's twisted-to-the-side smile, she realized her mistake. She coughed, raising her hands.

"To change! Neither of us are dressed to ride." Her face must be ablaze. She spun on her heel and raced back toward the manor.

Once they'd changed and Catherine could show her face to the stable hand again, they mounted their horses and followed the path Loftus rode almost daily. To be on Woodbine again and feel the wind running through her hair was akin to floating on air and swimming through clouds.

They found frogs, toads, and squirrels—even the elusive red deer she'd been trying to spot—but nothing could make her happier than being with the one she loved. The things she enjoyed were exciting—yes—but she no longer cared what she was doing as long as he was at her side.

They rode back to the manor and enjoyed each other's company for the rest of the day, neither straying far from the other's side.

Only the remembrance that dinner was soon had them moving to their separate chambers to change, though Catherine didn't care what Loftus wore—whether it be satin or a sack of flour.

Catherine met Loftus in the drawing room after she'd bathed and put on her finest gown—a dark green one that had arrived only three days ago from Madame Lisette's shop. It reminded her of the leaves on the plants he loved so much. Susan had arranged flowers among her curls—though not nearly as many as that day she'd covered her head with them to impress him—and she'd dabbed a little extra perfume on her wrists and neck. Her golden wedding band shone on her ring finger, the tiny leaf engraved on it reminiscent of the one Loftus had curled right around her heart.

Tonight, they would be married—both on paper and in spirit.

CHAPTER 37

*L*oftus's breath left him as Cate entered the drawing room, her dark-green gown shimmering in the candles set about the room. Her eyes glowed with warmth as she glided toward him, the same flowers she'd worn on their wedding day placed carefully in her hair. Did that have special meaning?

He held out his hand to her, and warmth crept up his arm as she placed her smaller one in it. He didn't think he'd ever cease to be affected by her touch—he hoped not, at least. Placing a kiss on the back of her knuckles, he pulled her closer, craving her nearness.

She stepped toward him, eyes curious. "What will happen to your mother and brother now?" Her voice was soft.

He knew this question would come. "The magistrate will decide. God will deliver their fate." He exhaled. "What matters is that they can no longer harm us." He gently tugged on one of her curls. "We may start anew."

She nodded, her whole body leaning toward him. "How do you feel?"

He squeezed her hand. "As long as I am with you, I am content. We are all the family we need."

Cate's lips quirked up and her eyes glowed. How had he managed to marry such a beautiful woman?

"You once asked me my favorite flower." He lowered his head near her ear. "Do you remember what I said?"

The corner of her mouth lifted in a smile. "You said there were too many to choose from. You couldn't name just one."

He nodded, playing with one of the curls that framed her face. "I've changed my mind since then." He brought his lips to hers in a brief kiss, sending a sweet pink hue to flush her face.

She pressed her hand to his chest, lips parted. "And what is it, then? Is it in the garden?"

He shook his head. "It is difficult to find, but most enchanting. I haven't found it in any other country but England— neither have I found it outside of Cumbria, though you might have seen it in London."

She tilted her head. "Perhaps at the botanical garden? The flower is very striking, then?"

His voice lowered to a murmur. "Oh, yes. You would not forget the petals had you seen them."

Her hand grasped his lapel, tugging on it ever so slightly. "I confess, Loftus, I do not remember seeing the flower of which you speak."

He quirked a smile. "Perhaps you have become so accustomed to seeing it that you are no longer affected by its appearance, but I believe I always shall be. The flower I most favor is the bloom in your cheek."

'Twas then the bloom appeared, those rosy petals unfurling within the creamy white of her skin. Loftus couldn't help the widening of his smile as Cate's lips formed an O and she ducked her chin, gazing at him through her lashes.

"You're bamming me, my lord." Her voice held laughter.

He traced his finger down the side of her cheek, making his expression earnest. "I am not, darling. I would not say such a thing if it weren't true."

Their lips were inches apart when dinner was called, and Loftus escorted Cate into the dining room on his arm, seating her and pushing in her chair before taking his own at the head of the table.

Cook had truly outdone herself with all of the scrumptious dishes that were served. Each was as good as the last, and conversation never dulled for a moment throughout the entirety of the meal. Loftus was able to relax in her presence as he never had been able to with anyone else. Even the silence between bites and discussions was enjoyable—simply knowing she was at his side and content.

When they'd finished with dinner, they went to the library. The mess from the day before had been cleaned, the spilled wine lifted from the rug, just as they would now replace the bad memories with good ones.

All the same, Cate did not lead Loftus to the settee they'd sat upon that evening. Instead, she took him to the two brocade chairs in front of the empty hearth, turning around with a smile as she reached them. "I'll read to you for a while."

He matched her smile and came around the front of the chair, waiting for her to fetch a book before settling himself into it. He didn't catch a glimpse of the spine but didn't have to look at the cover as Cate began to read, her melodious voice filling the space around them.

"If ever two were one, then surely we.
If ever man were loved by wife, then thee.
If ever wife was happy in a man,
Compare with me, ye women, if you can.
I prize thy love more than whole mines of
gold,

Or all the riches that the East doth hold.
My love is such that rivers cannot quench,
Nor ought but love from thee give
    recompense."

Warmth as though rays of sunlight were spilling down on him from above spread throughout his body as Cate read Ms. Bradstreet's words. He closed his eyes as Cate continued.

"Thy love is such I can no way repay;
The heavens reward thee manifold, I pray.
Then while we live, in love let's so persever,
That when we live no more, we may live
    ever."

After a moment of silence, Loftus opened his eyes.

Cate looked at him with a hint of concern. "Are you well, dearest?"

"I am more than well, love." His voice was hoarse when he pushed out his answer, his emotions getting the better of him. Here was this woman who was better than anything he could have dreamed of for himself, and she was his to have and to hold on earth and in heaven. This already felt like heaven, and it was all because of Cate. He blinked, the back of his eyes stinging. "Please, read on."

Cate read more poems of love and marriage as they sat there together. It seemed Loftus was not the only one affected by their recent admission of feelings for one another and the subsequent peace that came with doing so and requited affection. Not too much longer, however, and she set the book aside, her face turned toward him. The candles flickered off her features, turning her into some ethereal being—an angel with a glow around her head and gold cast on her neck and shoulders.

She leaned toward him. "When I first came here, I had no

idea how our marriage would be. I did not know how *you* would be. I believed all men were like my father or Lord Balfour—violent and insulting and dangerous. Always wanting their way." Her eyes pierced him, flickering between green and brown in the candle's dance. "But you, Loftus, are different. You taught me that not all men are the same. That not all men will treat me the same, because *you* treat me differently."

He didn't speak—only listened. This was her time to reveal what she felt she needed to.

She raised her hand to her cheek. "I was so scared at the beginning that you would turn out like them, but I feared for nothing. You could never be what they are. You are..."—she choked—"understanding and patient, kind, honest and... loving. I do believe God sent me here for you."

Loftus stood from the chair slowly, his heart thumping against his ribs. He'd felt the same since Cate had arrived at Blackfern, though he'd tried his best to ignore the feeling.

She rose as well and took a few steps toward him.

His breaths grew heavier the closer she came. "I'm not sure you were ever meant to be away from me."

She placed her hand on his arm. "I won't be ever again."

Her face tilted up to meet his in a sweet kiss, and his arms wound their way around her, holding her in a tight embrace. Her hands pressed against his chest, the warmth from them seeming to seep through her gloves and his waistcoat and right into his skin.

He tilted his chin to deepen the kiss and began plucking the pins from hair, dropping them to the carpet one by one. She melted against him, her hair tumbling around her shoulders like the elegant branches of the willow.

When they separated, both of their chests heaving, she grabbed his hand in hers and a candelabra in the other. He let her tug him up the stairs and down the corridor. Thankfully, it seemed the servants had all retired or were attending to late-night duties elsewhere.

When Cate led him toward her chamber door, he prepared to say goodnight, but she walked past it. His eyes widened. She stopped in front of his chamber door and opened it.

What was she doing?

～

*a*s Catherine pushed the door of Loftus's bedchamber open, his valet appeared, and she straightened her shoulders with a smile. "You may retire, Verne. Loftus won't be needing your assistance this evening."

The man nodded, his face a mask of polite indifference, and fled from the room.

Catherine set the candelabra aside and closed the bedchamber door.

She grinned at Loftus, who was looking at her askance. "Wha—"

"I should very much like to kiss you again."

His mouth closed, and she was in his arms in a moment, exactly where they'd left off in the library. Her heart raced, and her head felt light and airy.

Loftus scattered kisses on her temples and cheeks, her eyelids and nose, and all along her jaw. She lifted her chin, and he pressed his lips along her neck and behind her ear.

She began to lead him toward his bed, thinking he would not realize.

He did.

"You are trying to kill me, Cate." He blinked his dazed eyes.

She snorted. "Quite the opposite. I am trying to *love* you."

His eyes widened, and he grabbed her hand. "You said you were not ready."

"I did not believe I was, but I am. Let us take *you* and *I* and become *us*."

His breath quavered as he exhaled. "Are you certain?"

She lifted her chin. "I am."

He brought his lips to hers and thus began their union as husband and wife, bound in love for the rest of their lives.

EPILOGUE

Six Months Later

*C*atherine walked down the bright corridor leading to her husband's study, a smile pulling at her lips. On the way, she stopped at the library, entering the room and picking up a book that had been wedged in one of the shelves for a few months now.

She'd placed it there in autumn when the last of the flowers in the garden were fading in the hopes of taking it down for this very occasion, and now her stomach was all aflutter with excitement as her fingers touched the soft leather spine.

She held it to her chest, closing her eyes for a moment. It was so odd how all of her dreams had come true when—only a year ago—she'd been in the most terrible of situations.

Taking a deep breath, she opened her eyes and strode from the library. When she arrived at the study and gave a light rap on the oak door, Loftus's voice bid her enter. As she did, the smile on his face lifted her heart.

"Darling." He set his quill aside and pushed back his chair.

In a moment, he'd stood from behind his stately desk and moved around it, enveloping her in his embrace.

She breathed him in, relaxing against his solid form. There was not a place on earth she preferred to her husband's arms.

After a minute, he pulled away, his hands on her forearms. "You always know when I'm missing you the most, my dear— even if you're only a few rooms away."

Her pulse thrummed within her. Loftus never failed to warm her cheeks with his sweet words.

She brushed an errant lock of hair from his forehead. "I know we saw each other at breakfast, but I cannot stay away from you for long." She met his ice-blue gaze, her head becoming light.

His mouth twisted to the side in a smile. "I would not want you to."

Their faces were inching toward each other when Cate remembered she'd had a specific purpose in coming to her husband's study—one besides seeing his handsome face. She placed a brief kiss on his cheek and drew away before he could distract her further, for he certainly would if given the chance.

His eyes widened as she seated herself in the chair in front of his desk, arranging her lavender skirts. She set the book upon his desk, and he leaned against the edge to get a better view.

"*The Meanings of Flowers and Blooms*." He tilted his head. "I wasn't aware this was a topic you were interested in, love."

She nodded. "Oh, indeed. Do you know anything about it?"

He rubbed his jaw. "I cannot say I do. My interest until this point has been in the medicinal parts of plants and under what conditions they will grow. I do believe this tome to be my grandmother's."

He reached for it, but Catherine grabbed it before he could pick it up, clearing her throat. "I found the book a few months ago now. There are many interesting bits of information within it." She opened it to the page where she'd pressed the flower then and smiled to find its pink petals and green bit of stem perfectly preserved. "I put this in it." She handed him the flower for his inspection.

Loftus held it between his fingers, turning it back and forth in the light, his eyes narrowed. "*Dianthus caryophyllus*, is it?"

Cate ducked her chin. "If that means carnation, then you are correct."

He spun the flower between his thumb and forefinger. "And what meaning does a carnation have, my dear wife?"

Her breath hitched in her throat as he looked at her with such fondness. She ran her finger down the page. "Not only a carnation, but a *pink* carnation." She closed the book, setting it back on the desk as she spoke in a murmur. "It means motherhood."

The flower stopped spinning in Loftus's hand. As carefully as though he were handling an empty egg shell, he set it atop the book, his eyes remaining on hers. "Are you saying what I believe you're saying?"

Cate's head dipped in a nod. "We are having a child."

Loftus pulled her up from the chair, his eyes shining. Cate stepped forward and raised her hand to his cheek as a grin pulled on his lips.

A chuckle escaped him and soon spread to her as they reveled in their joy. Loftus pressed his lips to hers in a sealing of their fate. No matter the hardships or triumphs that would come, they would face them together—always.

Did you enjoy this book? We hope so!
Would you take a quick minute to leave a review where you purchased the book?
It doesn't have to be long. Just a sentence or two telling what you liked about the story!

Receive a FREE ebook and get updates when new Wild Heart books release: https://wildheartbooks.org/newsletter

Don't miss the next book in the Saving the Spinsters Series!

A Joy for Jane

ACKNOWLEDGMENTS

Thank you to everyone at Wild Heart Books who help to make this book happen. Without your knowledge and assistance, it would still just be an idea in my head or some words typed up with nowhere to go. This whole series has truly been a blessing from God, and above all, I thank Him for allowing me to work with some of the kindest people in the business. Thank you, also, to family and friends who always support me and give encouraging words. You know who you are.

AUTHOR'S NOTE

Dear Reader,

I hope you had as pleasant a time reading this book as I had writing it. Boy, did I learn a lot whilst doing so. I wouldn't be surprised if I'm on the FBI's watch list for potential criminals or something of the sort, given how many odd things I was looking up—especially when I was researching what poison I should have Gilbert use.

There were a few potential options. Arsenic is a classic, of course, but it wouldn't have given the hallucinations I wished for in Cate's symptoms. Morning glories would have, but they weren't in bloom during the time Cate was wandering around in the garden with Loftus, so that wasn't really going to work. That was when I stumbled upon the humble mandrake and all of the folklore that goes along with it—seriously, there's a lot of backstory to this plant.

I also learned of the native and not-so-native plants of the U.K. and Cumbria and their scientific names, the many herbs used for medicine at the time along with the scary implications of those, and the Latin names of certain animals. *Bufo bufo* for the common toad—I mean, isn't that adorable?!

Throughout my books, I always seek to make my characters relatable, with flaws and deep emotions and the like. I do not want static portraits without feeling, and I imagine you don't either. I hope you were able to relate to my characters in some way or were moved by the story or themes. Perhaps you simply found it entertaining. That is enough for me.

If you wish to get in touch with me, please feel free to do so. If you like this book, please feel free to leave a review, as well! Thank you.

My website: https://jackiekillelea.weebly.com/
Instagram: @authorjackiekillelea
Facebook: @AuthorJackieKillelea

ABOUT THE AUTHOR

Jackie Killelea is a born and raised small-town girl from Connecticut with a degree in English and Creative Writing. She started off her writing journey with poetry, soon shifting into novels and becoming hooked. On days when she's not busy with her nose in a book, she can be found typing away with a piece of chocolate in hand.

If you love historical romance, check out the other Wild Heart books!

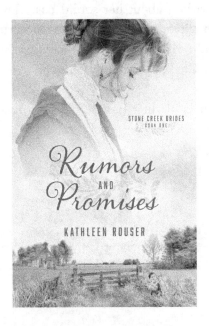

Rumors and Promises by Kathleen Rouser

She's an heiress hiding a tumultuous past. He's a reverend desperate to atone for his failures.

Abandoned by her family, Sophie Biddle has been on the run with a child in tow. At last, she's found a safe life in Stone Creek, Michigan, teaching piano. But when a kind, yet meddling and handsome, minister walks into her life seeking to help, Sophie is caught off guard and wary. When her secrets threaten to be exposed, will she be able to trust the reverend, and more importantly, God?

After failing his former flock, Reverend Ian McCormick is determined to start anew in Stone Creek, and he's been working harder than ever to forget his mistakes and prove himself to his new congregation—and to God. But when he meets a young woman seeking acceptance and respect, despite the rumors swirling about her sordid past, Ian finds himself pulled in two directions. If he shows concern for Sophie's plight, he could risk everything—including his position as pastor of Stone Creek Community Church.

Will the scandals of their pasts bind them together or drive them apart forever?

〜

A Summer at Thousand Island House by Susan G Mathis

She came to work with the children, not fall in love.

Part-nanny, part entertainer, Addison Bell has always had an enduring love for children. So what better way to use her creative energy than to spend the summer nannying at the renowned Thousand Island House on Staple's Island? As Addi thrives in her work, she attracts the attention of the recreation pavilion's manager, Liam Donovan, as well as the handsome Navy Officer Lt. Worthington, a lighthouse inspector, hotel patron, and single father of mischievous little Jimmy.

But when Jimmy goes missing, Addi finds both her job and her reputation in danger. How can she calm the churning waters of Liam, Lt. Worthington, and the President, clear her name, and avoid becoming the scorn of the Thousand Islands community?

~

Revealing the Truth by Lorri Dudley

His suspect holds a secret, but can he uncover the truth before she steals his heart?

When Katherine Jenkins is rescued from the side of the road, half-frozen and left for dead, her only option is to stay silent about her identity or risk being shipped back to her ruthless guardian, who will kill to get his hands on her inheritance and the famous Jenkins Lipizzaner horses. But even under the pretense of amnesia, she cannot shake the memory of her sister and Katherine's need to reach her before their guardian, or his marauding bandits, finish her off. Will she be safe in the earl's manor, or will the assailant climbing through her window be the death of her?

British spy, Stephen Hartington's assignment to uncover an underground horse-thieving ring brings him home to his family's manor, and the last thing he expected was to be struck with a candlestick upon climbing through the guest chamber window. The manor's feisty and intriguing new house guest throws Stephen's best-laid plans into turmoil and raises questions about the timing of her appearance, the convenience of her memory loss, and her impeccable riding skills. Could he be housing the horse thief he'd been ordered to capture—or worse, falling in love with her.